Measle looked around wildly, searching for somebody who could help him. There was an old man, leaning on a walking stick about ten feet away, watching him. Measle ran over to him and said breathlessly, "Did you see what happened?"

The old man sniffed. "Well, yes, I did, young fellow. There was this van—all black it was—and these people jumped out. They were all in black, too—funny-looking people they were. Their faces were so white they looked like corpses. They threw a bottle at that chap over there, and some funny-looking blue gas came out of it. Then they grabbed the lady and bundled her into the van and drove off. I saw the whole thing. Making a film, are they? Where's the camera then?"

Wrathmonks! thought Measle. *Wrathmonks have kidnapped Mum!*

MEASLE

and the

DRAGODON

IAN OGILVY

≜ HarperTrophy®
An Imprint of HarperCollinsPublishers

Measle and the Dragodon
Copyright © 2005 by Ian Ogilvy
www.harpercollinschildrens.com

Library of Congress Cataloging-in-Publication Data
Ogilvy, Ian.
Measle and the Dragodon / Ian Ogilvy.—1st ed.
p. cm.
Sequel to: Measle and the Wrathmonk.
Summary: Recently reunited with his parents, twelve-
year-old Measle Stubbs sets out to rescue his mother from
the Wrathmonk wizards who have kidnapped her, battling
an ancient dragon, as well as carousel horses and various
stuffed animals that have magically come to life, in an
amusement park.
ISBN-10: 0-06-058690-7 (pbk.)
ISBN-13: 978-0-06-058690-4 (pbk.)
[1. Amusement parks—Fiction. 2. Wizards—Fiction.
3. Dragons—Fiction. 4. Toys—Fiction. 5. Magic—
Fiction. 6. Humorous stories.] I. Title.
PZ7.O3435Md 2005   2004018284
[Fic]—dc22   CIP
                                                 AC

Typography by Amy Ryan

First Harper Trophy edition, 2006
First American Edition, 2005
First published in Great Britain in 2004
by Oxford University Press

For Barnaby and Matilda—again

CONTENTS

1

THE
SEARCHERS

The dingy, dreary street was still there, with its two rows of dingy, dreary houses. The houses were still abandoned and derelict, their doors and windows boarded over with rough planks of wood. Weeds grew tall in the sooty back gardens, and the fences that separated the properties sagged and rotted in the damp air.

Nobody had wanted to live there—not since Basil Tramplebone had moved in to the biggest and nastiest-looking house at the far end of the street, right down by the railway tracks.

1

And still they didn't want to live there, even months after Basil's death, when he and his pet bat, Cuddlebug, had fallen from their high attic window and splattered on the pavement below, and the nasty house itself had collapsed into a pile of rubble. There was still something about the street that made prospective house buyers turn away and go look for somewhere to live in another part of town—preferably a part of town that was as far away from that dingy, dreary street as possible.

And now, today, on this warm, late summer's evening, it seemed at first glance that the street was as empty of human life as ever. But if you looked a little closer, particularly there, down at the far end of the street, where a great rotting pile of black rubble—that had once been Basil Tramplebone's horrible house—lay by the side of the road, you might have noticed some movement.

On the pavement, in the shadow of the great rubble heap, two dark figures sat on a pair of folding camp stools. They held open umbrellas over their heads, and they huddled together under the rain that dribbled down on them.

The rain that dribbled down on them—*but on nothing else in the street.*

2

Elsewhere in the dingy, dreary street, the early evening sun cast a golden glow over everything. But over the two huddled figures there floated a strange object—a small black cloud in the shape of the figure eight. This odd-looking, little double cloud dribbled a constant stream of water over the two black umbrellas and the huddled figures beneath them.

Wrathmonks! Members of the third—and most feared—branch of sorcery. First among the sorcerers were the Wizards, who were kind and friendly and usually very secretive, living private lives and not bothering anybody very much; then the Warlocks—proud, ambitious, and a little greedy, perhaps; and last came the Wrathmonks, the most terrible of all the magical beings, for they were insane.

Besides the small movements made by the two Wrathmonks as they sat quietly talking to each other, there was other movement, too. Another pair of figures was scrambling about on the huge pile of dirty rubble. Their heads were down and their backs were bent and their hands were picking over the bricks, as if they were looking for something. Every now and again they would cast anxious eyes in the direction of the two figures under their umbrellas and then, just as quickly, they would avert their eyes and continue their search.

The pair of searchers were men, both in rough working clothes and heavy boots, with cloth caps on their heads. They looked frightened and exhausted—and a little puzzled, too.

They had been searching for a very long time and now, for a moment, each man took a few seconds to rest. They both stopped quite near to each other, and both straightened their aching backs and tried to rub a little of the dirt from their sore hands.

"Did I tell you to ssstop, Robert?"

The first man jerked at the sound of the hissing voice. He looked fearfully down at the figures on the pavement. One of them—a short, round, fat little blob of a person—had folded his umbrella and stood up from his camp stool and was now glaring at him from under hooded eyelids. The eyes were like two little black holes in a smooth expanse of white, white skin. There wasn't a single strand of hair on the shiny round head. The ears were small and round and lay close to the skull. The nose looked like a little ball of white wax. A pair of pale, pudgy lips occupied the lower half of the face and, below them, the chin sloped backward so that it looked as if he had no chin at all. Below the nonexistent chin was a nonexistent neck and, below that, a well-pressed black suit, a white shirt, a black tie, a pair of black leather gloves and, on the small feet, a pair of shiny black lace-up shoes.

"Well, Robert? I asssked you a quessstion, Robert."

The man on the rubble pile shook his head fearfully. "No, Mr. Gristle, sir—I wasn't stopping, Mr. Gristle, sir. I was just taking a breather, Mr. Gristle, sir. Won't happen again, Mr. Gristle, sir."

Griswold Gristle twisted his mouth into the semblance of a smile.

"No, Robert, it won't happen again. And would you like me to tell you *why* it won't happen again, Robert?"

Robert swallowed hard and whispered, "Oh, yes please, Mr. Gristle, sir."

"Well, Robert—it won't happen again because, if it does, you won't be taking a *breather*, as you call it, ever again. You won't be taking a *breather*, Robert—because you won't be *alive*, Robert, you'll be dead—and dead people don't do all that much *breathing*, you sssee. Hee hee." Griswold's fat little body jiggled up and down a

5

couple of times, and a wheezing sound slipped from his mouth. "Hee hee. Do you follow me, Robert?"

Robert nodded, lowering his eyes to the ground. "Yes, sir, Mr. Gristle, sir. Very, very sorry, Mr. Gristle, sir. Beg your pardon, Mr. Gristle, sir. Won't happen again, Mr. Gristle, sir."

Griswold wrinkled his tiny round nose in disgust. "Sssee that it doesn't. Well, get on with your sssearch, then," he muttered, and sat back down on his stool.

Robert didn't dare throw a look at his fellow searcher on the rubble heap. He simply stared hard at the jumble of bricks, crumbling plaster and rotting timbers beneath his feet and went back to his seemingly endless quest.

"Sssuch lazy creatures, these common working humans," hissed Griswold to his companion. "We let them sssleep at night, don't we? And they've only been sssearching for five days. That's nothing, Cedric—why, when I'm at my bank, I regularly work nonssstop for ten or eleven hours without even a break for doughnuts and lemonade—and I never, ever take a holiday."

Judge Cedric Hardscrabble nodded. "The average human," he said, "is an idle brute."

Judge Cedric Hardscrabble's appearance was the absolute opposite of Griswold Gristle's. Where Griswold was short and round and fat and as bald as a billiard ball, Judge Cedric was long and thin and twiggy, with a mass of pure white hair on his bony skull. It stood out from under his black bowler hat in a frizz, so that it looked as if he'd just touched a live electric wire and was still trying to recover from the shock. His face was the color of old candles. His ears were long and curiously pointed. His nose—which always had a drip of disgusting-looking greenish liquid hanging from the end of it—jutted from his face like the beak of an eagle and the tip bent down, as if trying to join itself with the pointed chin beneath. He wore a long, shabby black overcoat that completely covered the rest of his clothes, apart from the glimpse of a grubby white collar around his bony throat at one end and a pair of scuffed black shoes at the other.

Judge Cedric swiveled on his camp stool, moved his umbrella out of the way and peered up at the two searching men. "And what about you, Harry?" he called. "Are you working hard, Harry?"

"Working very hard *indeed*, Your Worship, sir," called Harry.

"Have you found what we are looking for yet, Harry?"

"Er—well, I can't rightly say, Your Honor, sir. Since—begging your pardon, Your Lordship, sir—we don't exactly know what it is we're looking for—"

"Sssilence, you insssolent creature!" snarled Judge Cedric. "It is not for you to know what it is we ssseek! It is enough that you sssimply obey your inssstructions!"

Harry swallowed hard. The last thing he needed was an angry Judge Cedric Hardscrabble. The last thing *anybody* needed was an angry Judge Cedric Hardscrabble.

"Yes, sir. Sorry, sir."

"You don't want me to *breathe* on you again, do you, Harry?"

"Oh—no, sir—please, sir—don't do that, sir—"

Judge Cedric had once breathed on Harry, and Harry had never forgotten the experience. In fact, he remembered it with horror. He'd done something wrong—he'd made Judge Cedric a cup of tea and put in three lumps of sugar instead of four—and then Judge Cedric had become very angry and had started *breathing* on him. The judge's breath had smelled horrible—of dead fish and old mattresses and the insides of ancient sneakers—but that hadn't been the worst part.

The worst part had been that within a few seconds, Harry's face and his hands—and then, moments later, his whole body—had suddenly become covered in disgusting and very painful, bright red, pussy boils, which had taken a whole month to clear up.

Harry didn't want that to happen again.

"We'll find it, Your Highness, sir! Don't worry, Your Greatness, sir! Robert and me—we'll search all night, all week, all month—but we'll find it, Your Supremeness, sir!"

"Sssee that you do, Harry. Sssee that you do."

Harry moved away, shifting bricks as fast as he could.

The two Wrathmonks sat in silence for a few moments. Then Judge Cedric sniffed and leaned a little closer to Griswold Gristle.

"Griswold, old friend—I've jussst had a thought."

"Really?" said Griswold in a surprised voice. In his experience, Judge Cedric hardly ever had any thoughts at all.

"Yesss. I was wondering, Griswold—when we find thisss thing that we ssseek—what are we going to *do* with it?"

Griswold Gristle sighed. He had explained all this several times to Judge Cedric but, ever since his old friend had been transformed from Warlock into Wrathmonk, Judge Cedric had become very forgetful. He had also become very stupid. Lately Griswold Gristle had begun to wonder whether being friends with Judge Cedric Hardscrabble wasn't, well, rather *pointless*.

Griswold decided he certainly wasn't going to go through the whole thing again—at least, not until they actually found what they were looking for. So instead, he just whispered into Judge Cedric's pointed, whiskery old ear, "*Do* with it, Cedric? Why, we shall do wonderful things. Wonderful, *wonderful* things."

Judge Cedric was about to ask *what* wonderful things when, from somewhere above them, there came a muffled scream, quickly followed by running, stumbling footsteps, then another muffled scream, then silence.

The two Wrathmonks looked at each other. Then Griswold Gristle said, "It would appear that they have found it, Cedric."

Judge Cedric smiled, revealing a mouth full of

brown and crooked teeth. The three upper teeth on either side of his mouth came to sharp points.

"Let usss wait a moment, to be quite sure," said Griswold.

The two Wrathmonks sat in silence, listening for any sound of movement on the rubble heap behind them. There was none.

"Robert?" called Griswold.

"Harry?" called Judge Cedric.

Silence, apart from the sound of the rain drumming against their umbrellas. Griswold got to his feet and rummaged in a leather bag by the side of his stool. He took out a small hand mirror and a pair of long barbecue tongs. "We mussst be very careful, Cedric."

Judge Cedric nodded and stood up, wrapping his long coat tight around himself. "Careful, yesss."

"You hold the tongs," said Griswold. "I shall manipulate the mirror."

"Do you have the container ready?"

"Of courssse," said Griswold, holding up a small cloth bag. "I have thought of everything, Cedric. Now let usss retrieve the preciousss thing forthwith."

Leaving their umbrellas by their camp stools, the

two Wrathmonks climbed up the rubble heap until they both reached the top. In front of them, about ten feet away, was a strange sight. Two gray stone statues of a pair of workingmen in flat caps and heavy boots were standing in a small pit in the brick rubble. The statues bore remarkable resemblances to Robert and Harry. Both were bent double at the waist, as if intent on some object on the ground in front of them. Both had their arms standing stiffly away from their bodies and their hands were splayed, fingers wide, as if trying to ward off some horror in front of them.

Griswold Gristle and Judge Cedric Hardscrabble approached cautiously. When they got within a few feet of the two statues, Griswold held the hand mirror in front of him, angling it toward the ground. He stared into the mirror, inching his fat little body forward step by careful step.

"Can you sssee it yet, Griswold?" whispered Judge Cedric, creeping slowly behind him.

"Not yet, Cedric. Be patient."

Griswold was now on the edge of the small pit, crouching between the two statues. His short, fat right arm, with the mirror clutched in his right hand, was sweeping backward and forward over the surface of the rubble. Slowly to the left, then slowly to the right. Then Griswold took a cautious step forward and swept his arm again, slowly left, slowly right.

He stopped. Very carefully, he moved his arm back a few inches.

"There!" he hissed. "Do you sssee it, Cedric?"

Judge Cedric stepped forward, his eyes glued to the ground in front of him.

Griswold seized his arm. "No, no, you fool! Look in the mirror! Look in the mirror!"

The two Wrathmonks stared intently into the little mirror. There, in the reflection, a small, gray, wrinkled object lay among the dirty bricks.

"Careful now, Cedric," whispered Griswold. "Bring the tongs forward—a little to the left—forward an inch—now a touch to the right—down a bit—down a bit—there! Now gently sssqueeze the tongs together—that's it—you have it! Now lift ssslowly— ssslowly—I have the bag ready—bring it ssslowly toward me—that'sss right—careful now—that'sss excellent, Cedric—keep looking in the mirror—a little clossser—good, good, you're now directly over the open bag—lower it ssslowly, ssslowly, excellent—now carefully open the tongs and—there! It'sss in the bag, Cedric! We have it! It'sss in the bag!"

A few beads of sweat stood out on the Wrathmonks' white foreheads. The drops of sweat were a pale green color, and instead of trickling down their faces (like ordinary sweat), these drops stayed where they were, as if stuck there with glue.

"A dangerousss business, Griswold," said Judge Cedric, his voice a little shaky.

"But worth it, wouldn't you agree, Cedric?" Griswold tightened the drawstring around the neck of the cloth bag and stuffed it carefully into his jacket pocket. "What was once Basil Tramplebone's is now ours! With thisss object, we have a mighty weapon at our disssposal—one that can ssstop an army in itsss tracksss! Imagine, Cedric—an entire army, all turned to ssstone before our very eyes!"

Judge Cedric looked a little confused. "And . . . what army would that be, Griswold?"

"Well, not necessarily *any* army, Cedric!" said Griswold sharply. "The point is, with thisss rare and preciousss object, we will be able—if we ssso choose—to *literally* petrify a large number of humans, whenever we want to!"

"*Petrify*, Griswold? Surely it does more than merely petrify?"

"The word has two meanings, Cedric," said Griswold with the air of somebody who is proud of his education and likes showing it off. "'Petrify' means to frighten—but it alssso means 'to turn to ssstone.' A preciousss object indeed! And, bessst of all, Cedric, it uses up none of our own magical powers!"

"We shall use it againssst my enemies!" hissed Judge Cedric excitedly. "My wicked, evil opponentsss! Twelve of them in particular—all mossst unpleasant persssons—they sssit in a sssort of box in my court-room and disssagree with everything I sssay!"

"You mean—the *jury*?" said Griswold in the sort of voice people use when they find it hard to believe what they've just heard.

"Indeed, yesss!" cried Judge Cedric. "The jury! We shall petrify the jury!"

"We could indeed," said Griswold carefully. "But firssst things firssst, Cedric. As I told you before, we mussst take our revenge againssst those who hurt usss the mossst!"

Judge Cedric grinned wolfishly. "The jury, yesss!"

Griswold Gristle sighed. Sometimes he wondered how his friend had ever managed to remain a judge at all.

"The jury, yesss," said Griswold patiently. "But later, Cedric—*later*. Firssst we mussst deal with the enemies of *all* of usss. Of all Wrathmonksss, wherever they might be. I am ssspeaking, of course, of those who persssecute usss! Who hunt usss down! I am ssspeaking of the family of Ssstubbs!"

Judge Cedric's thin, white face wrinkled in hatred. "The Ssstubbs family! Yesss! We mussst deal with the Ssstubbs family!"

"And in particular, Cedric, we mussst deal with the boy! That wretched child, Measle Ssstubbs, who murdered our beloved Basil Tramplebone! We mussst avenge poor Basil's death!"

"Yesss! Yesss!" cried Judge Cedric, dancing an unsteady little jig on the uneven ground. Then he stopped and leaned toward Griswold, his bushy eyebrows raised. "But how, Griswold? How shall we get our revenge?"

For a moment Griswold Gristle seemed at a loss for

words. He frowned, his fat face crumpling like a soggy cake.

"I am not yet sure, Cedric," he said. "I mussst think of a plan, and you shall help me. You and sssome others who will join usss. But ressst assured, Cedric, we shall find a way. Oh, yesss. We shall find a way! Now let usss leave thisss place—we have what we came for."

"And what about those two?" said Judge Cedric, inclining his head toward the pair of stone statues.

"Leave them, Cedric," said Griswold, beginning to scramble back down the rubble heap. "They have ssserved their purpossse. They are no ussse to usss now."

Judge Cedric sniffed and nodded. Then he took a couple of steps toward the statue that had once been his servant Harry. "Ssstupid, idle creature!" he sneered. He lifted one foot and kicked the statue hard. It teetered for a moment, then lost its balance and fell slowly sideways. It thudded against the statue that had once been Robert, and then the two stone figures fell together, down onto the jumbled bricks beneath them.

"Come along, Cedric!" called Griswold. He was down at the pavement level now, picking up his umbrella and folding his camp stool. "Come along! We have a plan to make!"

"A plan, yesss!" muttered Judge Cedric. His toes hurt a bit from kicking the stone statue, and he hobbled down the side of the rubble heap, retrieved his own umbrella and his own camp stool and then limped slowly after Griswold Gristle.

And the little black rain cloud, shaped like the figure eight, drifted along above them.

2

THE
ISLE OF SMILES

Measle Stubbs was having the time of his life.
It had all started the moment he'd come home.

Home to Merlin Manor.

It had taken Measle exactly three days, six hours and
seven and a half minutes to get used to living at Merlin
Manor. It's much easier to get used to things and places
and people if they're nice—and everything about
Merlin Manor was extremely nice indeed.

To Measle, who had spent most of his life living in a
really horrible house, with his really horrible Wrathmonk

guardian, Basil Tramplebone, Merlin Manor seemed to be nothing short of perfect. It was a big old house, way out in the countryside, made of warm red bricks. At the entrance to the estate was a pair of massive iron gates, then a long driveway made of crunchy gravel. A sweeping lawn in the front of the house. Tall trees at the back. Big stone urns, full of red, white and blue flowers, stood on either side of the front door. Inside the big old house, everything was just as good, with enormous, bright rooms full of soft, squashy furniture you could flop into, gleaming bathrooms with fluffy white towels and endless supplies of hot water, and a light and airy kitchen, out of which came the best food that Measle had ever eaten.

In fact, Merlin Manor was just about the most fabulous, comfortable and friendly house imaginable.

And it was Nanny Flannel who was partly responsible for making it so.

Nanny Flannel was small and old and round, with gray hair, pink cheeks and a pair of bright blue eyes that twinkled behind her wire-framed spectacles. She had helped look after Measle's father when he was a baby, and when he had grown up, she had simply stayed on at

Merlin Manor, cooking and cleaning and organizing everything. She had helped look after Measle, too, when he was a baby, so to have him and his parents—in fact, the whole Stubbs family—back again at Merlin Manor, after all this time, was just about the best thing that had ever happened to her.

So, what with Nanny Flannel fussing over him, and his father, Sam, and his mother, Lee, loving him so hard that sometimes Measle thought they all might burst from the strain of it, Measle couldn't have been happier.

"I say, Measle, isn't it about time you had a birthday?" said Sam, lowering the newspaper he was reading and peering at Measle over the top of it.

"Er," said Measle, who hadn't the faintest idea when his birthday was.

They were all sitting at the big pine table in the kitchen. Nanny Flannel was cooking sausages and bacon and eggs at the stove, and Lee was buttering a big pile of toast.

"Nonsense, Sam," said Nanny Flannel. "You know perfectly well when his birthday is. February the twelfth, and that's months away."

21

Ah, thought Measle, *February the twelfth. That's nice to know.*

"True, Nanny," said Sam thoughtfully. "But he's missed an awful lot of them. Let me see now . . . why, he's missed at least eight birthdays, hasn't he?"

"At least eight," said Lee, smiling happily at Measle. "And Tinker's probably missed a few as well."

At the sound of his name, Tinker, who was lying on the kitchen floor with his head resting on Measle's feet, wagged his stumpy tail. Like Measle, the little dog was having the time of his life, too. Oh, he'd been perfectly happy with his dear old lady—but life out here in the countryside, with the smelly kid to play with, was much better. (Prudence Peyser, the old wrathmonkologist, had given Tinker to Measle in gratitude for saving her life. Tinker was the best present Measle had ever been given.)

"I tell you what," said Lee, "why don't we have them all right away?"

"Have all what?" said Sam.

"All the birthdays, of course," said Lee, putting a big plate of buttered toast in front of Measle. "Over the next eight days, Measle and Tinker could have eight birthdays, couldn't they?"

"Terrific idea!" said Sam. "Eight days, eight birth-days. And, come to think of it, eight Christmas Days as well. They've missed them, too. We'll put them together and call them—um, let me see—yes, we'll call them their Birthmas Days. Oh, we *are* going to have fun." He turned to Nanny Flannel. "How about it, Nanny? All right with you?"

"Perfectly all right, Sam," she said. Nanny Flannel's eyes were twinkling behind her spectacles. "I'm all for a bit of fun. Eight Birthmas Days! That means eight Birthmas *cakes*! And a call to the butcher, too. Well, I *will* be busy, won't I?"

Over the next eight days, Measle and Tinker got a whole lot of birthmas presents. Tinker's presents were all bones—big beef bones, each one nearly as big as Tinker himself. (And, if Tinker was the best present that Measle had ever been given, then those big beef bones were the best presents that *Tinker* had ever been given). Tinker would chew each bone with passionate concentration for most of the day, until there wasn't a scrap of meat left on it. Then, in the evening, he would dig a hole under an ancient oak tree in the garden and carefully bury the bare bone among the tangled roots.

Measle's presents were the sorts of presents that a boy of his age might expect to get—a bicycle, a skate-board, a football, some new clothes—but he also got one very unusual gift indeed.

"Here you are, son," said Sam, handing Measle a small, oddly-shaped package, all done up in bright birthday wrapping paper, with a big blue bow on the top. "This used to be mine, a long time ago. I had a lot of fun with it when I was your age."

It was a strange little object, called a VoBo. It was shaped like a tiny trumpet and, like a trumpet, it seemed to be made of polished brass. But unlike a trumpet, which has three valves you can press, the VoBo had only one very small button set into its side. It also had a little, hinged sighting device—a ring of brass with a pair of crossed brass wires, one vertical, the other horizontal, set inside the ring. The device was fixed with a brass hinge on the top of the trumpet, and you could flip it up and down.

"Look," said Sam, "I'll show you how to work it. You hold the VoBo up to your mouth, press the button and then speak into it." Sam lifted the little trumpet to his mouth, pointed the sighting device at Lee and said, "Happy Birthmas Day, Measle," into the VoBo's tiny mouthpiece.

And, at exactly the same moment, Measle heard Lee say in her own voice, quite clearly, "Happy Birthmas Day, Measle."

The only thing was—she hadn't opened her mouth.

Sam grinned at Measle's look of astonishment. "The VoBo imitates voices. All you've got to do is point it at the person you want it to imitate, press the button and speak into the mouthpiece. The VoBo even makes the voice seem to come from their direction, too—and it's got quite a range on it as well. I used it on my math teacher once. I had her tell our whole class that we had the rest of the period off—so we all ran outside and played football on the playground."

"Don't give him evil ideas, Sam," said Lee, trying hard not to laugh. "I'm sure he'll think of some all on his own."

During each of the eight Birthmas days, the Stubbs family went on long car trips around the countryside to show Measle the interesting places nearby. Their car was—well—*different*. It was big and comfortable and

25

fast, but it didn't have the manufacturer's name on it anywhere and it didn't look like any other car on the road. It was long and low and sleek and painted a dark metallic green. The engine rumbled and roared like an angry lion and when Sam started it up, he didn't turn an ordinary, dull ignition key—he pressed a large red button in the middle of the dashboard. The big wheels had spokes like a bicycle, and the sides of the tires were painted bright red. The windows were tinted gray, so you could see out of them but it was hard for somebody on the outside to see in. But what Measle liked best about the car was the hood ornament: on the front of the hood, over the radiator grille, was mounted the skull of what (to Measle) looked like a giant lizard.

"It's a very small dragon," said Sam. "Actually a baby one."

"Oh, wow. Did you kill it?" said Measle. The idea that his father might have killed a dragon—even a baby one—was extremely cool.

"Oh, no," said Sam. "No, that's been dead thousands of years. There aren't any dragons around anymore. Pity, really. They must have been amazing creatures.

No, we were given that by the Wizards' Guild."

"Wow," said Measle. "That's so neat. They gave you a dragon's skull."

Lee laughed. "Actually, they gave us the *car*," she said. "The skull was already on it."

"The whole car. Wow."

"Yup," said Sam. "And what's really wow about it is that you never need to fill the gas tank. In fact, it doesn't even have one. The engine is—well, let's just say it's a bit different from the usual sort of engine. Apart from not needing any fuel, it's completely silent. The red button does two things—it starts it up and also makes the engine noise, so nobody gets suspicious, you see."

"Wow."

"And here's another wow about it. It's got a sort of autopilot. It remembers where it's been. So if I can't be bothered to drive, I just press the switch marked A/P, say the name of the place and it'll take me there. Of course, I have to sit in the driver's seat and *pretend* to drive, otherwise there could be all sorts of problems."

"Your dad refuses to use the autopilot, Measle," said Lee. "When it's turned on, the car behaves itself beautifully. It goes at *normal* speeds and obeys all the traffic rules."

"And where's the fun in that?" Sam laughed. "No, I like driving it myself. But it could be useful, I suppose, if you were really tired or something, and didn't *want* to drive."

"Wow. But *why* did the Wizards' Guild gave this car to you?" Measle asked.

Sam and Lee glanced at each other. Then Sam turned back to Measle and grinned.

"For services rendered."

Sam didn't explain what the services had been, and Measle had the sense not to ask. He'd been learning a lot about his mother and father, mostly from little snippets of information that they let drop now and then. Measle now knew that Sam and Lee Stubbs were Wrathmonk hunters, employed by the Wizards' Guild to ferret out Wrathmonks. What they *did* with the Wrathmonks when they found them, Measle didn't know. Once he'd asked his father, and Sam had winked and then changed the subject. One thing Measle *did* know—Sam and Lee Stubbs were the only ones around doing what they did.

On the last of Measle's and Tinker's Birthmas Days,

Nanny Flannel gave Tinker the biggest, juiciest bone he'd ever seen. Sam, Lee and Measle set off early in the morning for the Isle of Smiles.

"We've saved this until last," said Sam, weaving the big green car around a slow-moving truck. "Because it's the best. You're going to love the Isle of Smiles. It's by the sea—well, actually, it's sort of *in* the sea—and it's the biggest and the best amusement park in the country. It's got every ride you can imagine. There are carousels and water rides and haunted mansions and a Ferris wheel and spinning saucepans and bumper cars and a go-cart track and a whole lot of different sorts of roller coasters—"

"Those are the ones your dad likes best," said Lee.

"Well, of course," said Sam. "Everybody likes the roller coasters the best."

"Not me," said Lee. "They're too fast for me. Or at least they are when your dad's on them. I prefer the water rides myself."

"I bet I like them all," said Measle a little nervously. He'd never been on a thrill ride in his life, and he wasn't sure how he was going to handle the experience. He also wondered what Lee had meant when she said they

29

were too fast "when your dad's on them." He looked at his father. Sam was grinning, and Measle thought he looked as excited as a small boy.

Lee said, "This is your dad's favorite place in the whole world, Measle."

"And it'll be Measle's, too," said Sam. "I guarantee it."

They had been driving fast for some time along a motorway when Measle saw the sign—a billboard that read: ISLE OF SMILES—NEXT EXIT.

Sam swung the car into the slow lane and, a few minutes later, they left the highway and took a narrow road that led through thick pine woods. The trees grew dense on either side of them and cast a gloomy shadow over the road. But then Measle saw a bit of light ahead, which grew wider and wider as they came out of the pine forest. The great, gleaming green car roared out of the shadows, out into the blazing sun, and there, a little to the right and far below, between a dip in the distant hills, lay the sea.

They drove down a long winding road, descending steadily toward the ocean. There were a lot of cars on the road now, and Sam had to slow down and take his place in the line. Suddenly he lifted one hand from the steering wheel and pointed ahead. "See? There it is."

Measle saw a bay, with a little town and a harbor full of fishing boats. Starting by the harbor and extending right out to the middle of the bay was a broad causeway made of piled-up rocks. There was a wide, multilaned road on top of the causeway, and lines of cars inched their way along it toward their goal—a big, almost circular, rocky island set right in the very center of the wide bay.

"That's it," said Sam. "The Isle of Smiles."

Measle caught sight of the distant Ferris wheel and the loops and curves of a roller coaster, and he began to feel a growing excitement. Today was going to be *fun*.

And it was. The island was full of visitors and the park was crowded, but somehow Sam managed to lead them to rides where (at that precise moment) the lines were very short. So they never waited more than a few minutes, which seemed to Measle just a little bit— well, *magical*. And (with Sam Stubbs being his father), of course, it was.

They went on every ride at least twice and, on one or two of the more thrilling ones, three times. They rode all the water rides—the Crashing Rapids, the Log

Flume, the Giant Splash—and got very wet. They rode the tall Ferris wheel. They ate popcorn and hamburgers. They went on the Ghoulish Grange ride and laughed at the wailing ghosts and the clanking skeletons. They rode the Spinning Saucepans, which made Measle feel a bit sick. They took a turn on the old-fashioned carousel, riding the garishly painted, carved wooden horses. They tore around the go-cart track, and Measle won all three races. They shot air guns at paper targets, and Lee won a big, squashy, pink-furred hippopotamus.

And then they went on the roller coasters.

There was the Thunderer, a traditional wooden ride, which shook their stomachs and rattled their bones; then the Screaming Eagle, with tight loops and vicious curves that made them dizzy; the Golden Nugget ride, which plunged them into the darkness of a mineshaft and then out again into the bright sunlight; the Dinosaur Diver, which featured a life-size, animated model of a Tyrannosaurus rex that roared and lunged and snapped its massive jaws as the riders rattled by; and finally, the Big Daddy of them all, the Juggernaut.

The Juggernaut was a steel roller coaster, painted bright red. It rose to dizzying heights, dove to unspeakable depths, whistled around gut-churning curves and somersaulted and corkscrewed its riders so often that, by the end of the ride, they didn't know up from down or right from left. At the end of it, Measle felt like a piece of beef that had been through a grinder. His eyes didn't seem to be working properly, his spine was acting like a length of wet string and his legs appeared to be made of jelly. He loved it.

"Want to go again?" said Sam, cheerfully.

"Oh, sure," said Measle.

"Not me," said Lee, flopping down onto a bench. "I know when I've had enough. And besides, I don't trust you, Sam Stubbs. My pink hippo and I shall wait here for you two lunatics."

Sam and Measle managed to get themselves into the front seat of the leading car. As it clanked its way up the long incline, Sam said, "It was a bit slow last time, don't you think, Measle?"

"We-e-ell," said Measle, quite unable to imagine that anything could be faster than the Juggernaut—except perhaps light itself. "We-e-ell, maybe it was a bit slow."

"I thought it was *very* slow," said Sam, a small, wicked grin turning up the corners of his mouth. "We ought to do something about that, don't you think?" Then, before Measle could reply—and very quietly so that Measle almost didn't hear it—he muttered, "*Velocitum increasabile fractotum con seguridus.*"

The clanking sound of the chain-lifting mechanism underneath the cars had been going a steady *clank— clatter—clank—clatter.* Now, all of a sudden, it went *clankclatterclankclatterclankclatter*—and Measle felt a slight pressure on his back as the car began to speed up. "Er, Dad, we're going faster," he said a little nervously.

"So we are," said Sam. "Isn't that fun?"

"Er, yeah. Great fun. What did you say back there?"

"Oh, it's a little go-faster spell, that's all."

Measle swallowed hard. "Go faster?"

"Yup," said Sam airily. "And, if you think this is fast, wait 'til we get over the top."

"Er," said Measle.

Sam grinned down at him. "It's all right, Measle," he said. "We'll survive. I added a safety clause."

"Oh, good," said Measle. "I'm glad you added a safety clause."

They clanked their way rapidly toward the top of the long rise. Measle glanced behind him, taking quick

34

looks at the other passengers. They all seemed unaware of the increased speed of the car and were smiling and chattering among themselves.

Measle felt Sam nudge him in the ribs. "Don't look back, Measle, look *forward*. This is the fun part."

They had reached the top. For a moment it seemed to Measle that everything was going to be the same. Their car topped the rise and began to descend slowly on the other side, just as it had before, held back by the remaining cars in the rear, which were still on their way up the steep slope behind. But then the last car in the line reached the top and gravity took over—gravity, with a little bit of help from Sam's go-faster spell.

The car lunged forward. The wheels screamed. The wind tore at their hair. Their eyes watered with the blast of air that hit them. They howled down the first, impossibly steep precipice at terrifying speed, then ripped back up the short slope opposite, then screamed over the top (and Measle felt his bottom leave the seat by several inches, and he gripped hard onto the safety bar that held him down). Next to him Sam was yelling and laughing and waving his hands over his head. Then came the first loop, and Measle felt his body slam back into his seat as the centrifugal forces took over—then a rattling curve to the right—another to the left—then a sudden dive into the bowels of the ride and then up again into the blazing sunlight—and all this at such a dizzying speed that Measle wondered how the wheels could possibly keep their hold on the track. Sam seemed to read his thoughts, because he suddenly bellowed into Measle's ear, "Don't worry, Measle! There's that safety clause!" While that did manage to make Measle feel that perhaps they weren't actually going to die (at least, not immediately), it didn't stop his stomach from leaping about inside his body as if it was trying to escape through his rib cage. It only began to settle down into its proper position when they slowed down as the ride ended back at the station.

"Now that's what I call a *ride*," said Sam as the safety bar was raised and they climbed out of their seats. They both looked at the other passengers who were also emerging from the cars behind them. Most of them looked pale and a little startled, and one or two had faces the color of lettuce leaves.

When they rejoined Lee, she got up from the park bench where she'd been sitting and touched Sam lightly on his hand. Then she looked into Sam's face and said, so quietly that Measle almost missed it, "Sam Stubbs, you're a wicked little Wizard."

Sam laughed and gave her a quick kiss on her lips. "I know I am," he said, smiling happily down at her. "But it was a lot of fun."

Lee shook her head and tried hard to look disapproving. "If I wasn't here to recharge you—"

"But you are," said Sam. "You *always* are."

"Yes, but what if I'm *not?*" said Lee. Then, before Sam could reply, she turned and peered closely at Measle.

"I bet you feel sick," she said.

"No, not really," said Measle, although he did a bit. The thing was, he felt more *puzzled* than sick. What had that conversation between his mum and dad been all about?

They did every ride all over again, and when they boarded the Crashing Rapids water ride for the third time that day, for a joke, Sam thickened the water to the consistency of molasses, which meant that their raft floated v-e-r-y s-l-o-w-l-y down the stream and they didn't get wet at all.

"Very funny, dear," said Lee.

3

THE
SOMETHING

They had a wonderful time.

But had they known what was following them, they might have felt rather differently.

The *thing* (whatever it was) had started to shadow them since Sam and Measle emerged from the Juggernaut's exit. From then on it followed close behind, riding with them wherever they went. And none of the three Stubbses noticed.

It certainly wasn't human, because no human could do what this creature could do. The reason that Sam,

Lee and Measle failed to notice the creature was because it changed its appearance every few minutes. One moment it was an ordinary-looking middle-aged man in a blue tracksuit and a baseball cap. Then, in the blink of an eye, the creature became a ten-year-old girl with a freckled face and pigtails, then a fat woman in a cotton dress, carrying an ice-cream cone, then an eighteen-year-old boy with long hair and a spotty face and on and on, through a whole range of human disguises, each one being as ordinary and unremarkable as the last. The thing sat close behind them on every ride they took, and it stared at the backs of their heads with a strange, unsettling intensity in its deep, black eyes. Those eyes were disturbing things. There was no color to them, only the deep, black emptiness of outer space. The thing's eyes were the only feature that it retained each time it changed its appearance, and it was careful to hide them behind a succession of different sunglasses. Since it was a sunny day, at least half the visitors to the Isle of Smiles were wearing sunglasses, too. It was hardly surprising that the Stubbs family never noticed that they were being watched so intently.

And, for the rest of that wonderful day, wherever

they went and whatever they did—the *something* was never far behind them.

Then, that evening, when all three Stubbs family members were dog tired and ready to go home, the *something* made its move.

There was quite a crowd around the exit turnstile, and everybody was squashed together as they slowly filtered through the revolving gate. Sam was in the front, with Measle close behind him. Lee brought up the rear.

Behind Lee, and separated from her by a young mother clutching a sleeping toddler, was a thin woman with a pinched, sallow face. A pair of sunglasses, with rhinestones glittering on the frame, covered her eyes. As the Stubbs family inched forward, with the rest of the crowd pressed around them, the thin woman slowly extended her hand, past the mother with the toddler and on toward Lee's slim back.

"You'd think," muttered Sam over his shoulder, "that they'd have a few more exits working. This really is a bit of a squish—"

Then suddenly, behind him, Measle heard his mother gasp, as if somebody had trodden hard on her toes. Then he heard her voice, urgent in his ear.

"Push through, Measle! We've got to get out of here!"

Sam looked back. "What's the matter?"

"I don't know," whispered Lee, over Measle's head. "Something touched me—and now I'm—I'm—well, here—feel."

Lee extended her hand. Sam took it and a look of shock passed across his face.

"You're—you're *freezing*!" he hissed.

"I *know*, Sam. We've got to go now!"

Sam nodded. Measle saw that his face was looking a little pale.

"Come on," muttered Sam. He turned his body sideways and put his shoulder between two people who were in front of him and then pushed firmly through them.

"Excuse me, " he said, loudly. "Sorry—can you let us through? My wife's not feeling well—that's it, son, help your mother—thank you—thanks—"

The crowd parted obediently in front of him and the Stubbs family went quickly through the turnstile and out into the parking lot. Sam hurried them to the car, and they all got in quickly and locked the doors.

"What happened?" said Measle. "What's the matter?" His mother looked fine to him. She wasn't smiling like she usually did and there was a look of anxiety in her green eyes, but otherwise she seemed all right.

"Something touched me," she said, her voice a little shaky. "I think it was trying to take my mana."

"Your what?" said Measle.

"My mana," said Lee.

"It's what fuels magic, Measle," said Sam. He was holding Lee's hand and looking at her like a concerned doctor might look at his ill patient. "That's what separates us Wizards from the rest of humanity—the mana. Wizards have it stored inside them, and they use it up when they invoke magic. A big spell can use it all up instantly. It comes back slowly. After a major invocation, most Wizards have it back again after about twenty-four hours. Think of it as a sort of self-recharging battery, if you like."

"You mean Mum's a Wizard, too?" said Measle, looking at Lee with new respect.

Lee shook her head. "No, I'm not, Measle. I can't do any magic at all—and I don't want to, either."

"She's better than a Wizard," said Sam proudly. "She's much rarer than that. She's a Manafount."

"A what?" said Measle.

"A Manafount. There are only three others in the world—one in China, one in Australia and a third in Bolivia. They're all very old. Your mum's the only young one."

"But, what *is* a Mana—what you said?"

"A Manafount. Literally, a 'fountain of Mana.' Your mum has a constant supply of mana, which never runs out. Manafounts can't invoke magic themselves, but they can pass their mana on to somebody who can. But not just to anybody. They have to be married, you see. A husband Manafount can pass to his Wizard wife, or a wife Manafount can pass to her husband Wizard. That's us, of course. That's what she did when we came off the Juggernaut ride. She touched my hand and recharged me."

"I knew he'd done a spell, Measle," said Lee. "I could feel he'd used up all his mana, so I just put it back."

Sam gazed admiringly at Lee. "Let me tell you, Measle," he said proudly, "every Wizard and Warlock in the world wanted to marry your mum. Luckily, she chose me, which was very nice of her, since I'm a pretty minor Wizard. Of course, I was by far and away the best-looking one."

Lee leaned over and kissed Sam on the cheek.

"No, Sam darling, " she said with a smile, "you *weren't* the best-looking one. Justin Bucket was."

"Justin Bucket?" yelped Sam. "Justin Bucket was a total nerd! A geek! A dweeb! A dork!"

"Yes, Sam, darling," said Lee, stifling her laughter. "Justin Bucket was all those things. But he looked like a film star. He was easily the handsomest Wizard in the Guild. He was also the most *boring*. Not like you. You weren't boring at all. Of all the Wizards in the Guild, you were by far the most interesting. And you were certainly the *funniest*." Lee turned to Measle and said, "Your dad made me laugh, Measle—and I like laughing."

"You do, don't you?" said Sam happily. Then he turned back to Measle. "Anyway, a Wizard who is lucky enough to have a Manafount on his side can continue to perform spells without stopping, but there has to be an unbroken contact between them all the time he is doing the magic. That's why we work together, your mum and I. As I said, I'm not a particularly powerful

44

Wizard, Measle, but hand in hand with your mum, I can keep up a constant stream of small spells, while my enemy can only perform one big one at a time."

Sam broke off. He looked hard at Lee's small hand, buried in his big one.

"You're getting a bit warmer," he said.

Lee nodded. "Slowly, though."

"Thank goodness for that. What do you think happened?"

"Somebody—or some*thing*—touched me. I felt a finger tap me very gently on my back, and then—"

"How did it feel?"

"Very cold, very empty—like I had nothing inside me but icy air. Everything except my mana just sort of left me. All my emotions, all my feelings. We've been here all day, and I was getting a little tired and a little hungry, too—and then, when I was touched, even my hunger and my tiredness disappeared! How could that happen, Sam?"

"I don't know," said Sam, "but there's obviously something here—and I don't think we should stay to find out what it is." He stabbed his forefinger at the red button on the car's dashboard, and the engine rumbled

45

to life. He turned and glanced at Measle. "First rule of wizardry, Measle, if you don't understand what's going on, don't try to be brave. Run for the hills!"

Sam stamped hard on the accelerator pedal. The engine roared. The big car's rear wheels spun for a moment on the smooth asphalt of the parking lot. Then the rubber gripped the surface and the car leaped forward.

"Hold onto your hats!" yelled Sam, gripping the big steering wheel so hard that his knuckles turned white. "We're going to be breaking a few speed limits!"

"So what else is new?" said Lee.

Sam laughed. "Of all the rides we've been on today," he shouted over the roar of the engine and the squealing of the tires, "this one could be the most exciting!"

Sam spent the next few days locked in his study, head bent over his dusty old books. He also spent a lot of time on the telephone, talking to senior members of the Wizards' Guild. When at last he emerged, he looked tired and worried.

"Family conference," he announced. "Everybody into the kitchen."

Lee, Measle and Nanny Flannel sat down at the big pine table. Tinker lay down at Measle's feet, his ears pricked forward, so that it looked like he was listening. Sam sat at the head of the table, looking very serious.

"Did you find out anything?" said Lee.

"Not much, no. But, according to the Guild, the Isle of Smiles is something of a mana well."

"A mana well?" said Nanny Flannel. "And what, pray, is a mana well?"

"It's a rare, natural source of the stuff, Nanny," said Sam. "According to the Guild, the whole island is quite rich in mana. I must say, I wasn't aware of it myself, but the Guild has apparently known about it for years. They didn't know there was a magical entity actually living there, though. They think that whatever it is, this entity feeds on the mana, which means it probably can't leave the area, not without losing most of its powers. Whatever *they* may be. Meanwhile, until they've done a lot more research in the archives, nobody from the Guild is to go near the place—which means no more trips to the Isle of Smiles. Not that it makes much difference—they close the place next week, for the whole winter. Perhaps they'll have cleared up the

47

mystery by the time it opens again in the spring."

Later that same evening, they were watching the news on the television. At the end of the news came the weather forecast. It had been a hot day, and the whole screen was covered with little pictures of the sun.

"A glorious day all over the country," said the weatherman. "Record-breaking temperatures here—and here—a real Indian summer. Not a drop of rain anywhere—apart from one rather unfortunate little spot, right here on Borgrove Moor, where it's actually pouring rain right now. It only started a few minutes ago, but it's really bucketing down. A rather odd meteorological phenomenon, actually. A very small, localized low-pressure system that seems to have come out of nowhere and doesn't appear to be going anywhere, either. Very interesting and quite rare. Anyway, it's a forecast of what's to come, I'm afraid this lovely weather won't last, and by tomorrow afternoon wintry weather will be with us all over the country, with lots of wind and rain everywhere, just like what poor old Borgrove Moor is suffering at this very moment—"

Sam pressed the mute button on the television remote and the sound died. He turned to Lee and said,

"What do you think?"

"Well Wrathmonks, obviously," said Lee. "Must be rather a lot of them, too, for them to show up on the meteorological radar like that."

Measle felt a sudden chill. He remembered the rain cloud that had always been above Basil Tramplebone's house. On his own, Basil had been bad enough—but a whole bunch of Wrathmonks, all together in one place?

"What are they doing?" he said nervously.

Sam shook his head. "No idea, son. Nothing good, that's for sure. I'd better notify the Guild."

Sam got up and went to his study to telephone his superiors. Lee and Measle and Nanny Flannel were watching a game show when he came back.

"We're to sit tight," he said. "At least for the time being. They're keeping an eye on the place."

4

THE
CAVE

The air inside the cave was damp and cold. It was the kind of cold that slowly seeps into your body, chilling your toes and fingers first and then creeping gradually through your whole frame, numbing you until you can't even shiver anymore. It was dark in the cave, too; the only light came from a few guttering candles stuck in crevices in the rock walls.

Griswold Gristle sat uncomfortably on a narrow piece of rock that stuck out from the cave wall. The projecting rock was just high enough from the floor of the cave to give Griswold a small height advantage over Judge Cedric Hardscrabble, who stood next to him. This gave Griswold the look of a small, pale, fat king, sitting on his throne, with his trusty court chamberlain at his side.

In front of Griswold and Judge Cedric stood five figures of various shapes and sizes and ages. All were dressed in black, all had white faces and staring, fishy eyes—and all of them looked cold, uncomfortable and not a little irritable.

"But what I don't undersssstand, Griswold," said one of them, in a scratchy, self-important voice (he was a tubby man with a thin hank of long, greasy hair combed over his scalp in a futile effort to hide his baldness) "what I don't undersssstand, is who put *you* in charge? I don't remember usss holding any elections. Sssso who put you in charge?"

There was a murmur of agreement among the others. Griswold sighed. What was it about Wrathmonks that made them so quarrelsome? Why could they never agree about anything? *If only,* he thought, *we could all get along with each other—why, Wrathmonks could probably rule the world!*

"The reason I am ssspeaking for all of usss, my dear

Mr. Flabbit, is because it was I who called usss all together here on Borgrove Moor. It was I who found the thing—"

"I found it, too," said Judge Cedric, shooting a hurt look at Griswold.

"Indeed you did, Cedric," said Griswold in a soothing voice. "Cedric and I found it together. Found it in the ruins of the very houssse recently inhabited by our dear friend, the late and much-lamented Basil Tramplebone—"

"Get a blinking move on, Gristle," growled a deep, rumbling voice. All eyes turned to the back of the group, where an enormous figure stood. His hulking shadow wavered huge against the rock walls of the cave. His arms hung by his sides, and the tips of his black-gloved fingers (fingers as thick as bananas!) reached to a point half a yard below his knees. Everything about him—from his black hobnailed boots, to his bulky black leather jacket and on up to the shiny black motorcycle helmet on his bullet-shaped head—was oversized. Behind the helmet's visor, his eyes were dark and deep under his heavy brows, and his mouth was a wide slit in his flat white face.

"Ah," said Griswold, with a hint of nervousness in his voice. "Mr. Cudgel, my dear fellow——"

"Don't 'dear fellow' me," growled Cudgel. "It'sss cold in here, Gristle. It'sss cold and damp and dark and I don't care for it. The sssooner I'm out of here, the happier I shall be. Ssso jussst get on with it."

"I sssecond that," said Mr. Flabbit, nodding his head so violently that his long hank of greasy hair came unstuck from his scalp and flapped loose around his coat collar. "Ssstop patting yoursssself on the back, Griswold, and tell usss what you have in mind. And do it quickly——our merged rain clouds are sure to be noticed sssooner or later, and I don't want the Wizards' Guild knowing where I am, thank you very much."

Griswold ground his teeth with annoyance. He cleared his throat and started again.

"Fellow Wrathmonksss, we are gathered here to dissscusss a plan which will lead to the ultimate dessstruction of the evil Ssstubbs family——"

There was an immediate reaction. The Wrathmonks twitched and shook with rage, muttering and snarling like a pack of angry dogs: *"Ssstubbses! We hate the Ssstubbses!——"*

"They got my friend Hogsbottle!"

"They're Guild's pets!"

"Think they're better than usss!"

"Dangerousss, that's what they are!"

"Filthy, horrible beassstsss!"

"We'll get them!"

"Friends, friends!" shouted Griswold over the noise. "Lissten to me! That is why we are *here*! To devise a plot to rid oursssselves of these foul creatures! That is why Judge Cedric and I sssought the *thing*! For with the *thing* in our possession, we have a powerful tool which will aid usss in sssubduing the Ssstubbses! Basil himself sssubdued the Ssstubbses for eight years, using thisss very object that I hold in my hands!"

Griswold held out his two pudgy little hands, and the Wrathmonks shuffled forward to look. A small cloth bag lay on Griswold's sweaty palms.

"What's in there, then?" said a skinny young Wrathmonk, with long, wispy yellow hair and a scruffy, straggly, blond beard.

"A great treasure, young Draggle," said Griswold proudly. "It once adorned the head of Medusssa, a Gorgon. It is the mummified head of one of Medusssa's sssnakes."

"Yeah? But how do we know that'sss what it is?" said Draggle. "I mean to sssay, that could be anything in there, couldn't it? Like a pebble or something. Let'sss have a look at it."

Griswold hissed in disgust. *Really, what a sorry collection these Wrathmonks were! They had the brains of a herd of goats!*

"We cannot look at it, dear friends," he said with all the patience he could muster. "If we do, we shall be turned inssstantly to ssstone. That is what the Medusssa head does, you sssee. Merely retrieving the thing from the ruins of dear Basil's house brought Cedric and me to the brink of peril. However, if used properly, it is a fearsssome weapon againsssst our enemies. It is the firssst of many other weapons we shall use againsssst the hateful Ssstubbses."

"What sssort of other weapons?" asked a hard-faced, skinny woman in a long black dress. Her shiny black hair was scraped back from her long, thin face and tied in a tight little bun at the back of her head. Her nose was long and sharp and stuck out of the front of her face like the blade of a knife. Her mouth was caked thick with scarlet lipstick, and she had painted a pair of high, arched, jet black eyebrows on her white forehead.

"Excellent quessstion, Mrs. Zagreb," said Griswold, bowing slightly in the woman's direction. "We shall use the Medusssa head, of courssse, and also all our variousss individual powers, in particular our exhalation enchantments."

"He means our *breathing* magic, dear," said a short, dark man, standing by Mrs. Zagreb's side. The man had beady black eyes, thick, wavy black hair and a small, carefully clipped black moustache. His black suit was pressed and shiny, and he had several big gold rings on his fingers. He looked like a black beetle.

"I know what 'exhalation enchantment' means, Zag," said the woman, sharply. "Do you think I'm a fool?"

"Of courssse I don't, my dear," said Mr. Zagreb hurriedly. "On the contrary, you have a brilliant mind."

"I mossst certainly do," said Mrs. Zagreb, her scarlet lips drawing back from her teeth in a snarl of contempt. "A lot more brilliant than yours, that'sss for sure!"

Mr. Zagreb nodded nervously and decided to change the subject. "Our exhalation enchantment will come in very usssseful, I predict." He turned proudly to the other Wrathmonks. "Our breath is highly corrossive. Particularly my lady wife'sss. It can ssstrip paint from walls. It can remove varnish from furniture. We find it mossst ussseful when trying to dissslodge those annoying little price ssstickers you find on merchandise these days. One tiny puff from Mrs. Zagreb's lovely lipsss, and the thing almossst removes itssself!"

Griswold looked impressed. "*Mossst* ussseful, I'm sure," he said. "We shall certainly find a place for sssuch a talent—in my plan. For I have a plan, dear friends— and it'sss a fine plan. A wonderful, *wonderful* plan. My plan is to—"

And that was as far as he got before the other Wrathmonks started to interrupt him.

"I think we should get a really big mincing machine and grind them all up into hamburger meat!" shouted Draggle.

"Nonsssense, young Draggle!" snapped Flabbit. "Far too complicated. I propose we capture the Ssstubbs family, then buy a sssmall ship, sssail far out to sssea and then sssink it with them ssstill on board!"

"Don't be ssstupid, Flabbit!" roared Cudgel. "We'd all drown, too. And where are we going to get a ship?

No, but I sssuggessst we drop them from a helicopter ssstraight down into an active volcano—"

"I don't much care for flying!" squeaked Mr. Zagreb. "Nor does my lady wife. Here's an idea: we could get really big feathers and tickle them to death—"

"Don't talk rubbish, Zag!" barked Mrs. Zagreb. "Tickle them indeed! They might like it! No, we should put them in a cardboard box, full of ssscorpions—"

"We could make them eat coat hangers!" shrieked Judge Cedric Hardscrabble, who had been desperately trying to think of some horrible calamity for the Stubbses to experience and now said the first thing that came into his head.

Griswold was flapping his hands in frustration. "Friends, friends—I beg you—please be patient and lisssten to my plan—my wonderful, wonderful plan—"

BE QUIET.

The babble of the Wrathmonks stopped. All their movements stopped as well—their pacing feet, their flailing hands, their shaking heads—as if they had been somehow frozen in their tracks.

It wasn't a voice—or at least, not a voice that any of them heard with their ears. It was a sound *inside their heads*, a sound that had simply arrived in there without going through their ears at all. An icy sound, cold and hard and dark, like frozen blood. They all heard it in their heads at the same moment, and all of them felt a sudden, overwhelming impulse to stop their chattering and wait for further instructions.

The further instructions came almost at once.

REMAIN QUIET. REMAIN STILL. I AM COMING.

The Wrathmonks stood like stone statues, not moving a muscle.

There was a shimmering in the shadows, a movement of air and light—and then an extraordinary little figure drifted out of the gloom at the back of the cave.

It was a garden gnome. A perfectly ordinary little garden gnome, obviously made of painted concrete, with a tall, painted-on crimson hat and a little painted-on green jacket and a pair of painted-on shiny black boots with the tops turned over. The gnome's face was painted, too, with jolly red cheeks and a jolly red nose and a pair of sly little eyes with wrinkles at the corners. A clay pipe stuck out of the gnome's long white beard, which surrounded the little grinning mouth. The gnome floated a few inches off the rocky floor of the cave, drifting steadily toward the group of motionless Wrathmonks. When it arrived in their midst, it hovered for a moment, turning slowly in the cold, damp air, and then it settled with a small thump onto the rocky floor.

For several moments there was a stunned silence. Then Griswold Gristle found his voice.

"What is thisss? Is thiss sssome sssort of joke?"

NO JOKE.

Griswold's piggy little eyes blinked in astonishment. The gnome's mouth hadn't moved—well, how could it? It was made of concrete!—but Griswold had heard the words quite clearly, or rather, he hadn't heard them at all, they had simply appeared inside his head, clear as anything. . . .

"Who—who are you? *What* are you?"

I AM THAT WHICH YOU SHOULD FEAR THE MOST.

Griswold glared at the gnome. It didn't look particularly dangerous. In fact, it looked rather ridiculous, standing there with its fixed, concrete grin and its silly little clay pipe.

"I think," said Griswold, slowly, hopping off his rock ledge, "that it should be the other way around. I think *you* should fear *usss*."

There was a murmur of agreement from the other Wrathmonks, and they stared at the gnome with angry eyes.

"In fact," continued Griswold, his voice strengthening, "I think it would be bessst if you left immediately. Thisss is a private meeting. The guessst lissst contains the following names," Griswold said, pulling a folded sheet of paper from the inside pocket of his black jacket. He opened it and began to read in a pompous, official sort of voice. "Mr. Frognell Flabbit, Mr. Ssscab Draggle, Mr. Buford Cudgel, Mr. and Mrs. Zagreb, myssself as chairman of course, and Judge Cedric Hardssscrabble as vice chairman. But you—whoever you are—*you* are not here on my lissst. Therefore, whoever or whatever you are, you are not welcome and I sssuggessst you leave at once."

The gnome simply stood there, unmoving and silent.

Griswold began to feel a little foolish—he was talking to a concrete gnome, of all things!

"Very well," said Griswold, "I have given you fair warning. Gentlemen—lady—kindly deal with thisss intruder."

It was young Scab Draggle who made the first move.

He stepped forward and hissed, "*Zzzssychhherpsy herpsy globbershmuck!*" At the same moment, a pair of purple beams of light flew from his eyes and smacked the gnome clean in the middle of its forehead.

Nothing happened.

Draggle frowned. That was his best spell—his blow-up-like-a-balloon spell! The gnome's body was supposed to swell up, getting bigger and bigger and rounder and rounder and then, like an overfilled beach ball, burst with an enormous bang! But it hadn't worked! Now he was drained of his mana—at least until tomorrow. All he had left was his exhalation enchantment. He stepped quickly over to the gnome, bent over the short figure, took a deep breath and began to blow his stinking breath.

It seemed to last forever, this endless breathing out, and the only indication of any effort on Draggle's part was that after thirty seconds his eyes began to bulge a little with the exertion. After forty seconds there was still no change in the gnome's appearance.

"What is Draggle's exhalation enchantment sssupposed to do, actually?" whispered Mr. Zagreb into Frognell Flabbit's ear.

"Sssupposed to make all the hair fall out," muttered Flabbit, smoothing his greasy comb over into place.

"It doesn't ssseem to be working, does it?" said Mr. Zagreb under his breath.

"Well, it wouldn't," said Flabbit. "That'sss not real hair. Unlike yours and mine, Zag, old man." He broke off, stepped forward and touched Draggle's arm. "Here, that'sss not going to work, young Draggle. Let me have a go. Watch its nossse fall off!"

Draggle stepped aside. Flabbit took his place, glared at the gnome and said, *"Haarrrcky schnaarrrcky oichenblast!"*

A sizzling yellow flame splashed across the gnome's face, then blew out, leaving the gnome untouched.

"All right," said Flabbit, sounding a little disappointed. "That was my nose-falling-off enchantment and it doesn't ssseem to work. But look at *my* exhalation. In a couple of ssseconds, it'sss going to have the worssst toothache of itsss life!"

Flabbit bent over the gnome and began to breathe on its head. After a solid minute of blowing out without taking in any air at all, Flabbit was completely deflated and the gnome appeared to be perfectly fine, without any trace of a terrible toothache at all.

"Yeah well," said Flabbit, breathlessly. "It probably hasn't got any teeth, either."

One by one, the Wrathmonks tried their major spells and then, with their mana exhausted, they tried their exhalation enchantments. The only one that made any difference at all to the gnome's appearance was when Mr. and Mrs. Zagreb were breathing together into its face—after half a minute, a few square inches of paint on its crimson hat blackened and peeled away. Other than that, the gnome appeared quite unchanged. It stood there, grinning its sly little concrete smile, appearing to be rather enjoying the Wrathmonks' humiliation.

Then—

THANK YOU. I AM GRATEFUL FOR THE SMALL GIFTS OF YOUR MANA.

"Who—who—who are you?" stammered Griswold.

I? I AM—THE LAST.

"The lassst what?"

THE LAST—OF THE DRAGODONS.

They all heard it in their heads, and they all turned and stared at one another, puzzled frowns creasing their foreheads.

"Dragodon?" said Draggle.

"Dragodon?" repeated Mr. Zagreb. "Now where have I heard that word before?"

"Don't be a fool, Zag!" snapped Mrs. Zagreb. "*I've* never heard of it, ssso you *certainly* have never heard of it—and don't pretend you have!"

"Dragodon," muttered Flabbit, rolling the word around on his tongue. "No, doesn't ring a bell."

"It's a sssort of motorcar, isn't it?" said Judge Cedric.

Griswold Gristle shook his head impatiently.

"Ssso ignorant, all of you," he sneered. "The ssstory of the Dragodons is an ancient legend and, if any of you had ever bothered to visit the library of the Wizards' Guild and read the hissstory of our race, you would mossst certainly be aware of it. In the Golden Olden Days, the Dragodons were the keepers of the dragons. They possessed great powers, which they used to control the monsssters. It was sssaid that they could ssspeak to them, communicating directly with the creatures' primitive brains. The Dragodons were thusss sssupremely important and powerful Wizards, and no kingdom could exissst without employing the sssservices of one of them. Then, according to the legend, these Dragodons became arrogant and began to think they should have more power than even the kings they ssserved. They banded together and went to war, riding their dragons againssst the world of men. There were great battles and much dessstruction and losss of life. But then, ssslowly and with the help of the Wizards and the Warlocks and even sssome of the Wrathmonks, Mankind managed to turn the tide of battle againssst the Dragodons. One by one they were dessstroyed, along with their dragons, until there was not one left alive."

There was a long silence. Then Cudgel said, "I don't believe a word of it."

"Of *courssse* you don't, my dear Cudgel," said Griswold, smiling kindly at the huge Wrathmonk. "Nor do *any* of usss. It's jussst a ssstory. A legend. No truth to it whatsssoever."

IT IS THE TRUTH.

They all turned and looked at the garden gnome. Griswold opened his mouth to speak but the gnome got there before him.

LISTEN AND LEARN, LITTLE WRATHMONKS. THE STORY IS NOT A LEGEND. IT IS HISTORY. THERE WAS A GREAT WAR. THERE WERE MANY TERRIBLE BATTLES. AT FIRST

WE AND OUR DRAGONS WERE VICTORIOUS. THEN, LATER, THROUGH THE TREACHERY OF THE WIZARDS, WE BEGAN TO LOSE THE STRUGGLE. ONE BY ONE, WE FELL. OUR DRAGONS, OURSELVES. ONE BY ONE. EVEN MY OWN GREAT ARCTURION WAS FINALLY BROUGHT DOWN TO EARTH. HE FELL—AND I FELL WITH HIM, FOR I WAS ASTRIDE HIS GREAT NECK. TOGETHER, WE PLUNGED TO THE GROUND. THE FALL FROM THE SKY WAS LONG, AND THE ROCKS ON THE GROUND WERE HARD.

The words died away in the Wrathmonks' heads, leaving behind a slight aching feeling. Then—

BUT I SURVIVED THAT LONG, LONG FALL. I AM THE LAST. THE LAST OF THE DRAGODONS.

"A Dragodon?" sneered Griswold. "You? I hardly think—"

I KNOW. YOU RARELY DO, GRISWOLD.

"How do you know my name?" gasped Griswold.

I KNOW ALL YOUR NAMES. I KNOW EVERYTHING ABOUT ALL OF YOU. I CAN CRAWL INSIDE YOUR HEADS AND DIG OUT YOUR SECRETS. YOU CAN HIDE NOTHING FROM ME. I AM YOUR MASTER, AND YOU WILL OBEY ME.

"We mossst certainly will not!" spluttered Griswold. "The very idea! Expecting usss to obey sssome minor magical entity in temporary possession of a concrete garden gnome! Ridiculousss! Quite ridiculousss! And as for your claim to be the lassst of the Dragodons—well, I don't believe they ever exisssted!"

BE CAREFUL, LITTLE WRATHMONK.

Griswold drew himself up to his full height and looked down his nose at the garden gnome. "Huh!" he snorted. "If you're the lassst of the Dragodons, why don't you ssstop hiding in a sssilly little garden gnome and show usss what you *really* look like?"

DEAR LITTLE WRATHMONK. YOU TALK TOO MUCH. I WILL NOT SHOW YOU WHAT I LOOK LIKE—BUT I WILL SHOW YOU WHAT I CAN DO. I WILL SHOW ALL OF YOU WHAT I CAN DO.

A moment of stillness passed, then a tiny spark of green fire flashed from the bowl of the gnome's clay pipe. The spark darted across the cold, damp air of the cave and onto one corner of Griswold's thick lips. Then, like the needle of a sewing machine, it zipped rapidly up and down, moving steadily from one corner of Griswold's mouth toward the other corner. As it passed across his lips, it left behind blank, white skin. It was as if Griswold's mouth was being rubbed out by the little eraser on the end of a pencil, and replaced by—well, by *nothing*.

Griswold's eyes got very large and very round, and he tried to open his mouth to object to what was being done to him—but he no longer had a mouth to open, so he simply sat there, his snub nose twitching, and his eyes blinking.

Then, when the spark was finished, it left Griswold's face and hovered in the still damp air.

A DEFINITE IMPROVEMENT, GRISTLE. AND NOW FOR THE REST OF YOU.

The green spark zipped to the side of Judge Cedric's forehead. Judge Cedric said, "Ow!" loudly.

HARDSCRABBLE HANDS OUT FOOLISH SENTENCES. HE SHALL HAVE ONE OF HIS OWN.

The spark moved quickly across the skin toward the right side of Judge Cedric's forehead, writing in blue tattoo ink as it went. I AM A VERY STUPID OLD JUDGE, it wrote, and when it was finished, the green spark darted across the cave and hung in front of Draggle's frightened eyes.

WHAT CHARMING HAIR YOU HAVE, MASTER DRAGGLE. WE MUST PUT IT TO SOME USE.

The spark leaped forward and wound itself into

Draggle's long blond hair. It buzzed, like an angry bee, among the dirty locks, braiding them faster than the eye could see, plaiting them into a sort of loop over the top of Draggle's head. Then, when it was done, the spark attached itself to the top of the plaited loop and lifted Draggle off his feet. Draggle yelped with pain as he rose up toward the roof of the cave. The spark lifted him higher and higher and then dropped the loop over a small outcropping of rock that stuck out high on the cave wall.

The spark hovered briefly in front of Draggle's pain-filled eyes and then darted back to the cave floor. It paused there briefly, as if deciding whom to visit next. Then it zoomed through the damp air and landed an inch from Frognell Flabbit's nose.

FLABBIT BY NAME. PERHAPS FLABBY BY NATURE?

The green spark flew and, moments later, every bone in Flabbit's body was turned to a soft jelly and he collapsed in a shapeless heap on the cave floor. He looked like a pile of clothes with a head stuck on the top—and the head had a very worried look on its face.

Mr. and Mrs. Zagreb were next.

AH, THE PROUD ZAGREBS. THEY MUST BE TAUGHT

HUMILITY. THEY MUST BOW BEFORE US.

The spark sizzled to the Zagrebs' eyes. There was some yellow smoke, a squeal of pain from both of them and, when the smoke cleared, everybody saw that Mr. and Mrs. Zagreb's eyes had been moved from their usual place and put, instead, underneath their hair. This meant that, if they wanted to see what was going on in front of them, they had to angle their heads over and point their now eyeless faces at the ground—and that is what they now did, bending both their bodies into a bow before the little garden gnome.

Buford Cudgel was the last to receive the treatment. The green spark flew toward his great body and then paused there, hovering at the level of his broad black leather belt.

MR. CUDGEL WITH HIS GREAT BRUTE STRENGTH. PERHAPS, FOR MR. CUDGEL A LITTLE DAINTINESS? A SUGGESTION OF GRACE? A TOUCH OF DELICACY?

The spark flashed darted down to Cudgel's enormous booted feet. It zigzagged there for a couple of seconds and then began to move up toward Cudgel's helmeted head, moving rapidly from side to side as it went. As it did so, it left behind a transformed Mr.

Cudgel. The huge Wrathmonk's black boots morphed into a dainty pair of pink ballet slippers. The black leather trousers became a pair of shiny pink tights. Cudgel's thick belt turned into a frilly pink ballet tutu, which stuck out from his waist like a filmy ruff. His leather motorcycle jacket became a pink, lacy top, decorated here and there with pink satin ribbons, and the black helmet disappeared entirely and was replaced by a little coronet of soft, pink, downy feathers, which fluttered prettily every time Cudgel moved his head. Then the spark attached itself to the top of Cudgel's cropped scalp and lifted him up until he was resting on the points of his ballet slippers. Mr. Cudgel, with sweat pouring down his broad, flat face, could do nothing but hang there, quivering like an enormous pink blancmange.

There was a short, stunned silence from everybody, broken only by a nervous giggle from high up on the cave wall. For all the pain from his pulled blond hair, Scab Draggle still found the spectacle of Buford Cudgel as a pink ballerina just a bit funny.

A SMALL TASTE OF SOME OF MY LESSER POWERS. I HAVE OTHERS FAR GREATER. AND NOW, PERHAPS, YOU WILL ATTEND TO WHAT I HAVE TO SAY?

There was a murmur of agreement and a lot of nervous nodding of heads—except for Draggle, Flabbit and Cudgel, of course, who could not move their heads at all. Instead, these three mumbled that yes, they were absolutely prepared to listen to whatever was said and would, absolutely *certainly* agree with *all* of it—if only they could, perhaps, be released from their rather painful (and, in Mr. Cudgel's case, extremely *humiliating*) conditions?

VERY WELL. NOW, I UNDERSTAND YOU WISH TO DESTROY THE FAMILY OF STUBBS? EXCELLENT. SO DO I. HOWEVER, HAVE ANY OF YOU EVER MET THE STUBBS FAMILY?

There was more nervous shaking of heads.

I HAVE. THEY CAME TO MY HOME. THEY ARE POWERFUL, PARTICULARLY WHEN ACTING TOGETHER. FAR MORE POWERFUL THAN ANY OF YOU. BUT NOT, OF COURSE, AS POWERFUL AS I. NOTHING IS AS POWERFUL AS I. SO, IF YOU WISH TO DESTROY THIS FAMILY OF STUBBS, YOU WILL DO IT UNDER MY LEADERSHIP AND ACCORDING TO THE PLAN THAT I SHALL DEVISE. DO YOU AGREE TO THIS?

The Wrathmonks looked nervously at one another.

They were thinking that perhaps this thing, this creature—with its amazing resistance to their magic and its
enormous abilities with its own—would make a much
better leader than Griswold Gristle who, at the
moment, didn't even have a mouth with which to tell
them what to do.

They all looked back at the garden gnome and,
together, they all signified their agreement.

EXCELLENT. A WISE DECISION.

The green spark detached itself from Mr. Cudgel's
scalp, dropping the vast, pink ballerina heavily to the
floor. Then it zoomed around the cave, touching each
Wrathmonk as it passed by. Griswold's mouth
re-formed on his face, the tattoo on Judge Cedric's
forehead faded away, Flabbit's bones became hard again
and he slowly pulled himself back onto his feet, Mr.
and Mrs. Zagreb's eyes returned to their proper places,
Cudgel's pink satin became black leather once again,
and there was a sudden scream from high up on the
cave wall as Draggle's hair unwound itself from its
braid and released him from the rock peg he'd been
hanging on. There was a long, wailing cry as the young
Wrathmonk fell and then a loud thump as he hit the

rocky floor. For a moment Draggle lay still. Then, grunting with pain, he sat up, rubbing his back.

ARE YOU NOW READY TO OBEY ME?

There was much vigorous nodding of heads. Flabbit's hair flapped wildly and Cudgel's motorcycle helmet almost fell off his bony skull. Even Griswold reluctantly bowed his head in humble submission.

GOOD. MY FIRST COMMAND: I REQUIRE TO BE TAKEN HOME. NOW. THIS INSTANT. CARRY ME CAREFULLY. ONE CHIP AND I SHALL BECOME VERY ANGRY. VERY ANGRY INDEED. CARRY ME HOME, MY LITTLE MENIALS. I SHALL SHOW YOU THE WAY.

Slowly, and very fearfully, the Wrathmonks shuffled forward. With trembling hands, they lifted the garden gnome onto their shoulders. Then, carefully—as if they were carrying the coffin of a great, dead king—they moved toward the distant mouth of the cave.

5

KIDNAPPED

Ten days later the Wrathmonks struck.

It happened while the Stubbses were out shopping. The three of them, and Nanny Flannel, had bundled into the big green car and driven to the nearby town. Sam had parked in the parking lot of the local supermarket and then Measle, Sam, Lee and Nanny Flannel had gone inside and done the week's shopping, which meant that Nanny Flannel told everybody what to get and everybody did as they were told. When they were finished, they had two carts piled high with groceries.

Sam was pushing one and Lee was pushing the other. As they came out through the supermarket's sliding doors, Nanny Flannel suddenly turned to Measle and said, "Oh, Measle dear—I've forgotten the ketchup. We can't live without ketchup. Well, *you* can't live without ketchup. We'll have to go back for it. Come on, help me find it."

"Okay," said Measle cheerfully. He didn't mind going back for ketchup because it was true—he really didn't think he could possibly live without it. Measle had discovered that almost *everything* (except perhaps chocolate cake) tasted better with ketchup on it.

"We'll meet you at the car," said Sam, beginning to push his shopping cart toward the parking lot.

Lee smiled and started to follow him. "That's right, leave your dad and me to do all the loading," she called over her shoulder.

Measle and Nanny Flannel went back into the supermarket. It took them a few moments to find the ketchup and then another few moments to pay for it. Just as Nanny Flannel was handing over the money, they heard the sound of muffled shouting coming from the parking lot. Then there was a crash of glass, some more shouting—and then the roar of a car engine and the squeal of tires.

"Something funny's going on out there," said the checkout girl, craning her head around and trying to look out through the tall plate-glass windows. "Sounded like somebody was getting mugged or something."

Measle felt a sudden fear rush through his body like ice water. His mum and his dad were out there—and they attracted danger like jam attracts wasps! Without thinking, he began to run toward the sliding doors. By the sound of pounding feet close behind him, he guessed that Nanny Flannel had the same idea.

"Here—you've forgotten your ketchup!" shouted the checkout girl. But Measle was already through the doors and racing across the parking lot toward the car. Nanny Flannel followed as fast as she could, which, for an old lady her size and shape, was surprisingly fast.

When he got to the car, Measle skidded to a halt, panting hard. Sam was there, standing next to his full shopping cart. He was standing quite still with his mouth open and an odd, bewildered look on his face. At his feet there were some pieces of broken glass.

Near the front of the car, the other shopping cart—the one that Lee had been pushing—was lying on its side, with the contents scattered on the ground.

Measle tugged at his father's sleeve.

"What happened, Dad? Where's Mum?"

Sam looked down. He stared blankly at Measle. "What are you talking about?" he muttered. Then he frowned. "Who are you? What do you want?"

Measle stared horror-struck at his father's face. There was something strange about Sam's eyes—they were blank and empty, with no trace of friendliness in them. What was worse, there was no sign that Sam even recognized him.

Nanny Flannel joined them. "What happened?" she gasped.

"I don't know," said Measle. "Dad's gone funny. He doesn't seem to know who I am." He grabbed Sam's hand and shouted into his father's face, "I'm Measle, Dad!"

"That's an odd name," said Sam. "And I'm not your dad."

"Don't you know me?"

Sam shook his head. "No—no, I don't."

"But you must know who I am!" shouted Measle. "You *must*!"

Sam frowned with puzzlement. "I think I'd remember you if I did," he said slowly. "I mean——no offense—— but you do have the weirdest haircut I've ever seen. I think, if I'd seen you before, I'd remember you——and I don't. Sorry."

"Dad! I'm *Measle*!"

Sam gently removed his hand from Measle's clutches. "Measle, yes. You told me that. But why do you keep calling me Dad? I'm not your dad."

Measle stared up at Sam, his mind racing. Something terrible had happened here. Where was his mother? He looked at the overturned shopping cart. A few feet from it were a pair of black rubber skid marks on the pavement, and the ground there was wet, as if a very small shower of rain had fallen only on that particular spot and nowhere else in the parking lot.

Measle looked back at Sam. His father was staring off into the distance, a small frown creasing his fore- head. Measle grabbed his father's hands and shook them both hard, forcing Sam to look down at him.

"All right," said Measle. "If you're not my dad—— then *who are you*?"

Sam smiled—the kind of smile adults put on their faces when a kid asks them what they think is a really stupid question—and then the smile faded, and a frightened and bewildered look flooded his face.

"Who am I?" muttered Sam. "Who *am* I? I don't know. Why don't I know? And who are *you*? And *where* am I? And what's going on?"

"I don't *know* what's going on!" yelled Measle. "I heard some shouting, then a car driving away fast— and now Mum's gone and you don't know who I am!

Sam pulled one hand free from Measle's grasp and put it to his head. He rubbed his eyes and then blinked several times. Then he said, "I don't feel so good. I think I'd better sit down."

Measle opened the car door, and he and Nanny Flannel helped Sam into the front passenger seat. Then Measle looked around wildly, searching for somebody who could help him. There was an old man, leaning on a walking stick about ten feet away, watching him. Measle ran over to him and said breathlessly, "Did you see what happened?"

The old man sniffed. "Well, yes, I did, young fellow. There was this van—all black it was—and these people jumped out. They were all in black, too—funny-looking people they were, their faces were so white they looked like corpses. They threw a bottle at that chap over there, and some funny-looking blue gas came out of it. Then they grabbed the lady and bundled her into the van and drove off. I saw the whole thing. Making a film, are they? Where's the camera then?"

Wrathmonks! thought Measle. *Wrathmonks have kidnapped Mum!*

Measle wanted to ask the old man more questions, but he was already wandering away in search of a non-existent film crew. Measle ran back to the car. Sam was still sitting there in the passenger seat, with Nanny Flannel standing beside him. Nanny Flannel turned to Measle, a worried look on her face.

"I know what this is, Measle, dear. It's amnesia. Your dad can remember obvious stuff, like how to walk and talk, but he can't remember a thing about his life. It's a complete blank. He doesn't know he's a Wizard—and he doesn't remember either of us."

Measle swallowed hard. "What are we going to do?"

Nanny pointed at the overturned shopping cart. "Where's your mum?"

Quickly, Measle told her what the old man had said

and, by the time he'd finished, Nanny Flannel's pink cheeks had turned pale.

"We must get your father home," she said, her voice shaky. "That's the first thing we must do."

"But what about Mum?"

"We don't know where she is, dear. And we can't involve the police—not in wizarding business. That's the rule. No matter how serious, we have to deal with it ourselves. So, come on, never mind the shopping—into the car."

"But we can't just—"

"Yes, we *can,* Measle dear. We *must.* We don't know where they're taking her; we don't know what they want. What we *do* know is that we must get your dad home as fast as possible, and then we must tell the Wizards' Guild what's happened and *they* will get your mum back, because we certainly can't. All right?"

Measle thought quickly. Nanny Flannel was obviously right—what else could they do? It was just—well—it seemed so cold and unfeeling, just getting back into the car and driving away. . . .

Measle stared hard at the ground, willing himself not to cry. *This can't be happening,* he thought. *I can't lose my parents again! I've only had them back for a few weeks—and now—no! This can't be happening!*

But it was happening. And there was nothing he could do about it.

He felt Nanny Flannel's hand touching his arm. He took a deep breath and said, "All right, Nanny. We'll go."

Measle walked around to the other side of the car. As he was opening the door, his foot kicked against something that was lying on the ground. The object skittered away from his foot, making a small metallic sound as it skidded across the ground. Measle looked down. There were the shards of glass from the broken bottle—and there, a couple of feet away, a bottle cap. Without thinking, Measle bent and picked up the bottle cap and slipped it into his pocket. Then he slid into the backseat of the car.

Nanny Flannel had the engine running and, as soon as Measle slammed his door shut, she stamped down on the accelerator pedal and they roared out of the parking lot.

Three hours later Measle and Nanny Flannel were sitting on one of the big couches in the living room of Merlin Manor. Tinker, aware that something was wrong, lay on the carpet close to Measle, his head resting on Measle's feet. Opposite them, on the other big couch, sat two men. One was tall and lean and dark, the other short and fat and fair. Both wore dark suits and plain dark ties, both had shiny black briefcases resting on their knees and neither of them looked at Measle very much, even when they were talking to him.

The interview was not going well.

"How do you know they were Wrathmonks, Measle?" the tall lean man said sternly. "Did you see them?"

Measle shook his head. "No, but there was an old man there, and he told me what happened."

"He told you they were Wrathmonks?"

"No, but he told me what they looked like—and I used to know one and, well—it sounded a lot like Wrathmonks—and the ground was all wet and so I—"

"And so you jumped to a conclusion?" There was a note of accusation in the lean man's voice.

Nanny Flannel smacked her hand down hard on the arm of the couch. "He most certainly did *not* jump to a conclusion, Mr. Needle," she said angrily. "Measle's not a fool. He lived with a Wrathmonk for a very long time, as you well know. If he thinks they were

Wrathmonks, then they were Wrathmonks. And for what it's worth, I think they were Wrathmonks, too. Who else but Wrathmonks would do such a thing, I ask you?"

The short, fat, fair man grunted and said, "A professional gang of kidnappers, for one, Miss Flannel. They needn't have been Wrathmonks at all. And, if they weren't Wrathmonks, then there's nothing the Guild can do about it. Is there, my dear Needle?"

"Nothing at all, my dear Bland," said Mr. Needle.

"Well . . . but can't you find out where she is?" said Measle. "Haven't you got something you could look into?"

Mr. Bland shot a small smile in Mr. Needle's direction. Then he turned back to Measle and said coldly, "Something to look into? What sort of something?"

"I don't know—a crystal ball—or a—or a sort of revealing pool sort of thing, like they have in books and films."

Mr. Bland sighed with impatience. "The Wizards' Guild possesses neither a crystal ball, nor a—a sort of revealing pool thing. I'm afraid there is no magic available to show us the whereabouts of your mother."

"What about if it's raining—raining in one small place?" said Measle desperately. "Like the other day when Dad telephoned you about the rain on Borgrove Moor? If there was rain like that, well, then we'd know where they were."

Mr. Bland nodded toward the window. Outside it was dark, and Measle heard the spattering of rain against the glass.

"Unfortunately," said Mr. Bland, "it is now raining across much of the country and, according to the weather forecasts, it looks like it's going to keep raining for some considerable time. Ideal weather for Wrathmonks, I need hardly say."

There was a silence from everybody. Measle slumped dejectedly against the back of the couch and shoved both hands into his pockets. His fingers touched something hard, and he pulled out the object and glanced down at it. It was the bottle cap he'd picked up in the parking lot. He turned it over in his fingers. There was writing on the top. Measle brought the thing closer to his eyes and squinted down at the tiny writing—it read HAPPY DRINKING AT THE ISLE OF SMILES!

"I think I know where they've taken her," said

Measle quietly. "They've gone to the Isle of Smiles. Look, that bottle they threw at Dad, this is the top. I picked it up in the parking lot."

He held it out and Mr. Needle took it and examined it closely. "What do you think, Bland?" he said, passing it to his companion.

Mr. Bland peered at the bottle top. "Hardly conclusive, Needle. It could simply have been lying there in the parking lot, for goodness knows how long——"

"Oh, nonsense," snapped Nanny Flannel. "It's from the bottle they threw! Why can't you understand that?"

Mr. Bland changed the look on his face from one with a very small expression of interest to what was going on around him, to one of no expression at all. "Miss Flannel," he said smoothly, "you must understand that we cannot act unless we have absolute proof that this event happened as young Measle claims it did."

"And even if we had the proof," said Mr. Needle, "at the present time, we would still be unable to investigate any occurrence that involved the Isle of Smiles. The Isle of Smiles is off limits for now—and for the foreseeable future. The Guild is most concerned about that report that Mr. Stubbs filed concerning the alleged presence of an entity in the area, and we have an ongoing investigation into the matter."

"Ongoing *fiddlesticks*!" shouted Nanny Flannel loudly.

There was a short silence while the two officials glanced at each other. Each gave the other a tiny, almost imperceptible nod. Then Mr. Bland snapped his briefcase shut and rose to his feet. "Our business here appears to be concluded, does it not, Needle?"

"Indeed it does, Bland," said Mr. Needle, snapping shut *his* briefcase and then pushing himself out of his chair.

Measle racked his brain, trying desperately to think of something that might convince the two representatives of the Wizards' Guild that he was telling them the truth. But Mr. Needle and Mr. Bland were already at the door. Both turned and smiled coldly in Measle's direction.

"We are sorry about your loss," said Mr. Needle, not sounding sorry at all.

"Particularly in light of your past misadventures," said Mr. Bland.

"We trust that your mother will soon be back with you," said Mr. Needle.

"And that your father will make a swift recovery," said Mr. Bland.

Both men bowed slightly at the waist and said, in unison, "Good day to you."

The door closed behind them.

"Huh!" Nanny Flannel snorted. "I might have known it! Wizards' Guild indeed! Fat lot of use *they* are!"

"What do we do now?" said Measle, feeling utterly miserable. He'd been sure that The Wizards' Guild would solve everything in the blink of an eye, and all that had happened was that the Guild had sent along a pair of cold, dry officials who had flatly refused to do anything. His mother was gone, and his father was lying asleep in his bed upstairs, heavily sedated with some sort of tranquilizers that Mr. Needle had produced from his briefcase.

Nanny Flannel patted Measle's hand. "We wait, dear," she said sadly. "There's nothing else we can do. We wait and see what they want with her."

6

THE
CAR

Later that evening the rain became heavier. It was a cold, windy rain, and it drummed down on the manor's old slate roof and spattered against its leaded windows.

The rain went on through the night and the next two days. Measle and Nanny Flannel spent most of those days simply staring out of the window at the steady downpour. Every hour Nanny Flannel, Measle and Tinker would go up to Sam's bedroom and peek around the door, to see if Sam was still asleep. He always was.

"That," said Nanny Flannel as they returned downstairs for the umpteenth time, "was a very strong pill."

On the morning of the third day, Measle decided that he'd waited long enough.

"I'm going to go and find her," he said to Nanny Flannel across the breakfast table.

Nanny Flannel put down her cup of tea.

"What do you mean, dear?" she said, quietly.

"I'm going to go to the Isle of Smiles, and I'm going to find her. I'm going to rescue her."

Nanny Flannel looked at Measle, peering at him over the top of her spectacles, for several seconds. Then she said, "No, dear, you're not. You can't possibly. Do you have any idea what those creatures could do to you?"

"Yes," said Measle. "Yes, I do."

Nanny Flannel nodded thoughtfully. "Yes, I suppose you do, don't you? But Basil Tramplebone was just *one* Wrathmonk, Measle—and he very nearly killed you. This time there are *lots* of them. If they caught you— well, I dread to think what they'd do to you! And anyway, how can you be sure that they're on that island at all?"

"I'm not sure at all, but I've got to start somewhere. Besides, I've got a sort of a *feeling* that that's where they are. See, it's closed for the winter, Nanny, and it would be a great place to hide, because of the mana. Dad said there was a mana well there—and they'd like that, don't you see?"

"But you're just a boy, Measle! No, no—it's out of the question."

"But I *must* go, Nanny!"

"You *can't* go, Measle!"

Measle and Nanny Flannel sat, staring at each other for several moments.

Measle was thinking, *How can I get her to see that I have no choice? How can I persuade her to let me go? And, if I can't persuade her, how can I get away?*

Nanny Flannel was thinking, *There's a look in the boy's eyes that I've seen before. His father gets it sometimes, when he's determined to do something crazy. His grandfather had it, too. It's a look that says "Don't get in my way, because I shall do what I have to do, and neither you nor anybody else will stop me."*

Nanny Flannel sighed. She knew it was no use—and therefore she knew what she had to do. She got up from the kitchen table and said, "Come with me, Measle. There's something I think you should know."

She led Measle to the dining room and sat him down at the head of the long table. Then she went to the sideboard and opened one of its low doors. She reached deep inside and brought out a large, heavy glass jar. She set the jar on the table in front of Measle.

The jar was full of multicolored jelly beans.

"Now then," said Nanny Flannel, planting herself firmly next to Measle and peering at him fiercely through her little round spectacles.

This is obviously going to be very serious and very important, thought Measle, *and I'd better listen very, very carefully.* He put a serious look on his face and sat up a little straighter in the chair.

Nanny Flannel took a deep breath. Then she said, "What color is your least favorite jelly bean?"

"What?"

"You heard me, dear, don't pretend you didn't."

"But—but I thought this was something *serious*! Something about Mum and Dad! What's stupid *jelly beans* got to do with anything?"

Nanny Flannel clapped her hands together twice—

smack, smack! Then she glared down at Measle, real anger glinting in her eyes.

"Be quiet, Measle and listen. You only learn things if you listen. If you blabber and jabber all the time, you learn *nothing*—but everybody within earshot learns something. They learn that you're an idiot. Now I asked you a question, and I'd like an answer. *What color jelly beans do you like least?*"

"Er—I don't know—I like them all—er, the yellow ones, I suppose."

"Good. Yellow it shall be."

Nanny Flannel held out the glass jar. "Take out a yellow one."

Measle did as he was told.

"Good," said Nanny Flannel. "Now I want you to shut your eyes, stick your tongue out and put the jelly bean on the end of it."

Measle was about to say that he didn't actually feel very much like eating jelly beans at this particular moment—particularly not a yellow one and *particularly* not with his mum held prisoner by Wrathmonks on the Isle of Smiles and his dad lying in a sort of coma in his bedroom—but then he saw the glint of steely determination in Nanny Flannel's eyes. So he closed his eyes, stuck out his tongue and put the bean on the end of it.

"Good," said Nanny Flannel. "Now, when I say 'GO!' I want you to bite into it, chew it up and swallow it. Are you ready?"

Measle, with his tongue sticking out, could only nod.

"Good," said Nanny Flannel. "Right then, Measle—GO!"

Measle retracted his tongue and bit into the jelly bean. The familiar, sugary-lemony taste filled his mouth. Five quick chews and it was gone. Then he heard Nanny Flannel's voice again.

"All done? Good! All right, you can open your eyes now."

Measle opened his eyes. Nanny Flannel was still standing next to him—still looking down at him—but now her eyes didn't quite meet his. She was looking in the general direction of his face, but instead of looking into his eyes, she appeared to be staring at his right ear.

"Lift up your hand," she said to his right ear, "and look at it."

Measle lifted his hand and looked at it—or rather,

he looked at where it should have been—

It wasn't there.

Measle moved his hand frantically in front of his face. He felt the movement of the air as his hand passed through it, but where his hand should have been was—well—there was *nothing*.

"Look at your feet," said Nanny Flannel.

Measle looked down to where his feet should have been. All he could see was the carpet on the floor.

"What's happened to me?" he gasped.

"You tell me," said Nanny Flannel, still staring fixedly at Measle's right ear. "You're a smart boy, Measle, you should be able to work it out."

"I'm—I'm *invisible*?"

"Aha—you got it in one!" said Nanny Flannel proudly. "Invisible! You—and whatever you're holding onto at that moment. Invisible every time you eat a yellow jelly bean. Well, not *any* yellow jelly bean, obviously. These are—well—they're rather special. And only to be used in emergencies. They're not for fun, you understand. Besides, the effect doesn't last long—you should be coming out of it any minute now."

Measle stared at where his hand should have been and watched as his fingers slowly reappeared. At first they seemed to be made out of a thin gray smoke, but as the seconds ticked away, his fingers became more and more solid until, moments later, his hand was back to normal.

"It only lasts about half a minute," said Nanny Flannel. "But half a minute of invisibility can come in quite useful at times."

Measle thought about this for a few moments. Then he said, "Why did you teach me that, Nanny? I mean—why now?"

Nanny Flannel's face went pinker than its usual pinkness. She took her spectacles off her nose and polished them on her apron. "Well," she muttered, avoiding Measle's eyes, "you never know when it might come in handy." Then she stopped polishing her glasses. In one swift movement, she perched them back on the end of her nose and then peered over the top of them at Measle. "Just remember to keep a few of those yellow jelly beans in your pocket at all times, Measle," she said firmly. "*At all times*, remember. And use them—use them *when necessary*."

It was several hours before Measle realized what
Nanny Flannel had really meant by that remark, and by
then it was early in the evening. Outside the windows
it was dark. The rain had started again and was patter-
ing against the window panes.

And in Measle's mind a plan was beginning to form.

While Nanny Flannel was busy in the kitchen,
Measle went into the dining room. The jar of beans was
still on the table. He took the top off and began to take
out as many yellow jelly beans as he could find. He
counted them—twelve—and then he stuffed them
into his trouser pocket.

Next he went to his bedroom and took his warmest
coat from his closet. The coat was a leather jacket, like
the sort that fighter pilots in old war films wear. Of all
the new clothes Measle had got for his Birthmas presents, this jacket was his favorite.

Measle shrugged the jacket on. There was something
in one of the pockets. Measle reached in and pulled it
out. It was the VoBo. For a moment he stared at the
little brass trumpet, wondering whether or not to take
it with him. Then he stuck it back in the pocket. *It's*

small, he thought. *It won't get in the way—and, you never know, it might come in handy.*

Measle went out of his bedroom and crept downstairs. He heard the clanking of pots and pans from the kitchen. He moved silently across the dark hall to the front door. He opened it slowly to stop it creaking, and then he slipped out into the wet night.

The garage was off to the side of the big house. Measle hurried through the rain to the great sliding double doors. He pushed them aside and went into the garage. There it was: the huge, gleaming shape of the Stubbses' car. Measle went to the driver's side, opened the door and slipped into the seat. He paused for a moment, feeling the hammering of his heart in his chest. *Was he going to be able to do this?* He took a deep breath, placed the end of his forefinger on the big red button and pressed hard.

The engine rumbled into life.

Measle breathed a sigh of relief. That was the first hurdle, now for the second. He reached for the switch marked A/P and flipped it down.

Yes? What do you want?

The voice came from somewhere behind the polished wooden dashboard. It sounded tinny and very efficient and businesslike—and just a little impatient.

"Well," said Measle hesitantly, "I—um—I want to go to—"

Identify yourself.

"I'm Measle. Measle Stubbs."

There was a pause while the autopilot seemed to think this over. Then—

Measle Stubbs: youngest member of the Stubbs family. Identity accepted. Destination?

"Er—"

Ur—ancient city of Sumeria, located in what is now southeastern Iraq. Unable to comply with request, for the following reasons. First, there is a small ocean in the way. Second, the city of Ur no longer exists. Please state alternative destination.

"Um—"

Um—no such location known. Please state alternative destination.

Wow, thought Measle, *this machine is really picky.*

"The Isle of Smiles."

The Isle of Smiles—destination recognized. Please state magic word.

What? There's a magic word? And the car won't move with-out it? Oh, great! What on earth could this magic word be?

Measle racked his brains for all the magic words he could think of.

"Abracadabra?"

Unrecognized.

"Shazam?"

Unrecognized.

"Oogly-boogly?"

Now you're just being silly.

Come on—think! The magic word! What's the magic word? Oh, no! Could it possibly be as easy as that? Well, it's worth a try—

"Please?"

Finally.

And, the next moment, Measle felt the big car begin to move. The headlights came on, shooting twin beams of light out over the drive. The raindrops flashed through the beams and, as the car slid out of the garage, the windshield wipers came on automatically, flicking rapidly left and right. The huge wooden steering wheel turned slowly, and the big car veered away from the house, its tires crunching softly over the gravel. Slowly it began to pick up speed as they rolled down the long driveway, the steering wheel twitching this way and that as the autopilot made its small corrections. Moments later they were at the big iron gates that led out to the main road, and the car came to a stop. It waited at the junction for several seconds, almost like a pedestrian waits at a crossing. It seemed to be looking left and right, checking if any traffic was coming its way. Then it began to move again, turning slowly onto the main road. Once clear of the gates, it began to go faster, and Measle relaxed a little, sinking back against the soft leather. He glanced up at the rearview mirror. It was set for his father, who was a lot taller than Measle, so all Measle could see was a reflection of the ceiling of the car. He reached up and adjusted the mirror. There, in the reflection through the car's rear window, was a distant speck of white in the darkness— a speck of white that seemed to be following them— but the speck was getting smaller and smaller as the car accelerated away from it.

Measle turned around in his seat and stared back through the rear window.

There, far down the road, was Tinker, racing along

as fast as his short legs could move, desperately trying to catch up with them.

"Stop!" yelled Measle.

Stop? But we've only just started.

"I don't care! Stop! Please stop!"

I do wish you'd make up your mind.

The big car began to slow down. Seconds later it pulled over to the side of the road and rolled to a halt.

Measle opened the door, and a very wet and panting Tinker jumped into his lap.

"What are you doing here, Tink?" said Measle, trying to sound angry but not quite succeeding, because the truth was that he was very glad to see the little dog.

And Tinker was very glad to see him. It was good to get out of the rain—why, only minutes ago he'd been in the kitchen, sitting close by Nanny Flannel as she clattered about with her pots and pans. Then he'd heard, in the distance, the sound of the car engine rumbling to life and up had gone Tinker's ears. The old lady had looked down at him and said, "What did you hear, little dog?"

Tinker had whined softly and had gone to stand by the kitchen door, which led out to the backyard. Nanny

Flannel had joined him. She had opened the door a crack, and then both she and Tinker could hear the rumbling of the engine in the garage.

Nanny Flannel had looked down at Tinker. Her face was pale and her eyes were wide with worry. She said, "Go on then, Tinker. Off you go. And, whatever happens, look after him!" Then she'd opened the door a little wider and Tinker had galloped out into the cold, wet night and raced after the big green car as it crunched down the long drive. He'd almost caught it at the gates, but then the car had turned out into the main road and had picked up speed again. Tinker had strained every sinew in his body, charging after the red taillights, watching them get farther and farther away. Then the car had suddenly begun to slow down and then stop and the smelly kid (*well, he wasn't quite as smelly as he used to be, but that was all right, nobody's perfect*) had opened the car door and here they were, together again. Perhaps they were off on another adventure, maybe like the one when they were playing with that giant bug on top of the enormous table, which had been great fun and terrifically exciting. If that was the sort of adventure they were headed for this time, well then, Tinker was all for it.

"What am I going to do with you?" said Measle, scratching Tinker between his damp ears. "I can't take you back—I can't risk Nanny catching us. Oh, well, looks like you'll have to come along. Just be a good dog and do as you're told, okay?"

Tinker, being a dog, didn't understand a word of that. But whatever the smelly kid had just said, at least he didn't sound angry, so Tinker barked once, just to show that whatever was in store for the pair of them, he was game for it.

Measle pushed Tinker into the passenger seat, turned to face the dashboard again and said, "The Isle of Smiles, please."

Are you sure this time?

"Yes! I'm quite sure! The Isle of Smiles—*please!*"

Well, if you're quite sure, said the autopilot, in a slightly huffy voice. Then, a moment later, the car started to move again.

7

THE
GATES

The car behaved perfectly, driving itself at a smooth, sedate pace, obeying every traffic law and never breaking the speed limit. It didn't say anything, either, and Measle was quite pleased about that. There had been something in the tone of the autopilot's voice that had made Measle feel he was a bit of a nuisance.

For the first half hour of the trip, Measle had sat up very straight in the driver's seat, his hands resting lightly on the steering wheel, trying hard to look as though he was driving the big car. But, what with the darkness and the heavy, pounding rain, there was very little traffic. Measle never once saw a police car, but even if he had, the sharpest-eyed policeman on the force would still have had a hard time seeing through the dark-tinted windows of the Stubbses' car, so Measle began to relax. Tinker had curled up in the passenger seat and had fallen asleep, and eventually Measle felt his own eyelids getting heavy. So he let go of the steering wheel, closed his eyes and lay back against the soft leather of the seat. Quite soon, he, too, was fast asleep.

Measle woke up when the car stopped at a traffic light. He sat up, peering out through the windshield. The rain had stopped, and the wipers no longer flicked from side to side. It was dark outside, apart from the traffic lights, which now turned from red to green. The big car moved forward smoothly. Measle stared out of the side window at the passing houses. They were all dark, with not a single light showing through their curtained windows. Measle glanced at his watch. Just past midnight. They'd been on the road for over three hours—surely it didn't take that long to get to the Isle of Smiles? But then he remembered the speed his dad usually drove, which was a lot faster than the gentle pace the car had adopted for the long drive—so perhaps they *were* only just arriving? A moment later the car turned a corner and there, in front of them, was the little harbor and, beyond it, the long causeway stretching out into the bay. Far off, Measle could just make out the dark hump of the island itself.

Hanging over the island was a wide, black cloud, and Measle saw a faint, shifting haze hanging beneath it, which meant only one thing.

Rain.

Wrathmonk rain.

The Stubbses' car headed steadily through the small town toward the beginning of the causeway, and Measle realized that, unless he did something about it, the car would continue right up to the very gates of the park itself. He remembered that there was a small parking lot, right down by the sea, near the start of the causeway. It was used when there were too many visitors to the place, when the big parking lot on the island itself was full.

Measle leaned toward the dashboard and said, "The small parking lot, please."

The small parking lot. A wise choice.

Two minutes later the Stubbses' car rolled to a halt,

parking itself neatly in a marked space right by the lot entrance. The sound of the engine died away.

"Well," Measle said to Tinker, who was now awake and sitting up. "Here we are. Now what?"

Tinker wagged his stumpy tail. Measle scratched him behind his fuzzy ears and then peered out through the windscreen.

"It's so dark out there, Tink," he muttered. "I can hardly see a thing."

You might try looking in the glove compartment.

Measle realized that he'd forgotten to switch off the autopilot. And now the machine had made some sort of suggestion.

"What?"

The glove compartment, cloth ears. Honestly. I don't know why I bother.

Measle couldn't help grinning in the darkness. The idea of a rude and impatient car was kind of funny.

He reached over the passenger seat and opened the small door of the glove compartment. His hand fumbled inside——there was something there.

Measle pulled the object out of the glove compartment. It was so dark in the car that he found it hard to make out what was in his hand. It seemed to be made of soft leather, with two circles of smooth, hard stuff embedded in the material.

It was a pair of goggles. Old-fashioned goggles, like the kind pilots used to wear when they flew in ancient, open biplanes. Measle slipped the goggles onto his head and over his eyes.

Light! He could see! Quite clearly, as if the car was filled with ordinary daylight!

For a moment Measle actually thought that somehow nighttime had been banished and replaced with the day, but then he pulled the goggles up onto his forehead and, instantly, he was in darkness again. Measle slipped the goggles back over his eyes and the light returned. He looked about him. Everything in the car—and, indeed, everything *outside* the car—seemed to be lit by a soft, filtered light.

Measle pulled the goggles off his head and stared at them. Once again he couldn't make out a thing. Then Measle remembered that there was an overhead light in the car. He reached up and switched it on.

The goggles were odd. The leather was soft and brown, but it was the lenses of the goggles that were a little strange. They were dark and shiny and highly reflective, like a pair of small, round mirrors. *Obviously something to do with Dad's magic,* thought Measle. *Maybe he uses these goggles when he wants to be secret—perhaps when he has to drive without using the headlights? And maybe, just maybe, they might be a bit useful to me?*

Measle slipped the goggles over his head and hung them around his neck. Then he opened the car door, and he and Tinker stepped out into the night.

The air outside was cold and damp, and Measle was glad he was wearing his leather jacket. Tinker's wiry coat seemed to be keeping him quite warm, too, or, at any rate, the little dog certainly wasn't complaining. But he kept close to Measle's side as they left the parking lot. They padded together through the darkness down to the start of the causeway. Ahead of them the long, straight, multilane highway cut across the black waters of the bay.

It took Measle and Tinker fifteen minutes to walk the length of the causeway, and for the last two hundred yards, they both moved very slowly. When they were thirty yards from the gates, Measle slipped the goggles over his eyes and, with them, he could see clearly in the darkness.

That was how he spotted the Wrathmonk.

Scab Draggle was cold and tired and very damp. He was also rather irritable, because Frognell Flabbit was late. Flabbit was late for the third day in a row, and Draggle was fed up with it.

He and Flabbit had been ordered to guard the main gate, and that's what they'd been doing for several days, ever since they had captured the Stubbs woman and brought her down here to the island. The trouble was, Flabbit kept oversleeping—*or pretending to oversssleep*, thought Draggle. Flabbit was almost certainly being late on purpose, probably out of jealousy. Jealousy over the hair, of course. *I've got sssuch lovely long blond hair,* thought Draggle, hunching his thin body against the cold, damp air, *and poor old Flabbit is almossst completely bald, and he tries to hide it with that ssstupid comb-over! Well, jussst because I look nicer than he does, that'sss no reason for him to be late all the time!*

Draggle looked miserably around at his surroundings. He was sitting in one of the several ticket booths

113

at the park's entrance. Now that the Isle of Smiles was closed for the winter, most of the power was off, which meant that inside the ticket booth there was no heat and no light, either—which was why Draggle was cold and damp and very bored, too.

He turned to the stone statue that was sitting next to him and said, "When that ssstupid Flabbit fellow gets here, you jussst lisssten. I'll be giving him a piece of my mind, sssee if I don't!"

The statue stayed motionless, the blank eyes staring out through the small window of the ticket booth. It was a life-size statue of a woman, dressed in a sort of uniform. She had a badge on her lapel, which read "Susan." Underneath was written "Ticket Office: The Isle of Smiles."

When the statue failed to respond, Draggle kicked it irritably.

"Bet that took you by sssurprise, didn't it?" he sneered. "Of course, not as big a sssurprise as the one you got when we turned you to ssstone, eh? You and all the others we found here. Dear, oh, dear—you should have ssseen your faces! One by one, you all came running up to sssee what was going on, and one by one, well, thanksss to the Medusssa head, you all got *done*, didn't you? And now there's nobody here but usss!"

Draggle stopped suddenly and looked about him nervously. Apart from himself and the stone statue, there *was* nobody in the little ticket booth, but he knew that didn't mean a thing. The Dragodon could be anywhere—watching him, listening to him—he'd better be careful what he said and did!

Ever since they had brought the Dragodon to the Isle of Smiles, the Wrathmonks had grown more and more fearful of the creature. They had carried the little concrete garden gnome to the great red roller coaster and had deposited it—under strict instructions—at the foot of one of the massive, red metal columns that supported the rails. **LEAVE ME NOW** were the words the Dragodon had sent into their heads, and obediently, the Wrathmonks had turned away and left it there, in the shadow of the Juggernaut. Over the next few days, they had received detailed instructions—all of them hearing the words in their skulls at the same moment—and they had obeyed those instructions to the letter, for one very simple reason.

They were terrified of it.

When Mr. and Mrs. Zagreb failed to obey its instructions to bring an empty Isle of Smiles cola bottle to the base of the Juggernaut's metal pillar, they suffered the most horrible pain in their stomachs for the rest of that day. Later in the same week, Scab Draggle had failed to steal a particular kind of black van that the Dragodon had ordered—and the young Wrathmonk had spent the rest of that day writhing in agony on the floor of the ticket booth. All of them had been tortured like this, some for the most minor mistakes, and now they all trod very carefully indeed, living in constant fear of the creature—a creature whose true appearance they had never actually seen, whose whereabouts they didn't know and whose powers they could only guess at.

When Measle saw the young Wrathmonk all by himself inside the ticket booth, he wondered how on earth he was going to get past him.

That the creature was a Wrathmonk, Measle had no doubt whatsoever. The same white, white face as Basil Tramplebone's. The same cold, fishy eyes. The same long, bony fingers, the skin the color of old candles.

The same black clothes—yes, it was certainly a Wrathmonk and, if by some miracle it *wasn't* a Wrathmonk, then what was a sinister-looking young man doing there, sitting in a cold, dark ticket booth, at the dead of night, staring blankly out into the darkness?

And then there was the rain. Where Measle was now crouching, with Tinker pressed close to his side, the night air was heavy with dampness, but no rain was actually falling on them. But there, a hundred feet away, a steady downpour dribbled over the ticket booth, and as far as Measle could see, rain was falling in an unbroken shower all over the island. And that meant only one thing.

Wrathmonks. Lots of Wrathmonks.

Measle shivered—but not from cold. For the first time that night, Measle began to realize the danger he was in. He was sure now that he'd been right and that this was where the wrathmonks had brought his mother—*but now what?*

Tinker, sensing Measle's sudden uncertainly, pressed his cold nose into Measle's hand, as if to say, *It's okay, smelly kid—Tinker's here!*

To one side of the ticket booth there was a set of

roofed-over turnstiles, and Measle remembered from his last visit to the Isle of Smiles the clicking sound they made when he'd passed through them. He carefully scanned the whole area, looking for another way in. But the only entrance to the park was through those clicking turnstiles. Measle knew that if he and Tinker went in that way, the Wrathmonk in the ticket booth would be sure to hear them.

There was movement to one side of the booth, and Measle saw a tubby, balding man carrying an umbrella push the booth's door open and enter. Another white face. Another pair of cold, fishy eyes. Next to him, Tinker growled deep in his throat and Measle stroked his head and whispered, "We've got to be quiet, Tinker. Really, *really* quiet. Okay?"

The door of the ticket office burst open, and Frognell Flabbit stepped into the tiny room. He was holding a soaking wet umbrella, and he shook it violently, spattering Draggle with water.

"Here, do you mind?" whined Draggle, jumping out of his chair and wiping the drops of water off his greasy black coat.

"Whasssamatter?" said Flabbit, his pasty white face shining with moisture. "Ssscared of a drop of water, are you?"

"Now look here, Flabbit," muttered Draggle angrily. "You're late again."

"Yesss, well—I couldn't find my umbrella."

Draggle shook his head. "I don't care about your ssstupid umbrella, do I? I'm cold, and I'm tired, and I'm bored—"

"All right, all right," said Flabbit, flopping into Draggle's chair and stretching his short, fat legs out in front of him. "I'm here now, aren't I? Keep your hair on."

"Oh, I shall indeed," said Draggle, making for the door. "*I've* always been able to keep my hair on—which is more than can be sssaid for sssome of usss, eh?"

Flabbit nodded seriously. He had no idea that Draggle might be referring to *him*, since he'd always believed that his hairdo was completely convincing and that whoever looked at it would believe one hundred percent that he, Frognell Flabbit, was blessed with a fine and full head of hair. So he nodded and smiled in a superior sort of way and said, "Yesss, you mean poor old Grissstle, don't you? Poor old Griswold—why, he's

119

as bald as a billiard ball! But you and me, young Draggle, well, we've been lucky with our hair, haven't we? Oh, yesss, very lucky indeed—although I think you might be thinning jussst a little bit up on top—"

There was a faint clicking sound from somewhere outside, and both Wrathmonks heard it clearly through the drumming of the rain on the roof of the ticket both.

"Whasssat?" said Draggle, nervously. He was close to the door, and now he rather wished he hadn't jumped out of his chair so quickly. If he'd stayed where he was, old Flabbit would now be near the door.

"That's the turnssstiles, I think," said Flabbit. "Sssomebody's trying to get out—or get in. Why don't you open the door and have a look? Have you got the Medusssa head?"

Draggle patted his pocket. "It's right here."

"In the bag?" said Flabbit a little anxiously. The last thing he needed was for young Draggle to pull the thing out of his pocket, unshielded by the little canvas bag in which it was always kept.

"Yesss, Flabbit, *coursssse* it'sss in the bag. Think I'm an idiot, do you?"

That was *exactly* what Flabbit thought, but the look on Draggle's face stopped him short of saying so out loud.

"No, no, young Draggle. An idiot, you? Very far from it, young Draggle. Very far indeed."

Draggle nodded sourly. The whole business about who should have the Medusa head still irritated him. All the others had been given their turn with the thing, each one getting the chance to petrify a certain number of the park employees before passing it along to the next in line. Even old Judge Hardscrabble had been given a turn, and he'd been so clumsy with the thing that it had been pure good luck that he hadn't petrified *himself*, let alone the rest of them. By the time the Medusa head had come down to Draggle— the youngest Wrathmonk in the group and therefore the last to get it—there hadn't been a single park employee left to petrify. And that, thought Scab Draggle, was totally unfair.

But now there was this clicking sound from outside. Perhaps one of the park personnel had somehow managed to escape them! And now he, Scab Draggle, was going to get his chance to use the Medusa head at last!

121

Draggle cautiously cracked open the door and peered out into the wet night.

Measle froze.

He was halfway through the turnstile, with Tinker in his arms, when the door of the ticket booth opened and the young Wrathmonk's head appeared in the gap. Measle could see him clearly through the curtain of rain that fell between the roofs of the turnstile and the ticket booth. He had hoped that the Wrathmonks would be too busy talking to each other to hear the clicking of the turnstile, but the metallic sound had been very loud.

Measle stood quite still, wondering how much longer the effects of the yellow jelly bean would last.

He tried to do a sum in his head. He'd popped the jelly bean in his mouth at the very first sound of the clicking turnstile—about fifteen seconds ago. Now he'd been standing like an invisible statue for at least another five seconds, an invisible Tinker held tight in his arms, while the young Wrathmonk peered this way and that, his cold, fishy eyes sweeping over Measle's and Tinker's invisible bodies at least three times in the process. *How much longer before the effects wore off?*

"Anything there?" called a whiny, scratchy voice from inside the ticket booth.

"Can't sssee nothing, can I?" said the young Wrathmonk. "Mussst have been the wind."

Draggle paused for another moment, his eyes wandering suspiciously. Then, to Measle's relief, he shrugged his narrow shoulders and withdrew back into the ticket booth. The moment the door closed behind the Wrathmonk, Measle held his hand up to his face and watched as his fingers slowly reappeared. He looked down and saw Tinker's small black nose materialize and, a moment later, Tinker's eyes gleamed up at him from the folds of his jacket.

To Tinker, the whole experience had been only mildly interesting. First the smelly kid had insisted on carrying him into the little hut thing (and that was all right because Tinker quite liked being carried around, particularly when the ground was all wet like it was around here), and then the smelly kid had disappeared completely. Of course the smelly kid was still there, because Tinker could *smell* that he was still there (since he was a dog, smell was the only thing that mattered).

The rest was quite unimportant. If the smelly kid wanted to act like a window, that was fine by Tinker— *just as long as he didn't smell like a window, because windows don't smell much at all and that's not very interesting, now is it? Still, it's nice that the smelly kid can be seen again, because when he was like a window, you couldn't be sure which bit to lick and which bit to bark at—so now that he* could *be seen—*

Tinker swiped his tongue across Measle's nose and, for good measure, gave one, loud, high-pitched yelp of pleasure.

Frantically, Measle grabbed at Tinker's nose to stop him barking again. He dove his free hand into his jacket pocket, yanked out another yellow jelly bean and stuffed it into his mouth. At the same moment, he heard the sound of loud voices inside the ticket booth and, a second later, the door opening. Without looking back, Measle pushed his way through the last few clicks of the turnstile and hurried forward into the wet darkness.

"Oy!" shouted a voice behind him. Then Measle heard, "Quick, Flabbit! Look at that! There! Sssee that? Whasssat?"

How could it be anything? thought Measle frantically, *I'm invisible, aren't I?* He glanced down at his hand and saw, to his horror, that there was a kind of ghostly outline to his body—an outline that seemed to slip and slide, almost as if it was made of water.

Of course! It was the rain falling on him! In the turnstile he'd been sheltered by its roof. But now, out here in the rain, the water drops were hitting his body! The drops were actually stopping dead and then trickling over him—over his head, over his shoulders, over his jacket. Where they flowed, they made a perfect, watery sort of outline of his body, and that was what the young Wrathmonk could see.

"Oy! You! Whatever you are! Get back here, or you'll be sssorry! Come on, Flabbit—let'sss get after it!"

Measle heard the sound of flapping, squelching feet racing after him. He tightened his grip on Tinker, put his head down and ran. The rain spattered against his goggles, smearing the lenses and making it hard to see what was ahead of him, so Measle pulled them off his eyes and slipped them down round his neck.

He ran on, twisting this way and that, past the shadowy shapes of the park's attractions. The rides and the booths looked different in the darkness. The night washed away the bright colors they wore in the daytime, transforming them all into darkish gray lumps, and this, combined with their odd, angular shapes, made them somehow strange and a little threatening. Even so, Measle recognized them as he raced by: there was the Golden Nugget ride, there the Spinning Saucepans, and there, at the start of the Dinosaur Diver ride, huge and looming in the darkness, was the threatening shape of the enormous, life-sized model of the Tyrannosaurus rex. For a moment Measle felt a new fear grow in his chest. In the gloom, the monster seemed to be glaring down at him and even starting to move in his direction! But then he thought, *It's not moving, you idiot! It can't move, it's just made of plaster and plastic and steel, it can't hurt you. But there's something behind you that can!* So he ran faster, past the Log Flume and the Thunderer and on and on, right under the huge, spiderweb tracery of the Ferris wheel. Behind him he could still hear the sound of pounding footsteps, but only one pair now. Measle guessed that the tubby Wrathmonk was the one who had dropped behind—which meant there was only the thin, young blond Wrathmonk to worry about.

Measle raced around a corner and there, in front of him, was the ghostly shape of the carousel. The contraption was still and silent and dark, and even as Measle tore past it, there was something about those garishly painted horses, with their staring eyes and wide, flared nostrils that made him shudder. They looked alive somehow—as if, at any moment, they would leap from their painted stations and join in the chase.

"Oy! Cudgel! Zag! Anybody! There's sssomething loossse in the park!"

Measle threw a look over his shoulder. There, on the far side of the carousel, was the young Wrathmonk. He was standing still, his narrow chest heaving as he gasped for air, his fishy eyes looking frantically around, his wet hair hanging in straggly blond clumps over his white, white face. Measle ducked behind the cover of the carousel and backed slowly away. When he felt he was far enough into the shadows, he turned again and slipped around a corner, running on down the street as silently as he could. He ran until his lungs felt like they were about to burst. Then, gasping for breath, he risked a pause. There was no sound now, apart from the steady drumming of the rain. He glanced down at his hand. He was fully visible again—well, that was to be expected—he'd been running for at least a minute.

Measle looked about him, trying to get his bearings. He lifted the goggles back over his eyes and, in the resulting brightness, he saw that the nearest structure was the pay booth for the Giant Splash ride, and next to it was the back wall of what Measle guessed had to be part of the go-cart track. The alley between them might be a good place to take a rest.

Measle walked quickly into the narrow space. Through his goggles, he could see that the alley ended about fifty feet away, in a high, wire fence. Beyond the fence were the hulking shadows of some sort of electrical equipment, obviously part of the machinery that ran the nearest rides.

On one side of the alley was a small booth. There was a kind of awning there, made of red and white striped canvas. It hung over a glassed-in hatch. There was a picture of a bucket of popcorn painted on the hatch and Measle remembered getting a bag of popcorn and a soda right here, with his parents at his side, only a couple of weeks ago. In the shadows, on the back wall of the little booth, there was a shelf. On the shelf sat a familiar-looking pink hippopotamus.

A picture of his mum—a smiling, happy Lee sitting on a bench and holding her prized pink hippo in her arms—flashed into Measle's mind. He felt a sudden lump in his throat. He bent his head and put his mouth close to one of Tinker's fuzzy ears.

"She's got to be here somewhere, Tink," he whispered. "But where?"

Measle hurried under the awning, out of the incessant rain. He pulled Tinker out of the front of his leather jacket and put him on the ground. Tinker wagged his stumpy tail and then sat down and began to scratch his right ear with his back foot.

Slowly, Measle's breathing returned to normal, and he began to take stock of the situation. He counted the number of enemies that he knew of. There was the thin, blond Wrathmonk, the tubby one (Flabbit, that was what the young Wrathmonk had called him) and then a couple of other names that his pursuer had shouted out. "Cudgel," that was one of them. What was the other? Something like Zig, or Zug—"Zag," that was it! So there were at least four Wrathmonks and proba-bly several more. Measle felt in his pocket for the jelly beans. How many had he eaten already? Two—that meant he only had ten left! He would have to be care-ful if he wanted them to last.

There was the sound of pounding footsteps, and Measle huddled back into the shadows. A moment later, he saw the young Wrathmonk run past the entrance to the alley, his wet hair streaming behind him. Tinker huddled close to the ground and growled softly, and Measle quickly put his hand over the little dog's muzzle to quiet him. The sound of the slapping footsteps faded away, and Measle bent his head close to Tinker's and whispered, "You've got to be quiet, Tink. You can't growl or bark every time you see a Wrathmonk. You've got to be quiet all the time, okay?"

Tinker licked Measle's nose. He had no idea what the smelly kid had just said, but that was all right, wasn't it? *I could do without all this falling water, though—and it is nice and dry under this roof thingy.*

Tinker heard the distant voices before Measle did, and he growled again. Immediately the smelly kid wrapped his fingers around his nose, stopping any further sound from coming out. *Ah*, thought Tinker, *the smelly kid did this before—it happens when I give the smelly kid the warning-growly-business—the smelly kid wraps his paw over the old nose. Can't do the warning-growly-business anymore—so, the smelly kid doesn't want the warning-growly-business. Right then, I'll just keep quiet.*

Measle huddled deeper into the shadows under the awning as the voices came nearer and nearer.

Five Wrathmonks came into view at the end of the alley. Two of the Wrathmonks—one thin and blond, the other short and tubby—Measle recognized. The third Wrathmonk was huge. He looked to Measle more like a gorilla than a man—a gorilla wearing some sort of motorcycle outfit, complete with a motorcycle helmet on his bullet-shaped head. The last two Wrathmonks had glossy black hair and neat black clothes, and Measle noticed, with a start of surprise, that one of them was a woman. *Well, why not? Prudence Peyser had told them all, back there on Basil's tabletop, that women could be Wizards and Warlocks, too—but very few ever became Wrathmonks. This must be one of the rare ones.*

The small male Wrathmonk with the glossy black hair said, "You're quite sure it came thisss way, Draggle?"

The young blond Wrathmonk nodded impatiently. "Yeah, *courssse* I'm sure, Zag."

"But what did it look like?" said the skinny woman.

"I dunno, do I, Mrs. Zagreb?" snarled Draggle. "It was invisible, wasn't it? I only sssaw itsss outline because of the rain falling all over it."

"But did it appear to be *human*, Draggle?" said Mr. Zagreb. "That'sss what we want to know."

"Yeah," said Draggle, with growing confidence. "It was definitely human. It was a bit sssmall, though."

"The child!" said Mrs. Zagreb excitedly. "It must have been the Ssstubbs child!"

The Wrathmonk that looked like a gorilla grunted and said in a voice so deep that it sounded to Measle as if it was coming from an underground cave, "We ought to be sure, Mrs. Zagreb. It could have been anything. Knowing Draggle, it could have jussst been a big rat or sssomething."

"It was not a big rat!" shouted Draggle. "I know the difference between a big rat and a human being, don't I?"

The huge Wrathmonk took a step toward Draggle and put a fist the size of a soccer ball under the young Wrathmonk's nose. "Don't you raise your voice at me, young Draggle," he growled, and Draggle took a nervous step backward.

"I'm sure he didn't mean it, Mr. Cudgel," said Flabbit soothingly. "I sssuggessst we asssume it *wasn't* a big rat, though. Jussst for sssafety's sssake, eh? I mean to sssay, if it *is* the Ssstubbs boy—well, that'sss a bit of all right, isn't it?"

"Indeed it is," said Mr. Zagreb, "and we've got to find him! That was the whole point, wasn't it? The whole point of Grissstle's plan!"

Measle felt a sudden chill flutter down his spine. Gristle! Wasn't that the name of Basil Tramplebone's bank manager? Yes! Griswold Gristle! The one who had turned over all the Stubbses' money to his horrible guardian! Was he here, too?

"Right," growled Cudgel. "We'd better sssplit up. But I dunno how we're expected to find sssomething that's invisible. And come to think of it, how did he get to be invisible in the firssst place, that'sss what I'd like to know."

"It'sss a Wizard family, Mr. Cudgel," said Flabbit, nodding wisely. "There's no telling what they can do."

"Well, they can't do anything very much now,"

sniffed Mrs. Zagreb in a scornful voice. "Not without the woman—and we've got her."

In the darkness of the alley, Measle's eyes gleamed. He was right! His mum was here! Now it was just a question of finding her!

"Mr. Grissstle sssaid we could use sssome collective magic on thisss one," said Draggle. "He sssaid the Dragodon won't mind for once. What do you think we should do? Any ideas, Flabbit?"

Mr. Flabbit was busy trying to stick his loose hank of greasy hair back on his scalp. He smoothed it down with one pudgy hand. "I don't know any invisible-to-visible ssspells," he muttered. "Does anybody?"

All the Wrathmonks shook their heads gloomily. Then Mrs. Zagreb narrowed her small black eyes and smiled with her lipstick-caked mouth and said, "We could enlissst sssome help. Sssome *mindlesss* help."

"Sssome what?" grunted Cudgel.

"Come, I'll show you," said Mrs. Zagreb, moving away and out of Measle's line of sight. He watched as the rest of the Wrathmonks followed her. Their footsteps faded into the distance. Only when he could hear nothing but the steady dripping of the rain did Measle dare to relax a little. He took his hand off Tinker's muzzle and whispered, "Good boy," into one of Tinker's ears. Tinker wagged his stubby tail and managed a quick lick of the smelly kid's nose before Measle pulled his face away.

8

THE HUNT

There was a sudden flash of light in the sky, quickly followed by a low, rumbling sound. At first Measle thought it must be thunder, but the flash had been quite close and somehow lower in the sky than where lightning usually occurs—and the rumble wasn't quite the same as the rumble of thunder.

"I think they're doing magic, Tink," whispered Measle into Tinker's ear. "Big magic, too, by the sound of it."

Measle waited a few more moments, but there was

no further sound, apart from the drumming of the rain. He looked around at the dark alley. The pavement shone with wetness. There were scattered piles of used paper cups and paper plates and sodden paper napkins and there, down at the far end of the alley, the tall wire fence. The alley was a dead end. It was, Measle decided, a bad place to be holed up in—but, at the same time, he was reluctant to leave it. At that moment the alley seemed to Measle to be the only relatively safe place in the whole park.

Measle was wrong.

Sitting in the shelter of the awning, on the cold, damp ground, with his knees drawn up to his chin and his back resting against the wall of the booth, Measle was quite unaware that there was something moving behind him. The something was pink and fuzzy and *very* cuddly—until you looked a little closer and saw the nasty glitter in the thing's beady glass eyes.

The thing was creeping soundlessly along the shelves until it reached the glass window at the front of the booth. It bent its head and peered down at the figures of Measle and Tinker below. Then, quite silently, it began to push at the sheet of glass.

The booth's window was hinged at the top, so that it could be swung up and out when the booth was open for business. Bit by bit, the bottom of the window began to move outward, pushed by the steady pressure of the pink and fuzzy thing behind it.

Measle didn't discover the danger he was in until a pink, furry hippopotamus fell, with a soft thump, onto the top of his head.

Instinctively, Measle raised his arms and brushed frantically at the thing that was now clinging to his hair. His hands met softness—a furry, fuzzy softness—and he shoved hard at the thing and felt it lose what little grip it had. He pushed again, harder this time, and the thing flew off his head and landed several feet away, splashing into a puddle on the wet pavement.

Measle stared at the extraordinary object, his whole body frozen with shock. *How could a pink hippo—exactly the same kind of pink hippo as the one his mum had won the other week—suddenly come to life?*

Tinker wasn't frozen at all. Tinker was on his feet, the hair on the back of his neck stiff and straight, his lips curled back from his teeth in a snarl. Whatever this squishy-looking cushion on four legs was, Tinker didn't like the look of it at all. He'd seen it before: *it was the same nasty, squishy cushion thingy that the Nice Lady had brought home and I didn't like it then! Now here it is again—and now I like it even less! At least the one the Nice Lady brought home didn't move—but this one does! This one is stomping along on its fat little legs, lurching steadily toward me. . . .*

Tinker let out a succession of short, sharp little barks, and this brought Measle out of his shocked paralysis. He lurched forward and grabbed Tinker's nose and whispered frantically into Tinker's ear.

"Shhh, Tink! Not a sound!"

Measle pushed Tinker behind him and stood up, facing the oncoming creature. It didn't look very dangerous. Other than the disturbing fact that a pink, furry hippopotamus had somehow come to life, it was still just a soft, cheap, cuddly toy and, as such, could hardly do either him or Tinker any harm.

Measle took a step forward and reached down to pick the thing up.

And then the pink hippo's mouth split open.

A moment before the mouth had been a simple line of black thread, embroidered into the nylon fur, to give

139

the suggestion of lips. Now the threads parted and the mouth gaped open and, in the fraction of a second before the hippo lunged at his hand, Measle saw half a dozen gleaming steel needles lining the front of the open jaws. They looked like the sort of needles that a sewing machine uses.

The hippo's head darted forward, and the needles sank deep into Measle's outstretched hand.

The pain was bad. It was like being stung by six large and ferocious bees all at the same time. Measle gave a sharp cry and yanked his hand away and, at the same instant, the hippo released Measle's hand, opening its mouth to take another bite.

Measle kicked out at the horrible thing, and the toe of his shoe connected with the snout of the creature, hurling it backward into the shadows.

Measle hissed with pain and stared down at his throbbing hand. There was a line of six little pinpricks on the back of his hand, and from each tiny puncture wound oozed a small drop of blood. The stinging feeling was bad, but just about bearable if he didn't think about it too much. *That thing might* look *cute and cuddly*, thought Measle, *but it's really* dangerous.

And here it came again, waddling out of the darkness toward them, its mouth gaping wide, its little glass eyes glittering.

I've got to get rid of it! thought Measle. *I've got to stop it from coming after us!*

The creature's pace was slow. Its legs were only two inches long, and it lurched clumsily from side to side as it advanced. Measle walked quickly to one side and then watched as the hippo turned slowly to face his new position. The hippo's turn was a sluggish business, and Measle realized that he could, if he moved reasonably quickly, get behind the hippo before the thing would be able to face him again.

"Stay, Tink!" he hissed. "Sit!" Tinker, growling very quietly at the back of his throat, obediently sat down. Measle moved quickly around the hippo. Then, firmly pushing his fear aside, he darted forward and grabbed the creature by the scruff of its neck and lifted it off the ground.

It was heavy and damp from the rain. The fur felt slimy. The hippo wriggled weakly in Measle's hand, its head twisting from side to side, its mouth opening and closing, the tiny needle teeth gleaming faintly in the darkness. But, try as it might, it couldn't reach Measle's hand—or any other part of him, either.

Holding the writhing hippo at arm's length, Measle ran to the end of the alley. The high wire fence loomed over him. It was high—but not too high. Measle swung his arm back, then forward, releasing his grip when his hand was at the highest point of the arc. The hippo sailed through the darkness, turning end over end as it cleared the top of the wire fence. Then it fell among the electrical machinery with a faint and distant thump.

Measle pulled his rain-smeared goggles down from his eyes and ran back to where Tinker was still sitting.

"Come on, Tink," he whispered. "We'd better get out of here. I don't know if that thing can climb fences—I hope it can't—but I don't want to wait to find out!"

Measle and Tinker ran quietly toward the entrance of the alley. When they got there, Measle carefully put his head out. To the left was the go-cart track, the street beside it empty and stretching away into the darkness. To the right—also empty darkness.

No, not empty.

Something was moving in his direction. Some sort

of mass of crawling things, slow and low to the ground. It looked like the ground was swarming with movement.

Measle pushed his goggles over his eyes and rubbed both lenses with the cuffs of his leather jacket, clearing as many of the raindrops as he could from their mirrored surfaces. Then, in the soft light that the goggles revealed, he saw them.

Pink, squashy, furry hippopotamuses. At least fifty of them! And behind the pink hippos came a whole zoo of multicolored, cuddly toys—lime-green teddy bears, lemon-yellow camels, crimson monkeys, blue dinosaurs—all advancing steadily toward him, their glass eyes glinting menacingly.

It isn't just the one pink hippo that's been brought to horrible life, thought Measle. *It's every toy prize in the theme park! And, while I might be able to cope with one or two of the creatures, here's a whole regiment of them! And if I get surrounded by the things—a few more of those sharp, stinging bites and I'll be done for!* As he watched in horror, Measle saw four of the creatures break away from the main group and waddle off down a side street—then another four turned off and waddled in another direction.

Mrs. Zagreb had said something about getting mindless help.

These things didn't seem to be mindless at all.

They were searching the place.

Searching for *him*.

Panic suddenly seized Measle. He grabbed Tinker, ran back down the alley, and huddled under the awning once again. The front line of the army was passing by the alley entrance. Measle watched them as they went by. They marched in step with each other, a steady, pounding rhythm that Measle could hear through the drumming of the rain. *Thump, thump, thump.*

Then, to Measle's horror, two yellow camels, a green teddy bear and a small blue dinosaur broke off from the main body and waddled into the alley.

Tinker growled softly. Measle fumbled in his jacket pocket for a jelly bean and, as he did so, he lost hold of Tinker. The little dog wriggled free, jumped out of his arms and ran toward the advancing creatures, the hair on his back standing up straight and stiff. Measle, his fingers still searching frantically in his pocket, froze. But it was too late. The leading camel's head turned and its tiny, black glass eyes stared fixedly at Tinker, who was now advancing slowly on the small group, a low, rumbling growl sounding deep in his throat.

"Tinker!" whispered Measle hoarsely. "Come back!"

Tinker took no notice. *This is too important—what are these thingies? They don't smell like animals—they smell more like cushions—wet cushions—but, wet or dry, cushions don't walk and cushions don't look at you all funny, and if there's one thing I don't care for, it's being looked at all funny.*

The two yellow camels and the green teddy bear came closer. The little blue dinosaur paused and then turned and began to move back toward the alley entrance, where the tail end of the army of soft toys was just passing by.

It's going to report on what it's seen! thought Measle. *It's going to report that it's found us! I've got to stop it!*

Measle got up from his crouched position and ran toward the end of the alley. He passed Tinker, who was holding his ground, and he skirted by the three other creatures, whose attention was fixed on Tinker.

Measle caught up with the dinosaur just as it reached the alley entrance. He bent down and grabbed it by the back of its neck. It was surprisingly heavy and felt horribly cold and slimy. Measle realized that the steady rain had soaked right through the fur and into the stuffing of the toy, so that it was saturated with water.

Holding the horrible thing at arm's length, Measle ran back down the alley.

And then Tinker attacked his foes.

The little dog decided that walking cushions were objects that he simply couldn't allow. So he leaped forward, buried his teeth in the nose of the leading camel and began to shake the thing wildly from side to side.

The squashy wet dinosaur in Measle's hand was wriggling, its stumpy legs jerking backward and forward. Its mouth gaped open, its head twisting as it tried to find something to sink its needle teeth into.

Measle ran past Tinker to the end of the alley. There was the high wire fence and, beyond it, the dark humps of the electrical machinery. He hurled the dinosaur clean over the top of the fence. It landed with a squishy thump somewhere in the darkness. Then Measle turned to see how Tinker was getting on.

Tinker was in trouble. He'd been so busy trying to shake the leading camel into small pieces that he hadn't noticed the other two creatures closing in on him and, by the time he felt the pressure of their heavy, wet bodies against him, it was too late. The lime-green teddy bear lunged forward and snapped its steel teeth into Tinker's stumpy tail.

Tinker yelped, high and loud. The stinging in his tail was very painful, but it wasn't enough to make him lose his grip on the camel's nose. He held firm the camel's snout and went on shaking the creature from side to side with all the strength of his powerful neck muscles. At the same time, he began to circle faster and faster, trying to keep his rear end as far as possible from the snapping jaws of the other two creatures.

All the attentions of Tinker's attackers were on the little dog, so neither of them saw Measle approaching from behind them. The first thing they knew about it was when they felt Measle's hands grab the scruffs of their necks. A moment later they were dangling in midair. Tinker, free now to concentrate on the one enemy over which he had complete control, gave one more furious shaking to the camel in his mouth and, in a great shower of wet, fuzzy, nylon stuffing, the head ripped clean off the camel's body. The lemon-yellow torso flew several feet across the alley and landed in a pile of discarded food wrappers. Its legs waved feebly in the air. Tinker gave one more furious shake to the head and then let it go, and the head dropped away into the darkness.

Measle ran once again to the end of the alley. He hurled the camel over the fence and there was a *squish!* as it landed somewhere in the darkness. Then he pulled his arm back and hurled the teddy bear.

The teddy bear flew through the falling rain. Measle had let go of it a fraction early, so the thing went higher over the fence than the other three. It soared over the electrical machinery and then began to fall, hitting a high power cable on its way down. There was a sudden, blinding flash of blue-white light, a crackling bang, a great shower of sparks, and an explosion of white stuffing that fell out of the night sky like oversized snowflakes.

"They are doing too much magic!" screamed Griswold Gristle, peering out into the darkness through the office windows of the park's administration block. "I sssaid they could do *one* major collective ssspell, but they've jussst done a *sssecond* one!"

148

"How do you know that, Griswold?" said Judge Hardscrabble. The judge was sitting bolt upright in a swivel chair behind a big steel desk and pretending that he was in his courtroom, presiding over a very important case. "Where is your evidence, Griswold?" he said in his best judge's voice. "Where is your evidence that they are disssobeying you?"

Griswold turned away from the window. "There was another flash of light in the dissstance, Cedric," he said angrily. "A flash of light and a loud crash. Is that sssufficient evidence for you?"

"A flash of light and a loud crash?" murmured Judge Cedric, narrowing his eyes, in the hope that he would look intelligent and thoughtful. *He looks like a shortsighted old tortoise*, thought Griswold.

"Well, I mussst grant you, it is certainly a *posssibility* that they have cassst a further ssspell, Griswold."

"A posssibility?" yelped Griswold. "A *posssibility*?"

"It is certainly a *posssibility*," repeated the judge in his most pompous voice. "However, there is another explanation, Griswold. Have you consssidered that, what you sssaw could well have been caused by—the sssetting off—of a sssmall *nuclear device*?"

Griswold gritted his teeth. Of all the Wrathmonks he'd ever known, Cedric Hardscrabble was certainly the stupidest.

"It was *not* a nuclear device, Cedric, sssmall or otherwise," said Griswold. "It was magic! A fairly powerful ssspell, too—and very sssoon after the firssst one. Where they obtained the additional mana is anybody's guesss. I presume they mussst have been very near the sssource to recharge ssso quickly. And that could ssso easily upssset His Lordship the Dragodon! We cannot afford to disssplease His Lordship the Dragodon in thisss manner!"

"Well, what do you want me to do about it?" said Judge Cedric sulkily.

"We mussst go out there and take charge," said Griswold, seizing his umbrella and making for the door.

Judge Cedric didn't move. Instead, he settled himself more comfortably in the swivel chair, leaned back and clasped his hands behind his head. He had no intention of going anywhere. It was dark out there and cold and, of course, very wet. But here, inside the administration offices, it was nice and warm and dry. The only inconveniences were the twenty or thirty stone statues that littered the offices and the corridors and just got in everybody's way. The statues were all that remained of the administration staff and the security personnel who had been left behind to look after the Isle of Smiles while it was closed for the winter. Of course, the Medusa head had made short work of them! It had really proved its worth—it had been such fun watching them all petrify one by one.

"Well, come *along*, Cedric!" snapped Griswold, now standing in the open doorway.

"I thought I might ssstay here, Griswold," said Judge Cedric in a dreamy voice. The chair was so comfy. . . .

Griswold plastered a sickly smile on his little mouth and put on his most persuasive voice. "When we capture the intruder, Cedric," he said, "perhaps you would be ssso kind as to use your exhalation enchantment on him—before we kill him, that is. I would ssso love to sssee all those horrid boils popping out all over his body and his face! Would you do that for usss, Cedric?"

Judge Cedric was proud of his exhalation enchantment, and the thought of using it on a helpless captive was very appealing. He jumped to his feet. Then he took his old bowler hat and his umbrella from the coat stand in the corner of the room and joined Griswold in the doorway.

"Come then, Griswold," he said happily. "What are we waiting for? Let usss make hassste!"

Half a mile from the administration block, the other Wrathmonks were also on the move. They too had seen the flash of blue-white light and heard the sizzling crackle as the wet teddy bear had exploded in a shower of stuffing but, unlike Griswold Gristle, they had been close enough to realize that this was not magic. This was some kind of electrical short circuit—and it almost certainly had something to do with whatever it was that they were seeking.

They began to hurry back toward the alley.

9

GHOULISH GRANGE

Measle stood frozen to the spot as the stuffing fluttered down around him. Then, a moment later, the stinging pain in his hand brought him back to his senses. He hurried back down the alley toward Tinker, who was running in little circles, trying to catch up with his hurting tail. Measle scooped up the little dog in one smooth movement. Then he ran with Tinker in his arms to the alley entrance. He peeked out. To the left he could just make out the tail end of the soft toy army marching away into the darkness. To the right was the empty street—but that was the way the Wrath-monks had gone, and Measle was sure that the flash and the crackle would bring them back to the alley in a hurry. So, he would run in the opposite direction.

Holding Tinker, Measle slipped out of the alley. Silently, he trotted through the darkness. Quite soon he came to a side street, and he ducked into it. It was dark here, like the alley. But this was a proper street, with no high wire fence across it, which meant that Measle and Tinker couldn't be trapped here. They had a clear escape route, just so long as they kept going.

Measle tried to remember where this particular road led to. On his right there was a miniature carousel with brightly colored little cars and buses and trucks. Farther up the street, was a small railroad track that went in a simple oval. Standing silently in the miniature station was a little bright red locomotive. It had a happy, smiling face painted on the front of its boiler, just above the cowcatcher—and Measle realized where he was. This was the area of the Isle of Smiles where the rides were reserved for the littlest children. Somewhere close by, Measle remembered, was one of those blow-up castles. On the day he and his parents had come to the park, it had been full of squealing, laughing, bouncing toddlers. Yes, there it was, just around a bend in the road! It was still and silent now, and a lot of the air had leaked out, so that the castle drooped and sagged, almost as if it was made from melting ice cream.

There was a distant, clattering sound coming from somewhere behind them.

Measle turned and Tinker poked his snout out from the folds of Measle's jacket and sniffed the air suspiciously. The clattering sound was getting steadily closer. It was a very odd noise, as if a hundred wooden hammers were tapping away against the hard ground. The hammers tapped with no apparent rhythm, just a constant, irregular *tap—tap—tap, clatter—clatter—clatter.*

Measle couldn't smell anything other than the cold, wet air, but he could see through the darkness to the spot where the street joined the road they had just vacated. And there, just coming into view, trotted a brightly painted, wooden carousel horse.

It paused for a moment, and as it did so, it was joined by another horse—then another, and another— until a small crowd of the creatures jostled for space at the juncture of the two roads.

Measle watched in horror as the leading carousel horse flared its nostrils wide. Slowly, the yellow head turned this way and that. The mouth was open and gaping, and Measle could see the bright red, lolling tongue of the thing. Its eyes were wide and unblinking, and it moved its head with a certain stiffness, as if movement was strange to it. The pole that had attached it to the platform of the carousel was still upright in its body, sticking up from the middle of its back and down through its belly, the end just clearing the ground beneath.

Measle shuddered. The pink hippos and the lime-green bears and the lemon-yellow camels—they were bad enough. But these things were a lot worse. The hippos and the bears and the camels could bite and sting, but they were soft and light and (one by one, at least) fairly easy to throw over a nearby fence. But these horses were made of wood, and wood was heavy and hard! And then there was the size of the crea-tures—they were much bigger than Measle and dwarfed little Tinker completely! And last—but far from least—was their speed. *They may be made of wood,* thought Measle with growing despair, *but these are horses, and horses can run really fast!*

All the carousel horses were now turning their heads this way and that, their staring eyes peering through the rain and the darkness, their nostrils flared wide to catch any scent on the damp air. It was lucky for Measle and Tinker that it was a dark night and that the breeze was, at the moment, blowing in their direction, otherwise the horses would have been certain to see them and smell them. As it was, the horses went on milling around at the junction of the two streets, as if unsure which way to go next.

Very carefully Measle reached into his jacket pocket and took out a yellow jelly bean. Slowly, he raised his hand to his mouth and popped the jelly bean onto his tongue. A quick chew, and it was down his throat. Then Measle turned and began to run, as silently as he could, his invisible feet skimming over the wet road like a ghost.

He passed the drooping castle and headed fast toward a big dark building that loomed large at the far end of the street. It was a spooky-looking place with tall chimneys and a steeply sloping roof. Beneath the roof, the eaves were ornately carved, and the windows looked like the sort you see in old churches. The whole thing reminded Measle a little of the horrible house where he'd spent so many miserable years with Basil Tramplebone. There was a short path that led to the tall front door, and at the beginning of this path was a sign that read GHOULISH GRANGE.

For a moment Measle wondered if perhaps it was here that the Wrathmonks were holding his mother prisoner. Unlike the rest of the rides, here was an actual house—and it was grim and nasty enough to suit the Wrathmonks' purposes—whatever they might be. . . .

Measle's thoughts were interrupted by the sound of wooden hooves on the roadway—a sound that was getting rapidly louder and louder. Measle risked a quick glance over his shoulder—and there, not a hundred feet behind him, came the carousel horses at full gallop, heading straight for him! How they knew he was there, Measle couldn't imagine. Perhaps the wind had changed, perhaps they had seen his ghostly outline—but there was no time for thinking, there was no time for anything, except to run as fast as he could toward the only place that might offer him even the smallest degree of safety. . . .

Ghoulish Grange.

By the time he reached the short path that led to the front door, Measle felt that his lungs were about to burst. Panting heavily, Measle passed under the sign and staggered up the path. The sound of the wooden hooves was almost deafening—the carousel horses could only be a few feet behind him now! He reached the heavy door and slammed his shoulder against its wooden panels.

It didn't move. Measle rammed his shoulder against it again. Nothing. But how had it opened before? When he and his parents had been here it had just swung open as they approached, with a lot of amplified creaking and shrieking from its rusting iron hinges, and a ghostly voice had boomed out, "Welcome to Ghoulish Grange, my hideous house of horrors! Abandon hope, all ye who enter here!" Obviously, the whole thing worked on some sort of sensor beam that detected the approach of visitors, and now, with the power off all over the park, the beam wasn't working.

The clattering of the hooves was right behind him

and Measle turned, his back to the door. There, right in front of him, was the leading horse. Its wide, unblinking eyes bored into his and Measle realized, with a start of horror, that the effects of the jelly bean had worn off and he was no longer invisible. Even if he could somehow have reached into his pocket for another jelly bean, it was now too late. The horse was rearing up onto its hind legs, its front hooves pawing at the air. A shrieking, whinnying sound came from its gaping mouth. Then it lunged forward, its front hooves slicing through the air toward Measle's head. Desperately, Measle threw himself sideways onto the ground, and the wooden hooves whistled past his ear and slammed against the door. There was a groaning, splintering sound and then the whole door suddenly fell inward, torn from its locks and its hinges by the sheer weight of the carousel horse's attack.

The horse took a step backward and reared once more. In the moment before its hooves came smashing down again, Measle—clutching Tinker tight to his chest—scrambled on hands and feet through the opening and into the deep shadows of the building.

With Measle on all fours, Tinker found himself no

longer being held tight to the smelly kid's chest, so he wriggled free and slipped onto the concrete floor. He thought for a moment of turning back and confronting these strange, woody-smelling creatures that were attacking him and the smelly kid. *They look like horsey thingies and they run like horsey thingies and they even sound like horsey thingies, but they don't* smell *like horsey thingies and that's all that matters! Like, back on the tabletop, when that giant bug was after us, it had* smelled *like a giant bug, which was why there'd been no question about going after the nasty great thingy! But these horsey thingies smell of wood and paint and that isn't right! That's not the way things are supposed to be! And when things aren't the way they're supposed to be then, on the whole, running away is a good idea—a couple of quick barks first though, just to show who's really the big boss around here.*

Tinker yelped twice and then darted off into the shadows, and Measle scrambled to his feet and raced after him. There was a moment while the carousel horses seemed bewildered by the unexpected turn of events. Then the leading horse shouldered its way through the opening, its hooves sounding hollow on the fallen door.

161

In the house it was pitch dark, but Measle quickly slipped the goggles over his eyes, and now he could see exactly where he was and where he needed to go. In front of him were five rows of steel rails, set in the concrete floor, which channeled the visitors to the Ghoulish Grange ride. Measle remembered how it had been on the day they had visited the Isle of Smiles— this whole space full of happy, smiling faces, the sound of laughter everywhere around them. He remembered the slow, shuffling feet of the crowd as the line inched its way to the landing, where the passengers got on and off the little trains—little trains that were shaped like *coffins*, Measle remembered. At the time they had all found that quite funny, and Sam had even made a joke about *his* coffin being far too small for him ("Look at this, Measle! Fat lot of good this is! I can't even lie down in it!") but now, it wasn't funny anymore. Nothing was funny anymore. . . .

A loud clattering of wood on concrete jerked Measle back into action. Ahead, he could see Tinker blundering about under the steel railings. The little dog kept bumping his nose against the metal poles and then shaking his head and trying again. Measle realized that

Tinker, in this total darkness, couldn't see a thing.

The leading carousel horse stumbled into the area, its head jerking to and fro, its painted wooden eyes staring in the blackness. Behind it, the rest of the horses began to push their way forward, crowding the creature in the front, pressing against it, and the leading horse turned and snapped its wooden jaws at the noses of those behind it. When they didn't move away, it bucked and lashed out with its rear hooves, and there was a loud *crack!* of wood on wood.

Measle ran forward, away from the snapping jaws and lashing hooves. He scrambled over the first metal rail, then the second, then the third.

Behind him, he could hear a commotion of clattering hooves. He glanced back and saw the leading horse launch itself forward and up. It soared through the pitchy darkness, clearing the first barrier easily, and the second, and now it was dropping down and heading straight for where Measle was crouching!

Desperately, Measle threw himself under the fourth barrier, rolling across the narrow space under the fifth and last barrier. And, behind him, came a great splintering *crash!* as the carousel horse's body landed across the third line of rails. Measle saw that the wooden body of the creature, draped over the iron railing, had broken almost in half. There were jagged splinters of wood sticking out from around its painted saddle, and the vertical steel bar that had connected it to the carousel platform was bent almost double.

In the pitch darkness, the rest of the carousel horses had no idea of the dangers in front of them. All they could hear was the frantic snorting and whinnying of their leader, somewhere up ahead. One by one, they all leaped forward, crashing together in a great jumble of splintered wood. Three survived the collision and they began slowly to pick their way round the obstacles that lay between them and their prey.

Measle crawled forward as silently as he could. The three remaining carousel horses might not be able to see him, but they could certainly hear him, so the sooner he put some sort of barrier between the creatures and himself, the better. In front of him was the landing platform and the rails and a line of little coffins on wheels. The wheels rested on the narrow rail lines that led to a pair of tall, arched doors. The doors were made of iron and were massive, the kind you might find in a medieval castle, designed to keep out a whole army of invaders—the kind that could certainly stop a few wooden horses from breaking through. So that was where he should head for—but first, where was Tinker?

Measle looked around frantically and found the little dog, sitting right by the leading coffin, pawing at his bruised snout. Measle ran forward and scooped him up. Tinker gave a small yelp of surprise at being grabbed, without any warning, in this total darkness. Then, realizing who was holding him, he shot out his tongue and flipped it over Measle's nose.

"Shhh, Tink," whispered Measle, holding the little dog tight to his chest. He pushed his way past the line of coffins and reached the huge doors. He put his hands flat against them—yes, they were cold, like iron or steel!—and he pressed hard, but it was like pressing against a mountain. Nothing moved beneath his straining hands, and meanwhile, the clattering of the hooves was getting nearer and nearer.

There, on the other side of the rail was a sort of hatch in the wall! The hatch door was ajar and, beyond it, a rectangle of darkness. . . .

Measle scrambled over the line of coffins and knelt down by the opening. Holding tight to Tinker, he pulled at the small door with his spare hand and the door swung sideways, revealing a metal tunnel that ran for several feet before curving away into darkness. Measle guessed it was some kind of ventilation shaft, or perhaps an access tunnel of some sort. Without looking back, Measle crawled into the narrow space and began to inch his way forward. Where this shaft was leading, he had no idea, but it was away from the danger behind him, and Measle was pretty sure that horses—wooden or otherwise—couldn't crawl through tunnels as small as this one.

The tunnel bent to the left and then carried on a few more feet, before ending at a metal grating.

Measle pushed against the metal grating and he felt it bend beneath his hand. So, in an emergency, he could probably break through. With any luck, he wouldn't have to. This was as good a hiding place as any, and he certainly didn't fancy spending any time in the cemeteries and the tombs of Ghoulish Grange.

From the folds of his jacket came a soft growl.

"What is it, Tink?" whispered Measle, and Tinker

pushed his nose out of the depths of the jacket and sniffed the still air.

Wet cushion! Another stupid wet cushion! More than one, actually! And close by! Too *close.*

Tinker slipped out of Measle's jacket and onto the metal floor. Measle could see him clearly in the pitch darkness. The hairs on his back stood up in a ridge, and his ears were flattened on his skull. He was facing away from the grating, staring blindly back up the tunnel. Measle peered in the same direction—there was nothing there. But now Tinker was growling again, a low, menacing sound from deep in his throat. The curve in the shaft decreased the distance that Measle could see—only a few feet in fact—so he leaned sideways to look around the bend, and there, crawling steadily toward him, came three crimson monkeys.

Their nylon fur dripped with rainwater. Their mouths were stretched wide in silly grins, revealing the line of steel needles. Their big, round eyes were blind in the darkness. On they came, slowly feeling their way round the curve in the tunnel, coming steadily nearer and nearer. . . .

Tinker burst out with a flurry of short, sharp barks,

and the three monkey heads swiveled toward the sound.

Frantically, Measle turned and lashed out at the metal grating with both feet. He kicked again and again, and the flimsy lock on the edge of the grating gave way and the whole thing swung to one side with a tinny crash.

"Come on, Tink," hissed Measle, grabbing Tinker's collar and pulling him hard toward the rectangular hole.

Tinker wanted to stay and fight, but he couldn't see a thing and his paws couldn't get a grip on the smooth metal floor of the tunnel, and the pull on his collar was powerful—and the smelly kid sounded pretty determined So, reluctantly, Tinker turned away from the approaching monkeys and allowed himself to be dragged out of the tunnel. He and Measle landed with a tangled thump on the side of a plaster slope, and together they rolled down the little hill until they were brought up with a bump against a weathered, mossy tombstone.

For a moment Measle lay still. The wind had been knocked out of him by the fall, and he was having trouble getting his breath back, but Tinker was nudging at him with his nose. Then he heard the soft, wet shuffling sound as the three crimson monkeys slipped out of the tunnel and slithered down the low wall. He scrambled to his feet, grabbed Tinker and ran from the tombstone, until he was brought up short by an open grave in front of him. The grave was about eight feet long and five feet wide and it was deep. Measle's goggles showed him what was down there. A plastic skeleton, with red glass eyes, was lying in the bottom of the pit. Measle remembered the moment (it seemed so long ago!) when he and his parents had passed this way before. His mother had screamed when this same skeleton had suddenly reared up out of its grave as their little coffin had rattled by, its red eyes flashing and its long, bony arms waving over their heads. Lee had screamed, then laughed—and then screamed again when Sam had turned to her in the semidarkness, his face pulled into a monster grimace, his eyes crossed and his tongue sticking out and his teeth glowing white.

Behind Measle came the same slow, wet, slithering sound. He whipped around—the three crimson monkeys were coming toward him, carefully feeling their way in the pitch darkness. From the folds of Measle's leather jacket came a soft growl. Tinker could smell these three wet cushions. He could smell that they were coming closer and closer—*but how am I supposed to fight them if I can't see them? And all this being carried about everywhere—it's nice, but enough is enough! Doesn't the smelly kid realize I have legs? Perfectly good legs, too— and four of them, which is a lot better than two, thank you very much! Particularly when there are cushions to fight! So, let's do a bit of the old walky-walkies now, shall we?*

Tinker started to wriggle inside the jacket, trying to get free, but Measle tightened his grip, because Measle had just had one of his ideas, and this particular idea required Tinker to be unmoving and quiet, at least for a moment or two.

Measle tensed the muscles in his legs, pulled Tinker's wriggling body tight to his chest and leaped forward. In three steps he was running, and in four he was in the air, his jump carrying him clean over the deep pit. He landed with a thump safely on the far side, right by the narrow rail tracks. Quickly, he turned and crouched down and watched as the three monkeys crawled nearer and nearer.

Tinker managed to wriggle free from the folds of the leather jacket and dropped lightly to the floor. He was as blind as the monkeys, but his keen nose told him which way to face.

Tinker growled again and the growl ended in a little yelp, and the three crimson monkeys turned their heads toward the sound and came crawling forward, a little faster now.

The sound of their shuffling bodies, somewhere close by in the darkness, caused Tinker to break out in a series of sharp, furious little barks. *Here they come—nasty, wet crawling thingies that don't smell like anything I can remember ever smelling before—I'll let them know who's boss!* And Tinker let out another flurry of furious barks.

The three monkeys lifted their nylon front paws from the floor and stood up on their hind legs. They bared their steel needle teeth. Then, together, they sprang forward into a shambling, scurrying run.

They didn't see the gaping pit in front of them. The only indication that it was there at all was when they felt the ground disappear beneath their nylon feet—and then it was too late. One by one they dropped soundlessly into the black hole, landing with squishy plops on the skeleton at the bottom.

There was a moment of silence. Then Measle heard the soft, wet slithery sound again. He and Tinker cautiously approached the edge of the pit and peered into its depths. There, crawling over the long white bones of the skeleton, were the monkeys. They looked up, smiling their crazy smiles. Then they felt their way to the walls of the pit and reached up for a handhold of some sort with which to pull themselves out of the grave.

But the walls were smooth. The builders of the ride had known that the insides of the various open graves had to be invisible to the passing riders, so they had made the walls out of painted steel, which was impossible to climb, even for crimson monkeys with nylon paws. The three horrible creatures clawed and scrabbled and made little jumps into the air in order to try to catch hold of the edge of the pit, but all their efforts were in vain.

Measle edged away from the grave so he wouldn't have to look at the slithering, clawing, jumping things. Soon he couldn't hear them anymore, either, and that made him feel a bit better.

He turned and looked around at the cavernous

space. In the soft light of his goggles, Ghoulish Grange didn't look creepy at all. It was just a vast, open area, with a high domed ceiling, filled with obviously artificial corpses and skeletons and zombies, with crumbling bridges and tottering, ivy-covered walls and ancient graveyards—all made of painted plaster—with a looping pair of railroad tracks that wound backward and forward and round and about until they disappeared under another pair of tall, steel doors on the far side of the building. It was just a mechanical thing, a place designed to amuse.

Not even a bit scary.

Well, perhaps a little bit.

But it wasn't the plastic and plaster inhabitants of Ghoulish Grange that were making Measle nervous now. It was the rhythmic *clang—clang—clang* of wood on iron that was coming from the great steel doors nearby. Measle guessed that the remaining carousel horses had reached the doors and were hammering against them in unison, their wooden hooves crashing against the metal in a steady rhythm. Measle wondered for a moment if animated creatures like cuddly toys and carousel horses ever got tired? Or could they just keep on going and going until either they—or the thing they were assaulting—finally broke? Still the great steel doors—a pair at the entrance and another pair at the exit—reassured him. Nothing was going to get through them, which meant that he and Tinker were reasonably safe for the time being. Of course, with all this noise, it was likely that the Wrathmonks would soon be arriving on the scene.

Measle shuddered. He didn't want to think about that. Cuddly toys and carousel horses were bad enough, but Wrathmonks were another story. Measle felt a sudden weakness in his knees, and he sank down and knelt by the tombstone. Tinker stopped scratching his ear and plopped down at his side.

Measle felt the vibration several seconds before he heard anything. It was nothing more than a small shaking of the ground—so tiny, in fact, that had Measle been standing up, he probably wouldn't have felt a thing through the thick rubber soles of his sneakers. But through the thin skin of his bare knees, Measle felt it plainly.

Something heavy—something very huge and very heavy—was approaching. It was still some way off—

Measle had no idea how far, but he guessed at maybe a hundred feet—but the faint shuddering of the concrete under his knees was getting stronger and stronger, and now even Tinker felt it, because he was tilting his head and staring with a puzzled look in his eyes at the ground under his feet.

And then Measle *heard* it. At first it was quite faint, but it grew quickly louder and louder until it almost obliterated the clanging hooves. *Clang! Thump! Clang! Thump! Clang! Thump! Clang! Thump! Clang! Thump! Clang! Thump!* Then the clanging began to die away, as if the surviving carousel horses had also heard the sound and felt the vibration. Measle imagined three wooden heads turning slowly toward the approaching sound, their wooden nostrils flaring, their staring wooden eyes swiveling with fear—

And then all the sounds stopped dead.

There was a deep, dark silence. It was as if the universe was holding its breath. Measle held his breath too, his ears straining to hear something—anything!— because this utter silence was the most scary sound of all.

Until the long silence was finally broken, and Measle discovered what being *really* scared felt like.

The sound began as a kind of low, grumbling, muttering sort of noise—very faint at first so that Measle had to strain to hear it through the walls of Ghoulish Grange. Then it grew steadily louder and louder, rapidly becoming an earsplitting, mind-numbing, blood-freezing roar that made Measle's ears ache. It shook the whole huge building that surrounded him; it even dislodged dust from high in the domed ceiling.

The roar went on and on and on—and then there was a great thumping crash as a huge and heavy *something* hurled itself against the side of the building. Another great, thudding crash, and Measle felt the air around him shift as the walls of the building bent inward under the enormous weight of—of whatever it was out there. Measle's legs felt like they were made of jelly, and he hugged his knees tight to his chest and stared wildly toward the point on the distant wall where the attack was taking place. Tinker whined softly and huddled closer to Measle, and what was going through his doggy mind was something like, *This is a bit of not all right, this is—a bit too noisy and a bit too thumpy and a bit too much of the ground jumping about in a nasty way—not that I'm scared, of course, perish the thought! But*

it is better to be really close to the smelly kid, 'cause the smelly
kid may need a bit of support during these trying times.

A third shattering crash—and there, on the far side of the building, a small section of the concrete wall exploded onto the floor in a cloud of concrete dust. Another thudding smash, and a larger piece cracked away from the wall and fell.

And now the darkness inside was no longer the pitch darkness of before, because now a dim light from outside showed through the gaping hole in the wall. Through this jagged opening, Measle could see something huge moving. The thing was so big it completely filled the hole, and all Measle could make out through his goggles was the suggestion of brown lumpy skin.

And then there was a fourth shuddering thud against the distant wall and, this time, a whole section of the building simply caved in with a great, dusty crash. Measle could see an enormous pair of back legs, scaly back legs that ended in long, vicious-looking claws— and higher up, at least twelve yards off the ground, was a pair of little arms, completely out of proportion to the rest of the enormous body. Now the whole body of the creature bent, and a great rectangular head ducked into sight and poked its long, teeth-bristling snout inside and sniffed the dusty air.

It was the plastic and plaster and steel Tyrannosaurus rex from the Dinosaur Diver ride.

The huge head of the thing swung slowly from side to side. Its eyes were glowing a deep red and its jaws were bared, showing the double rows of long, yellow teeth. It peered into the darkness and a low grunting noise, like that of a gigantic pig, rumbled deep in its throat.

Measle kept very still. Even in his intense fear he realized that, in this pitchy blackness, it was unlikely that the dinosaur could see him—hadn't he read somewhere that scientists believed that Tyrannosaurus rex had pretty bad vision? He certainly hoped so, because now the huge creature was pushing its shoulders through the opening in the broken wall, causing more chunks of concrete to cascade around its scaly feet. It shoved its way through the gap and stood there, its head rearing up toward the ceiling, the claws on its little forearms twitching and clenching, as if the creature was desperate to get its talons on something—anything—just so long as it was alive and juicy, with lots of bones to crunch. . . .

Tinker stood up, his wiry fur bristling on his back. Then, before Measle could stop him, he ran forward and began to bark furiously at the great looming shape in the shadows. As far as Tinker was concerned, this thing had no business invading his space! How dare it! *Great big clumsy thingy, roaring and bashing about and making a mess all over the place—go on, get out of it! Get out of here, or I'll bite you to death—nasty great thingy with no proper animal scent—horrible, nasty thingy smelling of plaster and plastic and metal!*

Measle crouched by the tombstone, frozen with terror. His teeth were chattering, his tongue felt like a lump of stone and his eyes were wide and staring. He wanted desperately to call out to Tinker to make him come back, to make him be quiet, but no part of his body seemed to be working anymore.

Tinker was now standing just a few feet from the Tyrannosaurus's massive feet. Tinker's own little feet were planted firmly apart, his stumpy tail erect and bristling, his ears flat to his head. He glared up at the enormous shape in front of him and yowled furiously. The dinosaur lowered its huge head, its eyes glowing red in the darkness. Then it opened its mouth and snarled. The snarl sounded like canvas being ripped apart, and Tinker stopped barking for a moment, a little taken aback by the strange noise. The Tyrannosaurus lowered its head even closer to the ground. Then it cocked its head to one side, using one glowing eye to find and identify the little creature below. For a moment the T. rex and Tinker stood silently, staring at each other. Both seemed puzzled, uncertain what to do next. Then the Tyrannosaurus opened its mouth, revealing the double rows of gleaming teeth. It threw back its head and roared, and the sound crashed and thundered in the enclosed space. The earsplitting noise broke Measle's paralysis, and he instinctively put both his hands over his ears—but even then it was still deafening, and Measle could feel the air around him vibrating from the sound waves.

The effect on Tinker of this vibrating thunder was very sudden and very dramatic. He turned, in an instant, from a brave and fearless warrior dog into a quivering, panic-stricken little runaway. It was the sheer volume of the dinosaur's roar that did it; Tinker could cope with pretty much anything—*but not that sort of noise, thank you very much*—*that sort of noise hurts the old ears and we don't like being hurt. So, where's the exit? Right now, please—where's the rotten exit, 'cause it's time to go, indeedydoody—time to go somewhere else, anywhere else, just so long as it is far away from that horrible noise!*

And Tinker forgot all about the smelly kid huddled against the tombstone. All he could think about was his own safety and, with a sudden yelp of terror, the little dog tucked his tail between his legs and ran in the direction of the dim light that filtered in from outside. Without really being aware of what he was doing or even where he was going, Tinker ran between the huge feet of the dinosaur, ran right beneath the huge stomach of the creature, ran past the long tail that swayed back and forth three feet above his head, ran up and over the great lumps of fallen concrete, ran through the gaping opening in the wall and out into the cold and the rain and the darkness of the night outside.

For a moment the Tyrannosaurus rex stood frozen to the spot, as if it didn't understand what had happened to the little yapping creature at its feet. Then it bent its head and craned its neck around and peered shortsightedly behind itself. A little flicker of movement, a small shadow racing over the chunks of fallen wall: its prey was escaping! The huge creature heaved its body around, and one foot crushed a desk-sized piece of concrete to fine powder. Its tail swung in a great arc, smashing to dusty smithereens a long section of brick wall that enclosed a part of the cemetery. Then it was pushing its way back out of the broken building, its massive body dislodging more pieces of the outer wall of Ghoulish Grange. With a grunting sound, the dinosaur was through. It swung its head to the left and to the right and then, to Measle's relief, he saw the dinosaur lurch off in a stumbling, loping run.

But then came the sound of clattering hooves. Not against the iron panels—it sounded more like the start of some kind of chase. There was something determined in the distant clattering, something urgent. Maybe the carousel horses had been summoned somehow, to join in the hunt for Tinker! And that could mean that the entire regiment of cuddly toys, with their poisonous steel teeth, was even now turning in the same direction, all with a single idea—to hunt and catch and kill one small, frightened dog.

Measle had always been good at one thing—and that was knowing what to worry about and what *not* to worry about. He knew that the only things you ought to worry about were the things you could change. If you couldn't do anything about the problem, then it was a waste of time worrying about it. And right now, Tinker's running off into the night, with a whole horde of animated fairground creatures trying to hunt him down, was something Measle could do nothing about.

And that was the problem. What *should* he do now? *Well, what am I here for?* he thought. *I'm here to find my mum! If she's not here in Ghoulish Grange—and it doesn't look like she is—then where is she?*

Measle rubbed at his stinging hand. The pain seemed to be less intense now, which was something, he supposed. All the same, he really didn't want to get bitten again. (*Where's my mum?*) And next time, if there *was* a next time, he might not be so lucky. Next time he might be surrounded by the horrible things (*Where's my mum?*) and, if he was surrounded, he wouldn't have a chance.

Even as these thoughts were racing through Measle's mind, he heard in the distance the sound of voices. The voices were coming nearer and nearer, and Measle huddled back in the shadow of the tombstone.

The voices were very near now.

Some shapes—human shapes—jostled in the jagged

opening in the far wall. Through his goggles, Measle could see them as if it was daylight.

Horrible faces. The same horrible faces he'd seen in the ticket booth and at the end of the alley. There was the thin blond Wrathmonk (*Draggle, that was his name!*) and next to him stood the stout one with a long loose hank of hair hanging down his back (*that was Flabbit, wasn't it?*) and crowding in around them was the little black beetle and his skinny wife (*Zagreb—that was their name*) and the huge Wrathmonk who was called something like Truncheon—*no, not Truncheon—Cudgel, that was it!*—and there, behind this small, jostling crowd, stood two figures Measle didn't recognize. One was small and round, his head a pale blob of white skin, his tiny eyes two little black dots on either side of a short, round snub nose. The other was tall and thin, with a beaky, jutting nose and a pointed chin. A great mane of white frizzy hair stuck out from under an old black bowler hat.

Quickly, Measle counted—seven in all. Were there any more—and if so, how many?

"Do you think it'sss ssstill in there?" said Flabbit, his little piggy eyes squinting in the gloom.

184

"I dunno, do I?" muttered Draggle sulkily. "It'sss all dark, isn't it?"

"Your animated hunters have proved to be worthlesss," said a voice from the back. It was an oily, high-pitched, drawly sort of voice—one that Measle hadn't heard before. It made him shudder and shrink even farther into the shadow of the tombstone. It made the rest of the Wrathmonks turn toward it, and Measle guessed that this Wrathmonk was, in some way, their leader. The oily voice started again. "How foolish of you all to wassste your mana on such mindlesss creatures. All of them are now chasing after a harmlesss little dog—leaving behind the real prey! Which is—I have no doubt—ssstill hiding in here! Does anybody have a flashlight?"

There was a great patting of pockets as the Wrathmonks searched for flashlights—flashlights they obviously didn't have—and then a general muttering that, no, they didn't have a flashlight among them.

"Well, then," said the oily voice, "you will jussst have to enter and feel your way around—and, if there is anything in there worth catching, then you mussst catch it! Sssimple as that!"

"That'sss all very well," rumbled a deep voice (*That's Cudgel*), "but I don't sssee why it'sss jussst usss that has to go in there. Why don't you and the judge come in as well?"

A judge? The tall, skinny one with the frizzy hair was a judge?

The oily voice sounded a little irritated. "Come now, Mr. Cudgel—Judge Cedric and I are in *managerial* positions. Indeed, the word is part of my title—'bank manager.' That means, Mr. Cudgel, that I *manage*. I do not ssscrabble about in the darknesss, looking for a sssilly child. Neither does Judge Cedric. We are above sssuch things."

Measle's thin body tensed. A bank manager! This must be the Wrathmonk Griswold Gristle! And the other one, the judge—his name sounded familiar. Where had he heard that before? Was it a name his dad had mentioned once? They'd all been having breakfast one morning—yes, that was it! Sam had talked about the Wrathmonk judge, the one who had awarded Basil Tramplebone custody of Measle. He'd called him Cedric Hardscrabble! And here he was! Here they both were—Wrathmonk enemies of the Stubbs family!

Wrathmonk enemies from way back!

Mrs. Zagreb's voice sounded like nails on a blackboard. "I have no intention of wandering about in sssuch darknesss, Mr. Grissstle! Why, I might break one of my beautiful long fingernails! How could you asssk sssuch a thing of a lady!"

And then Measle felt it. A sudden, thudding sensation unheard by his ears but felt by every fiber in his brain. Each word vibrated in his skull.

HE DID NOT ASK. BUT I DO. AND I DO NOT ASK. I COMMAND.

The unheard sounds died away, leaving behind them a dull ache at the front of Measle's skull. Measle closed his eyes and rubbed his forehead. What on earth was that?

Then the sound of movement from the far wall.

Measle opened his eyes and peered through his goggles. To his horror, he saw that all seven Wrathmonks (without a single one of them voicing any kind of objection) had pushed their way in through the jagged opening and were now beginning to feel their way carefully across the huge space. They spread out in a line, their hands held out in front of them, their feet shuffling slowly forward.

Hurriedly, Measle crawled backward, putting the tombstone between himself and the slow-moving line of wrathmonks. Griswold Gristle and Judge Cedric held back, both making sure that Draggle was in front of them in case of a trap. Young Draggle blundered forward, waving his hands in front of his face, as if he was clearing away cobwebs. He was now well ahead of the others and then suddenly he stepped into nothingness, falling with a squeal of pain down into one of the open graves.

"Owwww!" he yelled, his voice echoing in the deep pit.

"What happened?" demanded Griswold Gristle, stopping where he was. He put his hand out and grabbed Judge Cedric's sleeve. "Ssstop, Cedric. There may be danger."

"I've fallen in a hole," yelled Draggle. "I've fallen in a hole and I can't get out! Help me!"

LEAVE HIM. CONTINUE SEARCHING.

Measle pressed his hands to his head. The words were like hammers, thumping inside his brain, and once again, he wondered where on earth (or out of it!) this unheard voice could be coming from. He peered around another tombstone and saw that the remaining Wrathmonks were back on the move again. There was no sound from the fallen Draggle. Cudgel was now the closest to him, with Mr. and Mrs. Zagreb not far behind. If he didn't do something soon, they would be on top of him!

Measle put his hand into his pocket and pulled out a jelly bean. Then he carefully and silently shifted his body into a crouch, his leg muscles tensed and ready. He peered around the tombstone and quickly worked out the path he would take—run around that open grave, along the wall, over the bridge, jump the far grave, up the hill of rubble—and out through the jagged hole in the far wall.

Cudgel was now only ten feet away. Measle could hear his heavy black boots shuffling over the ground—he could hear the sniffing sounds that the Zagrebs were making. . . .

It was now or never.

10

THE
FERRIS WHEEL

Measle put the jelly bean into his mouth and bit down on it. In the same instant, he began to run. There was no point trying to be quiet—speed was what he needed. Speed and the element of surprise.

"Sssomething's here!" shouted Cudgel, waving his hands backward and forward in the darkness. "Sssomething jussst ran passst me! Ssstop it!"

Measle took no notice. He could hear the pounding of his own feet, could hear the rasping of his own breath, and he knew that the Wrathmonks would hear it, too. But they couldn't *see* him, and that was all that mattered. He raced down the length of the wall, heading fast for the bridge. He saw, out of the corner of one eye, Flabbit slowly changing direction toward him. Then he was over the bridge and racing for the grave. Measle realized with start of sudden fear that the grave was the one that Draggle had fallen into—but it was too late to change his path now, so he ran straight for it and, at the last moment, jumped as high and as long as he could. He caught a glimpse of Draggle's startled face, peering up at the sound of some invisible thing whooshing through the air above him, then he landed on the far side of the grave, his legs propelling him forward in a frantic run towards the pile of rubble and the gaping hole in the wall.

"Quickly!" shrieked Griswold's oily voice. "Quickly back, all of you! It is essscaping!"

Measle glanced over his shoulder. He saw the Wrathmonks turning in his direction, saw them beginning to move toward him. They seemed to be moving more quickly now! There was less fumbling with feet, less groping with hands. Now they were stepping forward with more confidence, because they could see the dim shape of the hole in the wall, which gave them a point to head for.

Measle reckoned he had another five or six seconds of invisibility left. There wasn't a moment to lose! He tore toward the foot of the rubble pile and began to scramble over the loose chunks of concrete. Once he almost lost his footing, and for a couple of seconds, a small section of one trouser leg snagged on a piece of steel reinforcing bar that stuck out sideways from one of the concrete lumps. Measle yanked hard and felt the material give way—he was free again! He scrambled on. The rubble pile hadn't looked this big from the other side of the huge space—nor this steep! Just a few more feet to the top! The dim light from outside was very close now! Very close—but not close enough!

"There! Ssseee? In the hole in the wall!"

"It'sss that filthy boy!"

"He'sss getting away!"

"Quickly! After him!"

Measle threw a terrified look over his shoulder. He could see the Wrathmonks staring up at him. Griswold Gristle and Judge Cedric were each pointing at him. Then, together, all six Wrathmonks began to stumble toward him. He saw Cudgel pause by the open grave, lean over it and pull Draggle out of the pit by one arm. He saw Mrs. Zagreb trip over a tangled tree root and almost fall before Mr. Zagreb grabbed her around the waist and held her upright. He saw Mrs. Zagreb slap his hand away, he saw Flabbit begin a stumbling run toward him, and he saw Draggle fumbling in his pocket.

Measle turned away, forced his tired legs to move again and scrambled to the top of the rubble heap. Now he was in the gaping hole in the wall—two more steps and he was outside, feeling the cold drops of rain spatter on his head. Which way to run? The Tyrannosaurus had lurched off to the right. . . .

Measle took off fast down the left-hand street. He ran blindly, with no idea where he was going, just as long as it was as far away as possible from the muffled shouts he could hear behind him. The raindrops spattered against the lenses of his goggles, blurring his vision, so Measle pulled them down and they hung around his neck again. Now the raindrops stung his eyes, and his legs felt like a pair of lead weights. But he raced on through the night, turning left, then right, then dodging down an alley and then out again into a broad street. The theme park attractions flew by, their shapes looming in the shadows. His breath was coming in great rasps now and a pain was starting under his ribs. He had to stop—he had to find somewhere to rest, somewhere safe, somewhere quiet, where he could stop and think.

Something enormous loomed over him. It was tall and round, with spokes like a bicycle wheel—covered with a tracery of metal latticework, and all around the rim hung swinging wooden seats—it was the Ferris wheel!

Measle remembered the ride he and his parents had taken on it. It was one of the less exciting rides in the park, but the view from the top had been spectacular. You could see all over the island from the top of the Ferris wheel.

Suddenly Measle knew what he had to do. But he was going to have to do it quickly, because there, in the distance, were the sounds of urgent shouting coming nearer with every passing second.

Measle stared up at the huge Ferris wheel. His eyes took in the steel girders that braced the contraption— and the convenient-looking holes all the way up their lengths. These big girders were connected to smaller ones, so that everywhere he looked, there were hand-holds and footholds.

Measle ran to the foot of the great wheel and grasped the wet iron of the nearest girder. He pulled himself up—a foot in there, a hand reaching for the next one, up a yard, then another and another, hand over hand, foot over foot, up and up—hanging tight to the slippery metal, the rain bouncing on his upturned face. A sudden cold wind gusted by him and threatened to snatch him off this steel cliff. Far below him now, the voices were nearer. Perhaps they were coming out of the alley and starting down the road to the Ferris wheel? Would they see him, a little wet spider a third of the way to the top? Perhaps he should risk one more jelly bean?

Measle paused in his frantic climb and looked over his shoulder and down toward the ground. It was a long way to the base of the wheel—a very long way—and Measle suddenly felt a little sick and dizzy. His head swam for a moment, and his tired fingers began to lose their grip. He swayed, his eyes tight closed. Then he shook off the feeling and stared hard down the dark street. Yes! There in the distance, a group of black-coated figures hurrying through the rain! They would be here in half a minute! He mustn't be seen!

Measle locked one arm around the girder and pushed his free hand deep into his trouser pocket.

There was nothing there.

Well, there was *something* there.

A hole.

There was a hole in the bottom of his trouser pocket!

Measle could feel the skin of his thigh through the tear. Frantically, he pulled his fingers back into the ruined pocket and felt in all the corners.

Nothing.

The few remaining yellow jelly beans must now be scattered over the wet ground, somewhere between the Ferris wheel and Ghoulish Grange. Somehow he must have ripped his pocket in the wild scramble up the rubble pile! And now he'd lost his only advantage over the Wrathmonks! Without invisibility whenever he needed it, he was almost certainly lost! What to do? *What to do?*

The voices were nearer now, almost close enough to make out what was being said. Measle risked another quick glance down. The seven Wrathmonks were hurrying toward the foot of the great wheel! Measle could see that five of them were trying to shelter under a pair of umbrellas that were held by the remaining two—and that, at this precise moment, the five seemed more interested in getting out of the rain than in searching the dark, wet shadows that surrounded them.

There was still just enough time to do something.

Measle grabbed the girder tight and wriggled his body up and over the edge of it. Now he was on the *inside* of the girder and it was between him and the approaching Wrathmonks. The metal brace didn't fully conceal Measle, but it did hide a lot of his body from eyes on the ground, while still allowing him to climb the remaining two thirds of the wheel. He was just in time—the Wrathmonks arrived at the foot of the Ferris wheel only seconds later and stopped there, huddled together under the two umbrellas.

Measle kept his eyes firmly on the small group as he slowly inched his way upwards. He could hear them quite clearly, discussing what they should do next.

"I can sssmell the beassstly thing," said Mrs. Zagreb, the end of her sharp nose twitching like a hedgehog's.

"Ssso can I, dearessst," said Mr. Zagreb. "He is

certainly nearby. Perhapsss we ought to sssearch the area?"

"Well, of *courssse* that'sss what we ought to do, Zag!" snapped Mrs. Zagreb. "You always ssstate the incredibly obviousss, don't you?"

"My dear, I was merely sssuggesssting we—" said Mr. Zagreb, but Griswold Gristle interrupted him.

"We should ssspread out," said Griswold Gristle, clutching tight to his umbrella and wishing the other Wrathmonks wouldn't press against him so much in their eagerness to get out of the rain.

"Ssspread out, yesss," hissed Judge Cedric. "Ssspread out—and ssstick together!"

"How do we do that, then?" sneered Draggle, shaking the water out of his straggly hair. "How do we ssspread out—*and* ssstick together at the sssame time?"

"We do it by *doing* it, young Draggle," said Judge Cedric, in a superior tone of voice. Measle thought to himself, *That one isn't very bright, is he?*

"Judge Cedric was using a figure of ssspeech, Draggle," said Griswold, a note of impatience in his voice.

"It was a figure of *ssstupid*," muttered Draggle.

Griswold felt his temper rising, so he counted to ten

in his head and then said, gently, "What my learned friend Judge Cedric *meant* was—"

"Never mind what he *meant*, Grissstle," rumbled Cudgel who, being so big, was quite unable to fit under either of the two umbrellas and was therefore now soaking wet and very irritable. "Never mind what he *meant*. Let'sss jussst get on with it!"

"I sssecond that!" said Flabbit, nodding vigorously, so that his hank of wet, greasy hair flapped around his ears.

"Very well," said Griswold, in a soothing voice. "Let usss sssearch the immediate area. Mrs. Zagreb—how ssstrong is the ssscent? How far should we sssearch?"

Mrs. Zagreb sniffed the air. "Not more than fifty or sssixty feet, Mr. Grissstle," she hissed. "The beassstly thing is nearby."

"Thank you, Mrs. Zagreb." Griswold turned to the rest of the Wrathmonks. "Cedric, perhapsss you had better ssstay by my ssside. The ressst of you, sssspread out and sssearch. There are many nooksss and crannies here where a child might hide. And, when you find the horrid creature, sssing out! Sssing out loud! Very well—off we go!"

Measle heard all this as he climbed silently upward. By the time the Wrathmonks began to move off into the nearby shadows, Measle had reached the very top of the Ferris wheel and was now pulling himself up and into the topmost swing seat. He did this very slowly and very carefully—the seat was wet and slippery, and it shifted on its axle every time Measle moved against it. But eventually, Measle managed to pull his body up and into the seat. He lay still for a few moments, working the stiffness out of his aching fingers. The rain drizzled down on him and, for the first time that night, Measle realized he was soaked. Even his leather jacket was sodden with rain. His trousers were wet through, and he could feel water squelching in his sneakers. He was very cold. He was also very tired. His legs trembled from the effort of the long climb, and the muscles in his arms were sore and bruised. But at least the stinging pain in his hand had gone away.

Then Measle heard a distant roar. It was an angry, frustrated roar and, even at this distance, Measle knew that it had come from the throat of the Tyrannosaurus rex. Cautiously, he raised his head and peeked over the side of the seat, in the direction of the sound. There, in the distance, he could see movement—there, back near the go-cart track!

Measle slipped the goggles back over his eyes and swiped the palm of his hand across the lenses, wiping most of the raindrops away. He saw the top half of the Tyrannosaurus looming over the surrounding buildings—and the dinosaur was doing something very strange. It was turning slowly around and around, its ridiculous little arms waving uselessly, its jaws snapping furiously, around and around, in small circles. Then, quite suddenly, the creature reversed its direction and began to turn slowly in the opposite direction, around and around, arms flapping, jaws snapping, and another furious roar.

Measle guessed what was going on. Somewhere down there, hidden from his sight by the surrounding structures, was Tinker. The little dog must be running around and around his huge enemy, probably barking like crazy and nimbly jumping out of range every time the T. rex made a lunge for him.

The Tyrannosaurus suddenly stopped revolving on the spot. It roared again and then lurched off toward the distant loops of the Thunderer roller coaster. Tinker must have got bored of running in circles. Although he hadn't actually *seen* the little dog, the evidence that he was alive and kicking made Measle feel much better. Now if only he could somehow get rid of his own enemies—the prowling Wrathmonks, down there at the foot of the great wheel!

Something was digging into Measle's side—a lumpy object in one of pockets. Measle carefully rolled his body off the lump, put his hand in his pocket and pulled it out. It was the VoBo.

And then an idea jumped into Measle's brain—and, like all Measle's ideas that came to him in moments of extreme danger, this one was crammed with risks. But, like all Measle's crazy ideas, this one seemed (to Measle, anyway) to be completely brilliant, so he dismissed from his mind any thoughts that it might be a bit dangerous and began to think how he might make it work. Now, who among the searching Wrathmonks far below him should he start with? Nobody seemed to like Draggle, Cudgel was very grumpy, Mrs. Zagreb appeared to be irritable all the time, especially with her husband, whom she didn't seem to care for much— and besides, Mrs. Zagreb's twitching nose was the reason they were all prowling about in the shadows down there. So, if he could pull it off, Mrs. Zagreb would be the one he'd try it out on.

Measle peeked over the edge of the swinging seat and looked down toward the distant ground. He saw several shadowy figures poking about in the Ferris wheel's machinery—there!—close together, Draggle and Mr. Zagreb, on hands and knees, searching the narrow space under the Ferris wheel ticket booth! And ten feet away from them, Mrs. Zagreb, standing on her own by an ice cream stall, staring out into the darkness!

Measle lifted the VoBo to his lips, centered the crosshairs on Scab Draggle and pressed the little button on the brass tube. Then, very quietly, Measle spoke into the mouthpiece.

"I sssay, Zag—your wife'sss nose ain't half big, is it?" said Scab Draggle.

Only Scab Draggle hadn't opened his mouth.

Measle aimed at the distant figure of Mr. Zagreb, pressed the button and whispered a few more words into the mouthpiece.

"You're right there, young Draggle—it *is* big," said Mr. Zagreb's chirpy little voice. "I've ssseen filing cabinetsss that are sssmaller. And it'sss ever ssso sharp, too. The other day she tried to give me a kisss and I had to go to the emergency room and have ten ssstitches put in my lip!"

For a moment there was silence. Then, from the direction of the ice cream booth, a shrill scream of fury! Measle, peering cautiously over the edge of the swinging seat, watched as Mrs. Zagreb marched furiously toward Draggle and her husband, both of whom were staring at each other with puzzled looks on their wet, white faces.

"How dare you!" shrieked Mrs. Zagreb, pointing a shaking finger in their direction. "How dare you insssult me!"

"But—but—but—" stammered Mr. Zagreb, sounding a bit like a motorboat.

"How dare you sssuggessst that I have *ever* tried to kisss you!"

Measle swung the VoBo around and the crosshairs found the huge figure of Buford Cudgel.

"*And* she's ugly," rumbled Cudgel's voice. "She's ssso ugly, every time she looksss at her watch, it ssstopsss!"

Another shrill scream from far below. Measle

watched as Mrs. Zagreb turned on her heel and stomped in Cudgel's direction.

"You brute!" she shouted. "I shall breathe on you, Buford Cudgel, jussst sssee if I don't! Then you'll be sssorry!"

Griswold Gristle and Judge Cedric Hardscrabble came hurrying out of the darkness.

"What is going on?" bleated Griswold, waving his little arms about. "Why all thisss unpleasantnesss?"

Measle took aim at Griswold and whispered hurried words into the VoBo.

"Why be ssso nasssty to Mrs. Zagreb?" This appeared to come from Griswold's mouth—but his lips hadn't moved. Then, with his mouth still closed, Griswold cried, "Poor lady, she can't help it if she looksss like a chewed pencil!"

Another shriek of fury and now Mrs. Zagreb was advancing fast in Griswold Gristle's direction.

"Thisss is intolerable!" she hissed. "I am not ugly! I am beautiful! I shall breathe on all of you! One by one! I shall burn you all with my breath! You firssst, Grissstle—you usssselesss little blob! Ssstand ssstill and be breathed on!"

Griswold held up both his pudgy little hands and

backed away from the advancing woman.

"My dear lady," he squeaked. "I didn't sssay a word! It was sssomebody else!"

Again, Measle took aim with the mouthpiece.

"No, come on, Griswold," called the pompous voice of Judge Cedric. "It *was* you. I heard you clearly—and you're ssspot on! Mrs. Zagreb is ugly and ssskinny and ssstupid! In fact, she's even ssstupider than me!"

The crosshairs centered next on Flabbit's stout body, more words were whispered, and Flabbit's smug, scratchy voice came out of the darkness.

"Even ssstupider than Judge Cedric? Wow—that'sss really, *really* ssstupid!"

And now it was Mr. Zagreb's turn to speak without moving his lips.

"And that'sss sss*saying* sssomething!"

Mrs. Zagreb stopped suddenly where she was, closed her eyes tight shut and started to scream at the top of her lungs. Mr. Zagreb hurried to her side and tried to put his arms around her.

"My dear," he cried (and this time, his lips moved), "please try to calm yoursssself! I mussst insissst you *calm* yoursssself!"

Mrs. Zagreb shook off his hands and turned on him, her eyes blazing with fury.

"Oh, ssso it'sss not enough that you insssult me, Zag!" she hissed, her long fingers clenching and unclenching by her side. "It'sss not enough that you allow *others* to insssult me as well! Now you dare to tell me what to do?"

"No, no, my dear," stammered Mr. Zagreb, trying to back away—but Mrs. Zagreb had him by his wrist and her long red fingernails were biting into his skin.

"Jussst for that, Zag," she snarled, "jussst for that, I shall breathe on *you* firssst!"

"No, my dear—you mussstn't!" shouted Mr. Zagreb, trying frantically to free himself from his wife's iron grip. But Mrs. Zagreb only held him tighter. She opened her mouth and took a deep, deep breath.

"If you breathe on me," screamed Mr. Zagreb, "I shall be forced to breathe on you *back*, my dear!"

Mrs. Zagreb took no notice. She took one more deep breath—

—and Mr. Zagreb himself took a lungful of air—

—and, at precisely the same instant, they started to blow their stinking breaths towards each other's faces.

Measle stared transfixed at the scene far below. He had no idea what to expect. His only experience of being blown on by a Wrathmonk was when Basil had shrunk him down to a half-inch in height and dropped him in the middle of the great train set—and somehow Measle didn't think that was going to happen this time. Hadn't the woman said something about burning them all with her breath? Measle didn't want to see any-body—or any*thing*—being burned, but he found him-self unable to drag his eyes away from the extraordinary spectacle that was taking place.

Mr. and Mrs. Zagreb were steadily blowing out their horrible breaths toward each other and, where the breaths met, the air itself seemed to be turning into something else. At first it was just a thin, swirling mist. Then, rapidly, it became a thick, yellowish greenish brownish fog that rolled and twisted into a ball of gas. It thickened, turning to a darker brown and the fog was congealing into some sort of oily liquid that began, slowly at first, to drip onto the wet ground. Where the thick liquid hit, the ground began to sizzle and bubble and hiss, and a thin plume of smoke began to drift upward from the spot.

Neither Mr. nor Mrs. Zagreb saw this. All they saw was the infuriating fact that neither of their breaths seemed to be having any effect, other than making this stupid, rolling, dripping fog that hung in the air between them. So they each began to breathe out harder. Their eyes bulged with the effort and the tendons in their necks stood out like ropes and they blew harder and harder—and the only effect *this* had was to make the hanging ball of fog turn into the brown, oily liquid faster and faster, so that more and more of the horrible stuff was now dribbling down onto the ground between their feet.

Measle stared down, trying to work out what was happening. He was glad that neither Wrathmonk appeared to be getting burned but he could see the fog and the oily liquid, and he could hear the sizzle as the fluid touched the ground and see the little plume of gray smoke rising in the air. But what he couldn't see was what the liquid was doing to the ground, because Mr. Zagreb was standing in the way.

What Measle couldn't see was this: the corrosive fluid that was forming from the horrible, stinking breaths of the Zagrebs was actually digging a hole in the ground. Where it dripped, the asphalt lifted and bubbled and sizzled and then melted away, leaving a pit that had started out the size of an eggcup but was now rapidly approaching the dimensions of a mixing bowl.

The other Wrathmonks were as rooted to the spot as Measle was. This was amazing. None of them had ever witnessed the collision of two exhalation enchantments before, and all of them were fascinated to see what would happen next. Would Mrs. Zagreb's slightly more corrosive breath win the day—or would Mr. Zagreb overcome her small advantage with his slightly stronger lung power? Either way, it was an extraordinary spectacle, and none of the watching Wrathmonks had any intention of moving until it finished, one way or the other.

So Mr. and Mrs. Zagreb went on blowing their horrible breaths at each other, and nobody noticed the hole that was steadily growing between them. Finally Mr. Zagreb felt a slight movement of the ground under the toes of his right foot and felt the urge to glance down and see what was going on down there. But he stifled the urge immediately, because he knew that a moment of lost concentration on his part would mean the end of the battle—and in Mrs. Zagreb's favor. So he ignored the odd little crumbling sensation and blew even harder at his wife, who blew even harder at him.

And now the hole was almost the size of a toddler's wading pool.

And then, quite suddenly, the ground crumbled away from under the feet of both Mr. and Mrs. Zagreb. For a fraction of a moment, they both stopped breathing at each other. Their eyes, already popping with the effort, popped even further as they realized that the ground that had been supporting them simply wasn't there anymore!

And then they fell.

They fell quite silently, because neither of them had any breath left to scream. They just dropped down into the dark hole and the thin gray smoke closed over their heads—and they were gone.

There was a long, stunned silence. Then—

"Where did they go?" said Flabbit, leaning forward and peering down into the smoking hole with puzzled, piggy eyes.

"I dunno, do I?" said Draggle. "Why asssk me?"

"Mr. Zagreb?" called Griswold Gristle, taking a cautious step forward. "Mrs. Zagreb? Are you all right?"

"Oy! Zag!" bellowed Cudgel. His voice was so loud and deep that the vibrations from it made six inches of earth around the edge of the hole shiver and crumble and then fall into the darkness.

"Ssstand back!" shouted Griswold. "It'sss not sssafe!"

"But—where does that hole lead to?" said Flabbit, his hank of greasy hair hanging over his face. "Where'sss the bottom? How deep is it?"

"How should I know?" whined Draggle. "All I know is—they jussst disssappeared, didn't they?"

"It ssseems to me," said Judge Cedric, in his wisest voice, "it ssseems to me that an *aperture* has appeared in the earth."

"Yesss, Cedric," said Griswold irritably. "We *know* that. The quesssstion is, how deep is it and did Mr. and Mrs. Zagreb sssurvive the fall?"

There was a long silence as the Wrathmonks thought about this.

High on the Ferris wheel, Measle wondered what to do next. His scheme had worked brilliantly and now there were two less wrathmonks to worry about. Exactly what had happened to the Zagrebs, Measle had no idea—but the fact that they were gone was very encouraging. Perhaps he could try that trick again?

And that was where Measle made his big mistake.

He thought for a moment. Then he aimed the crosshairs at Judge Cedric Hardscrabble's long, bony face and whispered into the VoBo's mouthpiece.

"I sssuggessst we all hold hands and jump into the hole together and sssee where they went," announced Judge Cedric loudly. Unfortunately for Measle, at that precise moment, Griswold Gristle just happened to be looking at Judge Cedric and thinking that every time Judge Cedric opened his mouth, he said something really stupid, which made Griswold look even cleverer than he really was, and here was Judge Cedric saying something that was probably the stupidest thing he'd ever said—but he had said it *without moving his lips*!

"That'sss moronic," sneered Draggle. "You're a moronic old judge."

"Yeah," rumbled Cudgel, clenching both massive fists. "For once I agree with Draggle. You really are a sssilly old fosssil, aren't you?"

"Posssitively bonkers," muttered Flabbit.

"No!" cried Griswold, holding up both pudgy hands.

"No, no, my friends. It wasn't Judge Cedric who sssaid that!"

"Yesss it was," rumbled Cudgel. "I heard him with my own ears."

"But you didn't *sssee* him sssay it, did you?" cried Griswold.

"How do you *sssee* sssomebody sssay sssomething?" hissed Draggle. "You *hear* them, Griswold. Dear, oh, dear—you're getting as ssstupid as the judge, aren't you?"

"On the contrary, young Draggle," said Griswold, his voice rising with excitement. "I am cleverer than all of you put together. You sssee, unlike the ressst of you, I was *looking* at Judge Cedric'sss face when he ssspoke—and he never opened his mouth! Therefore, he couldn't have ssspoken! Don't you sssee? Sssomebody else is ssspeaking—in his voice! In fact, I sssussspect sssomebody else has been doing lots of voices! All those insssults about Mrs. Zagreb—I never uttered any—and I don't believe *any* of usss uttered any! It was sssomebody else!"

"Who?" said Flabbit, looking around uneasily.

"The boy!" hissed Griswold, lowering his voice to a hoarse whisper. "It mussst be the boy!"

"Where?" growled Cudgel, peering into the darkness.

"Sssomewhere clossse!"

"We looked everywhere!" muttered Flabbit into Griswold's left ear.

"Everywhere," echoed Draggle into Griswold right ear. Both he and Flabbit had moved closer to Griswold, and they were now squeezed tight against the fat little Wrathmonk, both sheltered by his umbrella and both close enough to whisper so quietly to him that Measle, high above them, could no longer hear what was being said.

Neither could Judge Cedric.

"What are you whisssspering about?" he demanded. "Don't you know it'sss very rude to whisssper? I once sssentenced a perssson to *ten years* for whissspering in my court—and he wasn't even the prisoner in the dock!"

"Come here, Cedric!" hissed Griswold. He stuck out a fat little arm and pulled Judge Cedric close to him. "You too, Mr. Cudgel—come closer! We mussstn't be overheard!"

The five Wrathmonks huddled together under the two umbrellas, and all Measle could now hear were their hissing whispers. They sounded like a nest of snakes down there and Measle shifted his position in the swing seat so that he could angle one ear in their direction.

Whether it was because all of Measle's weight was now on one side of the swing seat or whether it was because there was a sudden fresh gust of wind—whatever the reason, the seat swung suddenly backward and then forward and a loud *SQUEAK* came from its axle.

Both umbrellas rocked to one side and five horrible, wet, white faces stared up in his direction. Measle didn't even have time to pull his head back out of sight before Scab Draggle pointed one bony finger and screamed, "There! There he is! Up there!"

Measle jerked his head back and out of the Wrathmonks' line of sight, but then he heard Griswold Gristle's oily voice, calling up to him. "We sssee you, dear boy! We know you're up there! That was very clever, that little trick you played on usss! You mussst be a very clever boy indeed. We would ssso like to meet you and shake you by the hand—"

"Shake you by the neck!" roared Cudgel's thunderous voice.

"Take no notice of Mr. Cudgel, dear boy," called Griswold. "He'sss only joking! Please, come down here, ssso we can all be friends! What do you sssay, dear boy? Won't you come down?"

Measle had no intention of going anywhere. He huddled down in the swing seat. He didn't think any of the Wrathmonks were going to climb up to get him. They didn't look in any sort of shape to do that, so perhaps it would be the safest thing just to lie here and hope they would eventually go away.

Then Measle felt the swing seat jerk suddenly. It swayed backward and forward, squeaking on its axle. Measle peered forward and saw the seat in front of his was swinging, too—which meant only one thing: somehow, the Wrathmonks had got the Ferris wheel to turn! But it was turning in such an odd way—not smoothly, like Measle remembered from the time he and his parents had ridden it. No, this movement was a series of wrenching lurches, which set all the seats swinging on their axles. Measle could hear the whole massive wheel creaking and groaning under the strain. There was the sound of grinding steel cogs and then a screech of breaking metal, as one section of the central axle was sheared off. The whole wheel lurched a few inches to one side. Measle peered over the edge and stared down at the Wrathmonks far below.

Only they were not so far below now.

Measle was moving steadily downward—and what was moving him? What was moving the whole huge Ferris wheel?

It was Cudgel.

Cudgel's enormous hands, encased in their black leather motorcycle gloves, were grasping the steel rim of the Ferris wheel, and the giant Wrathmonk was heaving the whole contraption around and around in a series of jerks, and each wrenching jerk brought Measle closer and closer to the ground.

What can I do? thought Measle wildly. *Where can I go? Maybe I can get out of the seat, climb back up to the top, find another seat to hide in—but that wouldn't work, because the giant Wrathmonk would just keep pulling the wheel around and around and I can't climb that fast anyway. Think! Think! If only I had a jelly bean left! If only I hadn't tried that last VoBo trick! If only—if only—*

It was no good. With a great sense of despair washing over him, Measle sat quietly in the bottom of the swing seat and waited for whatever fate had in store for him.

11

THE
PRISONER

Tinker was beginning to enjoy himself.

At first sheer terror had made him run from the darkness of Ghoulish Grange and out into the falling rain, his feet a blur and his stubby tail tucked tight between his short legs. Behind him he could hear the *thump, thump, thump* of the great monster and the sound of clattering hooves.

Over the next ten minutes, he ran all over the theme park, and the three carousel horses and the Tyrannosaurus rex followed wherever he went.

Lagging far behind came the army of cuddly toys, moving very slowly now. They were so soaked with rainwater that they could hardly drag themselves across the wet pavement, and several of the horrible creatures were losing their stuffing through gaps in their seams, where the stitching had finally come loose.

But Tinker's initial terror eventually lessened to a point where he could pause and think. He discovered that there was a pattern to the chase, and he learned to use it to his advantage. The three carousel horses were the fastest of his pursuers, but they had a hard time running on the wet ground because their wooden hooves made them slip and slide and skid as if they were on an ice rink. Tinker found that if he let them come fairly close at full gallop, and then turned a corner sharply, the horses would lose all traction and fall and then slide on their sides across the slippery road until their bodies crashed into whatever obstacle was there on the street. One of them had lost one of its hind legs doing this. The wooden limb had splintered against a low brick wall, breaking off cleanly at the horse's knee, and now this lame one staggered along in the rear, trying desperately to keep up with its two fellows.

The Tyrannosaurus rex was also fast—but it was rather shortsighted and very heavy, so that it blundered about, crashing into things and knocking them over. When *it* came to a corner, it had to bring its huge body almost to a standstill before it could turn and change direction. So Tinker learned that as long as he kept moving at a reasonable pace and turned a corner now and again, none of these nasty things was going to catch him. At one point in the chase, at one of the park's larger crossroads, he'd even found enough courage to run in circles, barking his head off, around and around the Tyrannosaurus and even under the hooves of the carousel horses, and he'd only given up doing that when he saw, out of the corner of one eye, a slow-moving mob of blue dinosaurs waddling toward him from out of a side street.

Nasty, horrible wet cushions—nasty, horrible horsey thingies—and that nasty, horrible roaring thingy that obviously can't run very well. Hardly surprising, 'cause the horrible roaring thingy tries to do it on only two legs, and every sensible animal knows that it's better on four. Right, enough of this roundy-roundy running—quick, off down this road and then zip round this corner—ooh, that was a

221

nice sliding-crashing-breaking noise behind me! And here's the big roaring thingy again—better get a bit of a move on—wonder where the smelly kid is? Funny how I miss him when he isn't around—hope he's all right. . . .

Oops! Don't think! They're right behind me again! Run!

"Well, well, well," said Griswold Gristly, his oily voice even oilier with pleasure. "What have we here?"

Measle stared up at the circle of white, grinning, horrible faces that were looking down at him. He still lay on the floor of the swing seat, but now the swing seat was at the lowest point of the Ferris wheel's arc and the five remaining Wrathmonks, standing on the wet ground, towered over him.

"Young Massster Ssstubbs, isn't it?" said Griswold. His lips were stretched in a ghastly smile, and Measle could see the two sets of pointed teeth on either side of his tiny mouth.

"You—you'd better not come any closer," said Measle, in what he hoped was his fiercest voice. "My dad'll be along in a minute and he'll—he'll—"

"He'll what, dear boy?" said Griswold, raising his nonexistent eyebrows.

"He'll—he'll sort you lot out, that's what he'll do!"

Griswold thought for a moment and then shook his head. "No, I don't think ssso, dear boy. You sssee, we happen to know that the poor chap has lossst his memory. And how do we know that, dear boy? We know that because of what was in the bottle we threw at him. That bottle contained a concentrated dissstillation of His Lordship the Dragodon'sss breath, you sssee."

Dragodon? thought Measle. *What's a dragodon?*

"And that breath," continued Griswold, "like all great Wizards' breath, has a unique quality. Basil Tramplebone—who was a very clossse friend—Basil's exhalation enchantment was able to shrink a thing down to a tiny sssize. But of courssse, you know that, don't you? His Lordship the Dragodon'sss breath causes sssomething else entirely. His Lordship's breath causes complete and utter forgetfulnesss. Amnesia, in fact. How wonderfully brilliant is that? How marvelousssly refined! How sssuperbly sssubtle! Sssso dear boy, even if your dear father *was* here, without his memory he wouldn't be much ussse to anybody, would he?"

Draggle sniggered and Flabbit nodded in a satisfied

way, his lanky hank of greasy hair flapping around his collar. Measle saw that Judge Cedric Hardscrabble was simply staring at him as if he was a particularly nasty-looking bug, and the enormous Cudgel, panting slightly from the effort of dragging the Ferris wheel around, stood as tall as a small mountain, glaring at him from under the visor of his motorcycle helmet.

There was a sudden ominous creaking from the girders and braces of the Ferris wheel.

"Mr. Cudgel," said Griswold, staring up at the Ferris wheel. "Would you be ssso kind and lift young Massster Ssstubbs out of that ssseat. And then I think we should all move clear of thisss contraption. I fear you have done it sssome ssseriousss damage, Mr. Cudgel, and it is no longer sssafe. It could fall at any minute."

All the Wrathmonks—and Measle, too—peered up at the Ferris wheel. Its angle was no longer quite perpendicular. It now leaned a little to one side, and every now and then one of its supporting girders let out a small creaking sound.

Cudgel leaned down and took the collar of Measle's leather jacket between one enormous finger and one enormous thumb and carefully lifted him out of the seat. Then he and the rest of the Wrathmonks moved away from the Ferris wheel, putting themselves at least a hundred feet from the tottering thing.

"Thank you, Mr. Cudgel," said Griswold. "I think we are out of danger here." Griswold switched his eyes to Measle's dangling body and smiled. "Now dear boy," he said, obviously enjoying this moment. "It was *ssso* good of you to come. We all appreciate it ssso much. You have come for your poor dear mother, I sssuppose? You have come to the right place. She is here. But we have been ssso clever, my fellow wrathmonks and I. You sssee, we ssseparated your mother and your father because, *together*, they represent a ssseriousss threat to our little community. *Apart*, however, they are of little danger to usss. Thusss, the elimination of your dear father in the parking lot of the sssupermarket. As to which of them we should kidnap, well, that decision was made for usss by His Lordship, the great Dragodon himsssself."

"Yeah, well," said Measle, wondering desperately what in the world (*or out of it!*) a Dragodon was. Then he said defiantly, "His Lordship the—the Dragodon isn't going to like this, that's for sure."

"Really?" said Griswold, looking not in the least bit worried. "Oh, I don't think he'll mind at all. His Lordship the Dragodon had his own reasons for wanting your poor mother and has, no doubt, dealt with her in a thoroughly sssatisssfactory manner. He has no interessst in you—none whatsssoever! We, on the other hand, have an *enormousss* interessst in you. You sssee, it is our intention to take our revenge for the cruel murder of poor Basil Tramplebone. And, now I come to think of it, for the murders of poor Mr. and Mrs. Zagreb as well! All murders that *you* committed, dear boy. And now we have you—and, when we've finished with you, your father will be sssimple to deal with. And that, dear boy, will be the end of the sssinisssster ssspecies of Ssstubbs!"

Measle had stopped listening to Griswold's oily voice the moment he'd heard the bit about his mother. Griswold had said that she had been dealt with *in a satisfactory manner*—did that mean she was dead?

"What's happened to my mother?" Measle blurted.

"I have no idea," said Griswold, shaking his head and trying unsuccessfully to look sad. Then he turned to the other Wrathmonks. "Do any of you know what might have befallen poor Mrs. Ssstubbs?"

"Not a clue," said Flabbit cheerfully.

"Couldn't tell you," rumbled Cudgel, and Measle felt the vibrations of his deep, deep voice through the massive hand that still held tight to his collar.

"I dunno, do I?" whined Draggle. "Why asssk me?"

"*I* know what happened to her," announced Judge Cedric Hardscrabble, stepping forward. All the other Wrathmonks turned toward him with surprised looks on their faces—all except Griswold Gristle, who simply sighed and rolled his eyes toward the sky.

"I know what happened," repeated Judge Cedric. "Would you like me to tell you, boy?"

Measle nodded slowly, not sure whether he wanted to hear this.

"Very well, then I shall tell you," said Judge Cedric in his most pompous voice. "Thisss is what happened to your mother. We kidnapped her! There! What do you think of *that!*"

"Yesss, we *know* all that, Cedric!" squealed Griswold, flapping his arms irritably. Measle thought he looked like a fat little baby bird, trying unsuccessfully to take off. "We *know* all that!" he repeated. "Even the *boy* knows that! But what has happened to her *sssince*, Cedric?"

The judge stared blankly into Measle's eyes. "Ah," he said vaguely. "As to that, I really couldn't hazard a guesss. Perhapsss—perhapsss she has been ressscued?"

Griswold jumped up and down with irritation. "She has *not* been ressscued, Cedric!" he screamed. "She is with the Dragodon! His Lordship would never allow her to be ressscued! Why do you never think before you ssspeak?"

Griswold turned back to Measle, his fat, pasty face twisted with annoyance. "Anyway," he said, "We don't really care about what has happened to your mother, dear boy. Jussst as long as—*whatever* it is—it'sss very nasssty and ends with her death! That'sss what we want for the whole Ssstubbs family. A great deal of unpleasantnesss, leading eventually to death! And now that we have you, dear boy, we can make a ssstart! Ssso, what shall it be, eh? Shall we let young Draggle turn you bald? Shall we have Judge Cedric breathe his horrid red painful boils all over your body? Shall we allow Mr. Flabbit to give every tooth in your head the mossst terrible toothache? My own perssssonal exhalation enchantment is enormousssly effective—rather *too*

228

effective at times! And Mr. Cudgel's exhalation enchantment is also very impresssive. Why don't you tell our young friend all about it, Mr. Cudgel?"

Cudgel tightened his grasp on Measle's collar and lifted him higher off the ground, bringing Measle's face level with his own. Measle could see the giant Wrathmonk's hard eyes gleaming at him through the visor. Cudgel turned Measle's head sideways with his other massive hand and whispered in a voice that seemed to be coming out of the depths of the earth. "If I breathe on you, boy, all the microsssscopic germs that live on your body will begin to grow. They'll get bigger and bigger and bigger, until you can actually sssee them. They'll get as big as sssspiders, boy. You'll be completely covered in horrible, wriggling germs the sssize of sssspiders—and those horrible, wriggling germs have to eat sssomething, boy. They have to eat to ssstay alive, boy. Guesss what they'll ssstart with?"

"Thank you, Mr. Cudgel," murmured Griswold. "Mossst amusing. I am sure we should all like to sssee that. Now then, dear boy—which one would you like usss to begin with?"

They all sound horrible, thought Measle. His mind was

racing, desperately trying to come up with a way out of this terrible situation, but he couldn't think of anything! There seemed to be no escape!

Then, out of the corner of his eye, he saw Draggle put his hand in his pocket and pull out a small, cloth bag. At the same time, he felt Cudgel lowering him slowly toward the ground, right in the middle of the circle of Wrathmonks. When Measle's feet touched the wet pavement, Cudgel took his hand off his collar and took a ponderous step backward. Measle could feel the eyes of the Wrathmonks staring at him in excited anticipation—all except Draggle, whose hand was fumbling in the cloth bag. Measle saw the outline of Draggle's fingers close around something and his hand began to withdraw from the bag.

"Turn away, everybody!" shouted Draggle loudly and, instinctively, all the other Wrathmonks began to turn their backs to him. Halfway into his turn, Griswold Gristle realized what Draggle was up to and he screamed, "No! You idiotic youth! Don't use that!" But he was too late. Draggle's hand emerged from the cloth bag and the young Wrathmonk, his eyes now tight shut, held the object out toward Measle.

Measle had no idea what was going on. All he knew was that four of the Wrathmonks now had their backs turned to him, and the fifth Wrathmonk was holding something in his hand—something he apparently wanted Measle to see.

Two voices screamed in Measle's head—and they both belonged to him. The first voice yelled, *"Go on, have a look!"* The second voice shouted, *"No, don't! It could be dangerous!"*

The first voice won. It's very difficult not to look at something that is being held out for your inspection so Measle leaned forward and peered at the little, gray, wrinkled thing in Draggle's hand. It looked like a snake's head, a little, dry mummified snake's head.

And then a very strange thing occurred.

Nothing happened.

Griswold, with his back turned and his pudgy hands over his eyes, was shrieking, "You ssstupid fool, Draggle! A boy made out of ssstone is no use to usss! None of our exhalation enchantments will have any effect! What were you thinking, you cretinousss moron!"

While Griswold was screaming into the darkness,

Draggle was looking very puzzled. A bewildered frown was creasing his forehead. He still had his eyes tightly shut, but the fingers that were holding the mummified snake head were now moving all over the object, feeling an entirely new and unexpected texture to the thing. A few seconds ago, it had been rough and dry and a little soft—if you squeezed it, you could feel the bones of the snake's skull bend a little. Now it had changed. Now it was cold and smooth and hard, like a piece of polished rock. Draggle folded his fingers around the head, hiding it from sight. Then, cautiously, he opened his eyes.

Measle was standing there in front of him—a small, wet boy with sticking-up hair, his eyes obscured by a pair of old flying goggles. *But he ought to be a statue!* thought Draggle frantically. *A stone statue! But instead, here's a living, breathing and very obviously alive boy, without a trace of statue about him!*

Without thinking, Draggle opened his fingers and looked down at the small object in his hand. Then, realizing what he was doing, he slammed his eyelids shut again. But wait—he'd looked at it! He'd looked into the tiny dried up eyes of the thing—and nothing had happened to him! Cautiously, Draggle opened his eyes and peered down at the snake head again.

It had felt different. It certainly *looked* different too. Now it had the appearance of a lump of granite, carved into the shape of a serpent's head.

Draggle peered into the cold stone eyes of the thing and then shook it gently, as if it was a watch that had stopped. Then he looked back at Measle and the small wet boy with the sticking-up hair did something quite unexpected.

Measle grinned at him.

And a hundred and twenty miles away, at the end of a dreary, dingy street, the outer layers of a pair of stone statues (which had been lying like discarded toys on top of a huge pile of black rubble) suddenly cracked and flaked and splintered and then fell away in chunks, revealing, in an instant, two live men in dusty working clothes. Both men blinked and both sat upright, staring down in wonder at their grimy hands and flexing their fingers as if they didn't believe such a thing was possible. Then one turned and looked at the other.

"Is that you, Harry?"

"Yeah. Is that you, Robert?"

"I think so. What happened, Harry?"

"I dunno," said Harry. "I just know it's nice to be alive."

Robert looked around him fearfully and lowered his voice. "Where are our masters?" he muttered.

"Haven't the foggiest," said Harry. Then he pointed up to the sky and his voice took on a happier tone. "But they're not here, that's for sure."

"How do you know, Harry?"

"How do I know? Because the rain has gone, that's how!"

"So it has," said Robert, climbing to his feet. "It looks like we're free, Harry—and the sooner we get out of here, the better I'm going to like it!"

The two men scrambled down the rubble heap and began to run as fast as they could away from the dingy dreary street.

And there were other statues that came to life as well—and these statues weren't a hundred and twenty miles away.

They were much, *much* closer.

"What has happened?" squeaked Griswold, his back still firmly turned away from Draggle and Measle. "Is it sssafe to turn around?"

"Er—yeah," muttered Draggle, still staring at Measle with a dazed look on his thin white face.

Griswold and the other Wrathmonks slowly turned around. Flabbit was the first to see the little gray object in Draggle's hand, and he screamed and covered his eyes. "Put it away! Put it away!" he shrieked.

Griswold had also begun to cover his eyes, but then he saw Measle, standing there, quite unaffected, and so he slowly lowered his hands and took a step forward.

"What is thisss?" he whispered. "What has happened here?"

"It didn't work, did it?" said Draggle. "And now it feels all funny."

"Give it to me," said Griswold, holding out one pudgy hand. Draggle handed the snake's head to Griswold, and the little bank manager examined it closely.

"It appears to have turned to ssstone," said Griswold. Then he looked up at Draggle with fury in his little eyes.

"How did thisss happen, Draggle? What did you do to it?"

"I didn't do nothing, did I?" whined Draggle. "I jussst pointed it at him, didn't I? Everybody else has had a go with it, haven't they? And now it was my turn, wasn't it? And he should've turned to ssstone, jussst like all the others—but he didn't, did he? I dunno why not, do I?"

Griswold stared at Measle a little uncertaintly.

"What magic did you use, boy? Hmm? Why don't you tell your Uncle Griswold, eh?"

Measle knew what had happened—and he also knew that it wasn't magic at all. For several seconds he had been as puzzled as Draggle. But, the minute he'd guessed that the object was the Medusa head, he'd known what had happened. The same thing had occurred back in the train set when Basil had miniaturized him. Measle had ducked under the mirror at the precise moment when Basil Tramplebone had started his cockroach spell—and the spell had reflected off the mirrored surface of the lake and had bounced back into Basil's eyes—and Basil himself had been turned into the cockroach.

There was only one difference. That extraordinary

incident had been on purpose.

This extraordinary incident was an accident.

It was the goggles, of course. Those brilliant goggles that let you see in total darkness. The lenses were like highly polished mirrors, which reflected anything and everything that fell on their shiny surfaces, including the deadly stare of a dried-up, mummified snake's head from a long-dead Gorgon's skull.

"Ah," said Griswold, his voice shaking with anger. "I think I underssstand." He pointed with a fat finger at Measle's nose. "Mossst effective! I congratulate you, dear boy!" He turned to Cudgel. "Mr. Cudgel, would you be ssso kind as to retrieve the boy once again? And hold him tight, if you would be ssso kind."

Cudgel stepped forward, grabbed the front of Measle's jacket and lifted him off his feet.

"Thank you, Mr. Cudgel," said Griswold. "You can always be trusssted to do the right thing. Unlike *sssome*. Unlike sssome*one* in particular."

Griswold turned on Draggle. "You moron!" he screamed, holding the Medusa head in one shaking fist. "You cretin! You blithering idiot! You've *broken* it! It'sss *usssselesss*! Thisss preciousss object is now completely *unusable*! Because of your ssstupidity, we have losssst one of the raresssst magical articles in the entire *universssse*! You *donkey*! You *dunce*! You driveling *dunderhead*!"

Griswold had been steadily advancing on Draggle during all this, and Draggle had been steadily retreating from the little Wrathmonk's fury. What was making Draggle even more fearful was the fact that the other Wrathmonks had stepped in behind Griswold and were also pushing their way toward him—and they all had fury in their eyes.

"L-look here," stammered Draggle, taking another couple of steps backward. "I didn't *mean* to break it, did I? It was an accident, wasn't it? I'm ever ssso sssorry, honessst I am—"

"Ho, yesss," said Flabbit menacingly. "I'm sure you're sssorry. But you're going to be even sssorrier in a minute."

Draggle began to regret being so rude to everybody.

"I don't know how it happened, do I?" he whined. The Wrathmonks were getting closer, and Draggle took another pace backward.

"You're going to pay for thisss missstake," rumbled Cudgel. "And for laughing at me in the cave on

Borgrove Moor." He was holding Measle as if he was a sort of weapon and marching slowly but steadily in Draggle's direction.

Draggle realized—far too late—that laughing at Buford Cudgel was a mistake. He took another step backward.

"You shall pay indeed," hissed Judge Cedric, waving a bony finger. "You are guilty as charged, young Draggle! I sssentence you to a million years in the sssalt mines of Sssiberia!"

Griswold, still advancing steadily, suddenly glanced past Draggle, at something behind the young Wrathmonk. Then a gleam came into Griswold's piggy eyes. "Indeed, yesss, dear Cedric," he said. "An excellent punishment! We will sssend him down into the deepessst mine in the whole wide world! Into a great black pit! And we shall do it—*now!*"

As Griswold yelled that last word, he made a sudden jump forward and Draggle, startled, made a sudden jump backward—

—right into the Zagrebs' yawning black hole. Measle caught a glimpse of Draggle's horrified face and a second later, the young Wrathmonk was gone. But unlike the Zagrebs, Draggle had plenty of air in his lungs, so they all heard his long, wailing scream as he fell into the darkness. The scream went on for a very long time—and then, when it was very faint and far away, it stopped abruptly.

Griswold turned back from the hole and grinned unpleasantly.

"There," he whispered, "a very sssatisssfactory ending, I think. We cannot tolerate incompetence— and besssides, young Draggle was of little ussse. His exhalation enchantment, for example—making hair drop out! How pointlesss!"

"Well," said Flabbit, smoothing down his greasy hank, "perhapsss pointlesss for you, Griswold, sssince you don't have any. But for the ressst of usss—" Flabbit left the sentence unfinished. Griswold was staring at him with a very nasty look on his pudgy face, so Flabbit said, hurriedly, "Of courssse, it was a fitting end for the young fellow. Fancy allowing that to happen to the Medusssa head!" Flabbit frowned. "The only thing is, Griswold—how exactly *did* it happen?"

There was a murmur of agreement from Judge Cedric and Cudgel. Griswold didn't answer immediately.

Instead, he went up to Cudgel, who was still holding Measle by the collar of his leather jacket, so that Measle's feet dangled several inches off the ground.

"Lower the boy, if you would be ssso kind, Mr. Cudgel," said Griswold. Cudgel lowered his huge hand, bringing Measle back down to the ground. Griswold reached forward and snatched the goggles from Measle's head.

"Here," he said, waving the goggles in the air. "You sssee the lenses? Mirrors! The Medusssa head's ssspell was turned back on itssself! A very clever trick—and one that I sssusssspect the boy has used before! How else could he have overpowered our beloved Basil? He has no Wizard faculties of his own."

"What about all the disssappearing business he's been doing?" rumbled Cudgel, staring down at Measle angrily.

"A sssimple bit of Old Magic," said Griswold. "His father taught it to him, probably. I sssusssspect the boy eats sssomething. Kindly empty his pockets, Mr. Cudgel."

The next thing Measle knew was that he was upside down. His ankles were being held tightly in both of

Cudgel's massive hands, and he was being shaken up and down until his teeth rattled.

Clink went the little brass VoBo as it fell to the ground beneath him. Measle saw an upside-down Griswold toss his goggles next to the VoBo. Then Measle saw one of Cudgel's huge, booted feet lift up and stamp down on the goggles, smashing the lenses to tiny pieces. The same thing happened to the VoBo— *stamp—crunch—stamp—crunch*—and then Measle felt himself being turned right side up and felt his feet planted firmly on the ground.

"Thank you ssso much, Mr. Cudgel," said Griswold. There was a touch of sarcasm in his voice. "I can't help thinking that it might have been a good idea perhapsss to *examine* that sssmall brasss object that fell from the boy's pocket *before* dessstroying it. However, the deed is done, and I am sure he now poses no further threat to usss. Ssso now is perhapsss the moment to take our revenge for the death of our beloved Basil Tramplebone."

Griswold turned to Measle and smiled, revealing his sets of pointed teeth. "You will be relieved to hear, dear boy," he hissed, "that we cannot use any of our primary ssspells on you. Mr. Flabbit and Mr. Cudgel and the ressst of them expended all of their mana when they animated those variousss creatures—creatures that even now are (sssomewhat ussselesssly, I feel) chasing after one sssmall dog. Judge Cedric and I musset keep our mana in reserve, in cassse His Lordship the Dragodon should require it. Therefore, we can only use our exhalation enchantments on you."

Griswold brought his fat little face closer to Measle's, and Measle smelled on the Wrathmonk's disgusting breath the faint (but horribly familiar) scent of dead fish, rotten mattresses and the insides of ancient sneakers. Griswold whispered, "Would you like to hear about mine, dear boy?"

Measle was terrified, but he was determined not to show it. He shook his head firmly. "No, I wouldn't," he muttered, through clenched teeth.

"Oh, dear," hissed Griswold. "Well, never mind, I shall tell you anyway. I dry you out, dear boy. Everything that is wet inssside you, I dry it out. All your blood, all your tears, all your sssweat—all dried to powder! You become nothing more than a little dried bag of sssskin and bones! Dead, of courssse. Dead as a doornail—and jussst as dry, too! And, as my exhalation enchantment has thisss sssomewhat *final* effect, we shall leave it to lassst, I think. And then, when you are no more, we shall drop your poor little dried-up corpssse into that very convenient hole over there. Oh, yesss. Ssso, dear Mr. Flabbit, you shall be the first. Please, feel free to proceed!"

Flabbit smirked and stepped forward. Carefully, he smoothed back the greasy hank of hair. Then he bent down, his face close to Measle's.

"Sssuch pain," he whispered in Measle's ear. "In a moment or two, you will be ssscreaming."

Measle screwed his eyes tight shut and held his breath. He didn't know if holding his breath would be any use against the spell, but he certainly wanted to put off, for as long as possible, the horrible smell that he knew would be coming his way.

A few seconds ticked by.

Then he heard Flabbit taking in a deep, deep breath.

Here it comes!

STOP.

For the second time that night, Measle felt words jolting in his head. So powerful was the effect of that unheard word, that had he been doing anything other than waiting with his breath held and his eyes shut, he would have stopped whatever he was doing in an instant. And, in fact, everything seemed to have come to a stop, because nothing seemed to be happening.

Cautiously, Measle opened one eye.

Flabbit was looming over him, his fishy eyes wide and his flabby cheeks bulging. A few beads of greenish colored sweat had popped out on his forehead, and Measle realized that Flabbit was having to make a serious effort to keep all that poisonous air inside himself. Flabbit's pasty skin was changing color, too. His face was turning a faint shade of purple and his stout body was beginning to shake slightly, which made the jowls under his double chin wobble.

EXPEL THE POISON, FLABBIT—BUT AWAY FROM THE BOY.

Flabbit turned his head, opened his mouth and let out a great whoosh of stinking air. Unfortunately for Judge Cedric, Flabbit had turned in his direction.

"Ow!" screamed Judge Cedric, clapping his hands over his mouth. "Ooooh! My teeth! They hurt! Ooh— the pain!" Judge Cedric glared furiously at Flabbit.

"You will pay for thisss, Flabbit!" he muttered through his fingers. Then he took a deep breath and blew out hard, right into Flabbit's horrified face.

This time it was Flabbit's turn to clap his hands to his face.

"Ow!" he yelped. "That hurts!" Flabbit took his hands away from his face and Measle saw that horrible red boils were now popping out all over his nose. More followed on his cheeks and his chin and his forehead, until Flabbit's entire face was covered in a rash of lumpy, red, painful spots.

STOP—THIS—NONSENSE!

Everybody froze instantly. There was silence, apart from a faint moaning from Judge Cedric and a quiet sniveling from Flabbit. Then Griswold said in a voice that shook with fear, "Oh, Your Great Lordship—what would you have usss do?"

BRING ME THE BOY.

"The boy? Oh. Y-yesss indeed, Your Lordship," stammered Griswold. "The boy. Immediately, Your Lordship." Griswold paused, his eyes swiveling wildly in their sockets. He had no idea what to do next. The Dragodon wanted the boy—but *where* was the

Dragodon? There was only one way to find out and that involved some risk.

"We shall bring him at once, Your Lordship. B-but, O Great Lordship, *wh-where* shall we bring him?"

THE JUGGERNAUT RIDE. BRING HIM TO THE JUGGERNAUT RIDE.

"Immediately, Your Lordship!" cried Griswold. Then he turned to the other Wrathmonks. "Well, you heard His Great Lordship!" he shouted. "Cedric, ssstop moaning! Mr. Flabbit, don't be sssuch a baby! Mr. Cudgel, please be ssso kind and carry the boy—we mussst bring him to the Juggernaut ride. Quickly, everybody! As quickly as you can!"

Cudgel reached out, swung Measle under his arm, and began to run. Griswold was already halfway down the street, his short legs pounding the wet pavement. Judge Cedric, nursing his jaw, was close behind him, his long skinny legs jerking up and down, and Flabbit, tears of pain coursing over his lumpy face, was trotting in the rear.

A few minutes later, Measle felt Cudgel slow down and come to a stop. Then he felt the iron band that was Cudgel's huge arm lift away, releasing him from its

247

tight grip. Measle fell to the ground with a thud. He lay there, not daring to move anything but his eyes.

He was inside a small surrounding circle of Wrathmonks. All the Wrathmonks were staring up at the something, so Measle lifted his eyes and stared up, too.

Above him, the great looping steel rails of the Juggernaut roller coaster floated in the darkness. In the gloom, the crimson rails had lost all their color and now looked, to Measle, like the coils of a huge black snake. The coils were supported here and there by gigantic steel pillars that rose from massive concrete blocks set deep in the ground.

There was a long moment of silence. Measle peeked at Griswold's face and saw uncertainty there—and a lot of fear, too. The little Wrathmonk was peering about in the darkness, and Measle realized that he had no idea what to do next.

Griswold whispered, "O Great Lordship? Are you there, O Great Lordship?"

I AM NEAR, LITTLE WRATHMONK. I AM NEAR.

"Wh-what would you have usss do now, Your Great Lordship?"

PLACE THE BOY IN THE LEADING CAR OF THE RIDE, GRISWOLD.

"The leading car? Yesss, indeed, Your Great Lordship! Immediately, Your Great Lordship!"

Griswold waved bossily at the other Wrathmonks and Measle felt himself being hoisted up once again under Cudgel's arm. This time he managed to raise his head a little. Cudgel was following Flabbit, Judge Cedric and Griswold, and the Wrathmonks were threading their way through the steel barriers that led to the ride's twin platforms. Moments later they were there, gathered in a small group right by the rails. There was a line of the Juggernaut's cars waiting by the platform and, at a nod from Griswold, Cudgel lifted Measle from under his arm and planted him firmly into the seat at the very front of the train. Then Cudgel stepped back to rejoin the other Wrathmonks and, together, they all stared down at him with expectant looks on their faces.

Measle wondered what was going to happen next. *The ride won't start up, surely? Not without any power! It can't!*

But it could.

There was a sudden *clang!* as the tubular steel safety bar, padded with foam rubber, swung up from the floor. It pushed Measle back into the seat, pressing

249

hard—and a little painfully—against his stomach. Measle didn't remember the bar coming back that far, but it was back that far now, and it was holding him so firmly that he didn't think he could wriggle free even if he tried.

"Quite comfy?" said Griswold, staring down at him with hungry eyes.

Measle didn't reply. Instead, he looked straight forward and tried to grin, as if he was looking forward to the ride. *I'm not—but I'm going to make them think I am!*

HOLD TIGHT.

The power of the command in his head was so strong that, instinctively, Measle grabbed the safety bar in front of him. Out of the corner of his eye, he saw all the Wrathmonks flex their fingers, as if they too were trying to hold on tight to something. There was something so ridiculous about this pointless, collective movement that Measle's pretend grin turned into a real one and a little laugh, almost like one of Tinker's barks, jumped out of his throat.

"Ho! Laugh at usss, will you?" said Flabbit furiously. His face was now so red and swollen and lumpy that it looked like a big plate of raspberries, with two little eyes gleaming in the middle of it. He stepped forward, his pudgy fist clenched. Cudgel growled, and Judge Cedric took one hand from his aching jaws, clenched it into a bony fist and shook it angrily at Measle.

Then there was a sudden jerk that threw Measle's head backward with a snap. They were off! Measle saw the platform slide past much faster than he remembered. Certainly much faster than the first time he and his father had ridden it and it was even faster than their second go on it, when Sam had invoked his go-faster spell. The Wrathmonks were being left behind, and now there was a sudden uptilting of the leading car and Measle felt himself pressed back into the seat as they began to climb the long, steep ascent to the top. This time, though, there was no *clank——clatter——clank——clatter* from the chain-lifting mechanism underneath. This time, apart from the thrumming sound of the wheels on the rails, there was an eerie silence. Measle realized that, whatever was powering the Juggernaut, it certainly wasn't the normal sort of mechanism. It was something quite different.

He was halfway up the steep hill now and rising fast. Measle threw a quick glance over his shoulder, down to the group of Wrathmonks far below. He could hardly make them out in the gloomy shadows of the Juggernaut's station, but he could see that they were still there, their white faces staring up at him. He thought he saw Flabbit shaking one fat little hand.

Measle turned back and stared at the rapidly approaching crest of the slope. In just a few seconds, he would be up there—*and then what?* The air up here was chill, and a stiff breeze was blowing. It threw the rain sideways against Measle's face, stinging his cheek. A slight vibration from the whirling wheels beneath him was making the soles of his feet tingle and his hands, clenched tight to the padded safety bar, began to ache with the cold.

And then, directly in front of his leading car, the rails disappeared from his view and Measle realized that he was at the top of the long, steep slope.

And now there was nowhere to go but down.

12

THE
DRAGODON

This time Measle didn't feel what all riders of ordinary roller coasters feel when they reach the top of the first hill. If you're in the front, there's always an odd sort of pause as the leading car moves over the crest and starts down on the other side. At first the leading car seems almost to hang there, because it's being held back by the rest of the cars behind it, which are still being dragged up the final few feet. Then, when the last car crests the summit and starts down the other side, the leading car suddenly picks up speed and the ride really begins.

For Measle, the ride had really begun with that initial jerk. Then there had been a steady acceleration as he rode toward the top, and no pause or slowing down whatsoever as his leading car slid over the summit. Instead, there was one smooth, continuous speeding up, which continued as he began the long, howling plunge into the darkness below.

The wind blasted against his face and whistled in his ears. It blew his spiky hair straight backward from his forehead and, without the protection of his goggles, it stung his eyes until he felt tears squeezing out of the corners. This was fast—faster than ever before! What would happen when they reached the bottom and started up the other side? Would his body be able to take the force?

The wheels screamed. The cars rocked. Down, down they plunged into the blackness, gathering speed as they fell. Somewhere ahead—and coming up very soon—was the bottom of this long, steep drop. Measle tried to remember what happened next—*there was a bit that goes up, then a level bit, then a sudden uptilting as you go into the first loop.*

The screaming of the wheels and the howling of the wind went on.

And on.

And on.

And on.

No! thought Measle, *This is impossible! We must have got to the bottom by now! Nothing takes this long—certainly not the Juggernaut's first drop! No roller coaster in the world has a drop this long! It's impossible! Completely, utterly, totally imposs—*

Measle dragged his eyes away from the pitch blackness in front of him and looked sideways, expecting to see something flashing by—a pylon perhaps, or a section of rail—something, *anything*, that would show him where he was. But the darkness that was in front of him was exactly matched by darkness that was at his side.

Nothingness rushed past him.

Nothingness lay ahead.

Blackness everywhere. Only the incessant wind blasting into his face and the screaming of the wheels battering against his eardrums told Measle that he was still moving forward at a terrific speed. An idea sprang into his bewildered mind. He twisted his body around as far as the safety bar would allow and stared back toward the way he had come.

Black nothingness there, too—but, in the middle of the nothingness, a faint circle of *lighter* blackness! And this circle was getting smaller and smaller, just as Measle had thought it would.

It was a hole far, far above him.

Which meant only one thing.

He was underground! And, because the distant hole was getting smaller, that meant he was going deeper and deeper with every passing second!

Measle shuddered with terror and twisted back in the seat, once again facing forward.

There was light ahead.

A pinprick of light, that grew into a tiny circle. The edges of the circle expanded steadily, and now Measle could just begin to make out the shapes of the steel rails stretching out in front.

The hole grew bigger and bigger, and the light that streamed from it had a strange quality. It seemed not so much the sort of light you get from a lamp, or even from a sun obscured by clouds. It was more like the kind of light you see coming from the hand of a luminous

256

watch—a soft, greenish glow, rather than a hard, yellow beam.

The circle of light was coming fast toward Measle now, and he gripped tight to the safety bar, tensed his body, and he was through the hole in a flash. The greenish glow was all around him, lighting dimly the vast space that now enclosed him.

It was a cave.

An enormous cave, thousands of feet across and just as high. Measle looked ahead and saw the roller coaster rails stretched out below until they met the floor of this huge space. There were hills and valleys down there, making ripples across the surface of the ground and, far below, beyond the point where the tracks bent to meet the floor, the rails leveled off and ran for several feet across the ground.

And then Measle saw something that made his mind freeze with terror.

The rails stopped.

They simply came to an end, there in the middle of this vast, undulating floor and Measle knew that, at this headlong speed, his car and all the others behind him would shoot off the end of the rails and run, uncontrolled, across the ground. They'd hit one of those low hills and would probably shoot into the air—tumbling end over end and then crashing in a heap of splintered plastic and steel and wood. His chances of surviving that devastation were hopeless.

And now the ground was coming up fast. Measle gritted his teeth, closed his eyes, curled both hands tightly round the safety bar and waited for the end.

The wind shrieked. The wheels screamed.

He felt the sudden sensation of his body being pressed down into the seat. Now he must be racing along the stretch of level rails—the stretch that had looked so very, very short from way up there.

Measle clenched his fingers on the bar and squeezed his eyes as tight as he could get them.

Any minute now . . .

There was a sudden, smooth and powerful deceleration. Measle felt his chest being pressed hard against the padded bar. He braced his feet and, as he did so, he felt the wind die down to a whisper. The screaming of the wheels in his ears became a hiss, and then a silence as the Juggernaut train came to a gentle halt. Then there was a clang as the safety bar sprang from his chest and returned to its slot in the floor.

Measle opened his eyes.

There, a few yards in front of his leading car, the rails stopped. It looked as though whoever had laid them had simply got bored with the process and had gone off to do something else.

GET OUT.

There was no way Measle could disobey those thudding words in his head. He scrambled out of his seat and stepped out onto the softly glowing ground.

STAND ASIDE.

Measle stepped away from the rails. As he did so, he saw the empty cars begin to move backward. He watched in astonishment as they accelerated smoothly away from him, gathering speed as they raced back toward the roof of the cave. There was something very odd about those rails and, for a moment, Measle couldn't work out what it was. Of course! There were no supports! No great red steel pillars set in concrete, holding the rails up! Instead, these rails simply hung there in the glowing green air, stretching down in a long, unsupported curve from the tiny black dot in the ceiling of the cave (and, of course, the tiny black dot was the hole from which he'd emerged only half a minute or so ago).

Measle watched as the cars soared upward, getting smaller and smaller, until they disappeared into the tiny black hole in the cave's ceiling.

And then there was a slithering sound by Measle's feet. He looked down and saw that the steel rails themselves were now sliding along the ground! The two ends slipped past him, gathering speed as they did so. It was as if somebody was pulling the rails along behind the cars. Measle watched in bewilderment as they retracted quickly and now they were off the ground and were hanging in the greenish glow, the ends disappearing upward and, moments later, the rails were dragged up and through the hole in the ceiling, which then closed with a faint and distant *pop*!

There was no escaping now—at least, certainly not the way he'd come in.

His heart sinking with despair, Measle looked about him. The huge cave seemed to generate its own illumination. The strange green glow that shone steadily from the floor and walls, but not from the ceiling. Up there, the surface appeared to be made up of jagged black rock, which was in sharp contrast to the rounded green hills and valleys of the cavern floor. The walls, too, were made of this luminous material, and they also had rounded shapes and indentations, almost all the way up to the roof. Here and there, on the floor and on the walls, tall outcroppings of bare black rock pushed through the pale-green covering. There were several of these rock projections scattered across the enormous floor and one large one that stuck out from the wall closest to where Measle was standing. It was about twenty-five feet up the wall and Measle saw that there was some sort of opening in the wall at the point where this particular rock jutted out from the surface. As Measle was staring at this rocky spur, he suddenly noticed movement in the opening, and a strange little figure appeared, stepping out of the darkness and onto the rock platform. The figure moved to the very edge and then stared down at Measle.

Whatever it was, it was very old.

Very, *very* old. Measle shuddered. He didn't think he'd ever seen anybody—or any*thing*, that was as old as this creature. Its face was an ancient face, covered with a mass of wrinkles that crisscrossed the yellow skin in every direction, making the whole thing look like the bottom of a dried-up lake. Even the wrinkles had wrinkles of their own, and they extended all over the creature's scalp, which was mottled here and there with ugly patches of brown skin. Scattered across this crinkled scalp were little clumps of thin white hair, very long, that straggled down on either side of the creature's head. Measle saw, with a start of horror, that the thing appeared to have no nose. There were two dark slits where the nose *should* have been, and above them, a pair of blank, black eyes. And what was really horrible about the creature's eyes was the fact that the entire eye was black, with no trace of white anywhere. Its ears were nothing more than a couple of little withered scraps of yellow skin, and its mouth was a wide, lipless gash that slashed across the lower half of its horrible face like a scar. It had a long, scrawny neck, covered with folds of loose skin, and below the neck, a dusty black robe that covered the thing's body completely. But the robe didn't conceal the fact that the creature's body was hopelessly out of proportion to its head. Measle saw immediately that, whatever the *shape* of the thing was underneath its robe, its frame was no bigger than Measle's own frame—and quite probably a bit smaller.

"Welcome, Measlestubbs."

The gash in the lower half of the thing's face had opened like a letter box, letting out the words in a reedy, husky croak. The sound made Measle think that the creature hadn't spoken for a very long time.

The creature's mouth was still open and, quite suddenly and without any warning, two black pointed things, the size of pencils, slithered out of the opening and twitched in the still air. Then they slid from side to side and, a moment later, pushed their way even farther out of the creature's mouth. Measle saw (and this was worse than the thing having no nose) that the two black pencils were joined at the base and so, what he was looking at was, in fact, a tongue that was forked just like a snake's tongue.

The twin black tongues flickered for another moment and then slid back into the mouth and disappeared. Then the creature cleared its throat.

"I hope you won't object if we converse normally?" it said, its thin voice drifting down in the still air. "I find the projection of my thoughts into the minds of others tiring after a while and, since we are in reasonable proximity to one another, there is no reason why we cannot dispense with telepathic communication and simply hold an ordinary conversation."

The creature's mouth stretched into an unpleasant smile. "Well," it added, its voice coming more smoothly now, "as ordinary as is possible, under these *interesting* circumstances."

"Who—who are you?" stammered Measle, pretty sure that he knew the answer already.

"Who am I?" said the thing, its black eyes boring into Measle's. "I think you know who I am, Measlestubbs. We have spoken already. I am the Dragodon."

There was a long pause. It was as if the Dragodon seemed to be expecting some sort of response from Measle. He wondered what to say. There was really only one thing on his mind.

"Where's my mother?"

The Dragodon stared down at Measle. For several moments it said nothing. Then the gash in the lower part of its face opened.

"Do you not wish to know what the Dragodon is, Measlestubbs? Or why the Dragodon has brought you here? Or what the Dragodon intends to do with you? Do you have no curiosity about your fate?"

Measle stuck a thoughtful frown on his face and pretended to think about all these questions. Then he shrugged his shoulders and said, with more bravado than he really felt, "No, sorry, not particularly. But I would like to know where my mum is and if she's all right?"

The Dragodon glared down at Measle, looking like somebody who has just been on the receiving end of a mild insult. Then—

SIT DOWN.

Measle's legs folded under him and he sat down with a thump.

The Dragodon took a deep, rasping breath.

"I have forgotten how impertinent humans can be," it said. "It has been so long—so very long—since I spoke to one. And, when I finally get the opportunity, I find myself conversing with a *child*. And this child expresses no curiosity, other than wanting to know the whereabouts of its *mother*. This lack of curiosity betrays the child's dullness of mind. This child is an ignorant child and must be educated. So sit quietly,

265

Measlestubbs, sit quietly and listen!"

And then, in a quiet and measured voice, the Dragodon told Measle his story. It was the story that Griswold Gristle had told the other Wrathmonks in the cave on Borgrove Moor. It was the story written in the first great volume of Wizard history, a huge leather-bound book that lay on a forgotten shelf, deep in the library of the Wizards' Guild. It was the story of the rise and the fall of the Dragodons—the great battles and the great defeats—and the story ended with the last of the dragons and the last of the Dragodons.

"We fell, Measlestubbs. My beloved Arcturion and I. We fell from the skies."

The voice stopped. Measle opened his eyes with a start. The images from that slow, measured voice that had crowded his mind had been so vivid, so real, that Measle had completely forgotten where he was.

"What?" he managed to stammer, staring up at the Dragodon with bleary eyes.

"The last valiant dragon was my beloved Arcturion. His great wing was crippled. It was enough to bring us down. I survived. But it was the end of us all. The Dragodons and their dragons. The kings and their allies, those treacherous Wizards, they all decided that, for me—the last of our breed—eternal imprisonment would be the fitting punishment. They found this island, they extended the great cave beneath it and they sealed me inside. Here I have slept for many a thousand years, my only visitors the flocks of seabirds that nested here on the rocky shores. And then, one day, long after we and our deeds were all forgotten, men returned to the island and began to build. And what did they build? A great castle? A palace for an emperor? A fortified city? No! They built a playground for children!"

The Dragodon paused. Measle saw that it was breathing heavily, its narrow chest moving up and down beneath its dusty robe. Its black eyes were narrowed, and its slit of a mouth was turned down at the corners. *It's angry!* thought Measle. *Angry with what had become of its island.*

The Dragodon lifted its scabby head and spoke again.

"Whether it was the thunderous sounds of construction, or the foul and filthy insult to my dignity, whatever the reason, I awoke from my endless sleep. The men above were careless. The ground up there is thin in places. They broke through while building one of their ridiculous creations—the thing they called the 'Ferris wheel'—and I found a way out of my prison. Oh, the careless men quickly sealed up the hole they had made, but I found another within one of the great iron pillars of the Juggernaut ride. I began to move freely—but always on the island. I cannot travel far beyond my source of mana. I can contain my thoughts within an object and I can send that object far and wide—but I myself am trapped here."

The Dragodon paused. Then:

"At least, I was."

The Dragodon smiled, and Measle saw that the thing had no teeth. Its gums were black and its forked tongue flickered between them. *Well, at least it can't bite me to death,* thought Measle. He waited, while the silence between them grew longer and longer. *It's waiting for me to say something!* he thought.

"Well—what's all this got to do with me and my mother?" he said.

"With *you*, Measlestubbs? Very little," said the Dragodon. "I have no great interest in you, other than a passing admiration for your courage and resourcefulness, both of which are remarkable in one so young. I was mildly curious to meet you, which is why I removed you from the clutches of those ridiculous Wrathmonks. I have no interest in your father, either. He is a minor Wizard and is therefore no threat to me. However, those foolish little Wrathmonks were intent on some sort of revenge against your family, and I saw a way to use this to my advantage. You see, the only member of your family that has any significance for me is your mother."

"Why?" said Measle. He pulled himself to his feet. "And where is she, anyway?"

"She is here, Measlestubbs," said the Dragodon. "We *all* are here. All four of us—here in this great cave."

Measle was about to shout, *Where? Where is she?*—but something the Dragodon had said stopped him short. The Dragodon had said, "All four of us."

"Four of us?" said Measle, looking around.

"Indeed, yes," said the Dragodon. Measle saw that he was smiling very broadly now, his black gums exposed and his forked tongue flickering between them. "Indeed, yes—you, your mother, myself—and Arcturion, of course. I have not been alone in my prison. Arcturion has been at my side all through the

269

long, dark ages of our sleep."

"Arc—Arcturion?" stammered Measle. "You mean—your dragon?"

"Yes, Measlestubbs. My beloved dragon is here with us."

Measle looked wildly around the great cave, searching for some sign of scales, or teeth, or vast bat wings. There was nothing—only the undulating walls and floor, glowing a luminous pale green. Measle felt a little of his courage returning. If the Dragodon thought that a silly, obvious lie was going to frighten him.

"Where?" said Measle loudly. "I can't see any dragon!"

"Use your eyes, Measlestubbs."

Measle stared again, searching the walls and floor and ceiling. *Perhaps there's a tunnel somewhere, leading to another cave—no, nothing—*

"I don't see anything!" shouted Measle. "You're lying—there's no dragon here!"

"But there *is*, Measlestubbs."

"Where?"

"Why, Measlestubbs," said the Dragodon, his reedy voice almost a whisper, "you're *standing* on him."

13

ARCTURION

Griswold, Cudgel, Flabbit and Judge Cedric were still waiting patiently on the Juggernaut's platform when the command from the Dragodon slammed into their minds.

They had been waiting for something to happen. For some time, they had stood watching the section of rail that entered the platform area from the rear, expecting Measle's train to come hissing back from its journey around the ride. But when a full five minutes had passed, Griswold Gristle had turned to Judge Cedric and said, "It would appear, Cedric, that the boy is not coming back."

"Ah," muttered Judge Cedric, frowning with pain. His hands were still pressed to his aching jaws. "Then he mussst have essscaped usss, Griswold."

Griswold sighed. Really, he must find himself a more worthy companion in the future! "No, Cedric," he said, with as much patience as he could muster. "No, the car he was traveling in has not returned either, which can only mean one thing."

"It has exploded?" said Judge Cedric hopefully.

"No, Cedric. It means that His Lordship the Dragodon has him now and will, no doubt, be dealing with him in a mossst sssatisssfactory way."

"His *Lordship* has him?"

"Yesss, Cedric."

"You mean—I won't be able to breathe on him, Griswold?"

"It would appear not, Cedric."

"But—but my lovely boils!"

There was a snarling sound from Flabbit, whose face was now even redder and lumpier than before.

"They're not *lovely*, you ssstupid old plonker," he

muttered. "They *hurt*. I jussst hope my toothache hurts you worssse."

Judge Cedric sneered at Flabbit and opened his mouth to say something, but Griswold stopped him. He reached up and patted Judge Cedric's bony shoulder. "Ressst assured, my dear Cedric, His Lordship the Dragodon will punish the boy far more effectively than we ever could—"

He broke off, because here, sliding steadily and silently backward down the first slope of the Juggernaut ride, came the missing line of cars. They slipped between the two platforms and hissed to a stop. All the Wrathmonks stared at the front seat of the leading car.

Measle wasn't in it.

"There, you sssee?" said Griswold. "The child has been removed and is, I imagine, caught fassst in the clutches of His Great Lordship!"

"Ssso it would ssseem, Griswold," rumbled Cudgel. "What do we do now?"

The answer came, but not from Griswold.

YOU ARE RELEASED, LITTLE WRATHMONKS. I HAVE THE WOMAN. I HAVE THE BOY. THEY ARE MINE AND WILL

BE—EXTINCT—WITHIN MINUTES. I LEAVE THE FATE OF
THE STUBBS MALE IN YOUR HANDS. YOU ARE FREE TO
GO—SO GO!

That final command was the strongest one they had
ever received. Without a word, and with their heads
buzzing from the sheer power of the Dragodon's order,
the four Wrathmonks turned and walked quickly,
under the drizzling rain, toward the distant gates.

Measle's legs didn't seem to be working. Sheer
terror was paralyzing his muscles. He couldn't move
his feet—they seemed to be stuck fast to the ground.
But it wasn't the ground at all! It was—it was something else!

When the Dragodon had said, "You're standing on
him," Measle had immediately looked down at his feet.
Beneath them was the glowing green surface, rolling
into the distance like gently billowing waves in mid-
ocean.

"Of course, exactly which *part* of Arcturion you are
presently standing upon, I couldn't say," said the
Dragodon coolly. "Perhaps toward the tail? He has
grown considerably over the centuries—his great size

has increased by many thousandfolds—and his coils have extended over the floor and walls until even I, his master, can no longer tell the difference between neck or tail, wing or claw. Only when he raises his head will I be able to know for sure which end is which."

Measle's legs were numb with fear, but his mind and his mouth still worked.

"Wh-wh-why isn't it moving?" he stuttered. "Is—is it *dead?*" he added hopefully.

"Not dead. Far from dead. He is asleep, Measlestubbs. He has been asleep ever since we were imprisoned here. His injuries were extensive, and sleep was the only cure. You cannot put a bandage on a Great Worm."

"G-Great Worm?"

"Another name, Measlestubbs. Occasionally he wakes, if there is food, but he quickly sleeps again."

"Is—is it g-going to w-wake up soon?"

"Oh, yes. He will awake—but only when I tell him to. Not before. So you need have no fear for a few more minutes. You may move freely. Arcturion cannot feel your insignificant weight."

Measle stared out at the rolling green hills and valleys before him. The strange shape of the landscape now began to make some sort of sense. If you could imagine a faintly luminous, pale green snake, coiled around and over and under itself, it would, perhaps, look a bit like this. But the snake's coils would have to be *huge*, each one at least the width of a football field.

Measle bent down and put his hand to the glowing surface. It was hard as stone, but it wasn't cold like stone. There was a faint warmth that rose from within, lifting the temperature of the surface just enough to notice. And then Measle thought he felt a faint movement, that tingled against the tips of his fingers.

"Put your ear to his side, Measlestubbs," said the Dragodon.

Measle bent further and pressed the side of his head against what he still thought of as the ground. Faintly and from far, far away, came an almost inaudible sound. *Thud*. Ten seconds ticked by, and there it was again. *Thud*.

"His heart, Measlestubbs. You are hearing the beating of one of his great hearts. He has four altogether."

Measle rose slowly, his own heart beating ten times faster. *I've got to play for time!* he thought desperately.

"Where—where's its head?"

"Buried somewhere deep beneath the coils of his body. When he sleeps, Arcturion prefers the darkness."

Quick, another question! Keep the Dragodon talking! "And—and what does it—I mean *he*—what does he eat?"

"Whatever he can get, Measlestubbs. Three foolish little Wrathmonks fell through my ceiling a short while ago and I thought Arcturion might like a snack, so I woke him. He snapped them up quickly enough and seemed to enjoy them. Then he buried his beautiful head beneath his coils once again and returned to his slumbers. But soon his rest will come to an end. That, Measlestubbs, is where your mother enters the picture."

"My mother?" said Measle, resisting the urge to stare wildly around in search of her. Instead, he kept his gaze on the Dragodon. "What's my mother got to do with it?"

"Why, *everything*, Measlestubbs," said the Dragodon. "Would you like me to explain?"

Measle nodded. *I've got to keep this going,* he thought, *and for as long as possible.*

The black forked tongue slithered between the black gums.

"Great Worms generate great mana," said the Dragodon slowly. "Their masters, the Dragodons, were able to draw from this mana and use a small part of it for themselves. Thus, our almost limitless powers. But an injured Great Worm is a helpless creature, and its ability to generate mana is reduced almost to zero. There is but a small trickle—barely enough to keep the creature alive and, for its master, hardly enough for a dozen spells a decade. The Great Worm must sleep until his injuries are healed and only then will his full strength and mana return. I have waited patiently for Arcturion to recover, but the process has proved to be a lengthy one. At this rate, it will be another two or three hundred years before his strength and mana fully return. But I do not intend to wait that long, Measlestubbs."

The Dragodon paused, its blank, black eyes sweeping over the hills and valleys of the vast cave. Then it took another breath and said, "I knew there had to be a solution to my problem. When men came to my island, to build their childish amusements, I was able to move among them. I saw, at once, a means to escape for both myself and for Arcturion. These foolish men had built a bridge—a path—between this island and the main-land. A path that would allow us to escape our prison. You must know, Measlestubbs, that there was a *reason* the kings and the Wizards placed us on a piece of land that was surrounded by water. You see, ocean water is death to a Great Worm. It cannot swim across it. Neither can it fly above it. Ocean water is both a bar-rier and a weapon against the Great Worms. And that is why our enemies put us here. But now—now there is a road."

The Dragodon paused again. Now he was staring down at Measle and the black forks of his tongue were flickering faster.

"I was there that day when you came to my island, Measlestubbs. You and your father and your mother. I sat behind you, I walked behind you, I watched all three of you closely. I brushed against you, I touched your father's shoulder. I learned much, but then, at the end of the day, I managed to make contact with your mother. And, in that instant, I found my answer. Your mother, Measlestubbs! What power! What great reserves of power! A well of mana—a well that never runs dry!"

The Dragodon was panting now, its narrow chest heaving up and down beneath the dusty robe. *It's very old,* thought Measle. *And very weak.*

"But she's no use!" Measle blurted. "Not to you!"

The Dragodon turned its head and pointed its blank, black eyes down at Measle.

"Why not, Measlestubbs?"

"Because you've got to be *married* to her! My dad told me that! Otherwise it doesn't work!"

"*Married?*" said the Dragodon, slowly. "Are you quite sure, Measlestubbs?"

"Of course I'm sure!" yelled Measle. Then, realizing that he ought, perhaps, to deal more cautiously with this creature, he lowered his voice and said, in a small, pleading voice, "So, if she's no use to you, why don't you just let her go?"

The Dragodon seemed to consider this idea for a moment. Then it shook its wrinkled head.

"No, no," it said quietly. "No, I couldn't do that, Measlestubbs."

"Why not?"

"Because it is not I who needs her, Measlestubbs. At least, not directly. Your father was perfectly correct—I cannot use her mana. But another can."

"Who?" said Measle, looking around the great cave.

"Why, you foolish boy, Arcturion, of course," said the Dragodon, stretching its scar of a mouth into a wide, black-gummed smile.

Measle stared, bewildered, at the Dragodon.

"What for?" he said. "What's a dragon need my mother's mana *for*?"

The Dragodon sighed. "I thought I had explained that, Measlestubbs. If Arcturion can absorb your mother's mana—her endless supply of mana—all his strength and power will return instantly."

"Yes—but *how*?" said Measle. "You can't have a dragon getting married! And anyway, she's married already!"

"There are other means by which Arcturion can link himself to your mother, Measlestubbs."

"Yeah? How?"

The forked tongue flickered.

"Why, by *eating* her, of course."

The four Wrathmonks were pushing their way through the clicking turnstiles of the exits when they heard the sounds behind them.

They all turned together and saw, advancing toward them through the rain, a small crowd of people. Most of the people wore uniforms of some kind and several of them seemed to be holding rough weapons. One man had a broom in his hands, another carried what looked like a garden fork, and the faces of everyone in this small mob looked very angry indeed.

"There they are!" yelled a man, with the words *Administration Assistant* across the front of his peaked cap. "That's them! They're the ones who froze us! Let's get 'em!"

The crowd surged forward. As they came nearer, the Wrathmonks were able to read the words on the various badges that adorned their chests and caps. *Security,* said one; *Caretaking,* said another.

Griswold Gristle hissed, "Of *courssse*! Thisss is that fool Draggle's fault! With the dessstruction of the Medusssa head, the park'sss persssonnel have revived! Well, we are releasssed from our duties to His Lordship, and therefore, we can use our mana on these interfering fools! Leave thisss to me!"

Griswold took a deep breath and opened his pudgy little mouth.

"Pedoschkin asssphaltissscoop sssuctobolusss!" he screamed. Instantly a pair of orange beams shot from his tiny eyes. They flashed, sizzling across the gap between himself and the advancing crowd and then hit the ground around the mob. Wherever the orange beams touched, the thick black asphalt softened and then slithered up the mobs' legs to just below their knees, so that the advancing crowd was no longer advancing at all. They were held fast now, with nothing left to do but shout angrily at the Wrathmonks and brandish their weapons over their heads.

"Hah," said Griswold, a smirk of satisfaction on his plump lips. "My tar-trap ssspell! They are helplesss now!"

"Can I breathe on them, Griswold?" asked Judge Cedric hopefully. His teeth ached terribly and the only thing that was going to make him feel better would be to cause a lot of pain to a lot of horrible humans.

"No, Cedric," said Griswold firmly. "There is no time—and besssides, we have other fish to fry."

"Fish?" muttered Judge Cedric. "Fry? But—do we have a pan?"

"I mean Sssam Ssstubbs, Cedric!" snapped Griswold,

pushing his way through the turnstile. "Sssam Ssstubbs is at our mercy now!"

Cudgel and Flabbit grinned wolfishly. Judge Cedric took his hands from his aching jaws and looked puzzled.

"Sssam Ssstubbs is a fish?" he said, his bushy white eyebrows raised so high that they furrowed his forehead.

Griswold Gristle clucked his tongue impatiently. He reached back through the turnstile, and grabbed Judge Cedric by the hand. "Never *mind*, Cedric! I shall explain on the way! Come, we have no time to lose!"

The other two Wrathmonks followed Griswold and Judge Cedric through the turnstiles, and then, without a backward glance at the furious shouting from behind them, they began to hurry together across the long causeway.

And the only comfort for the park's personnel, who soon gave up the hopeless struggle against the clinging asphalt, was that the rain had stopped falling at last. The heavy black clouds moved off the island and drifted along the causeway, hovering steadily over the heads of the four Wrathmonks as they headed toward the distant town.

Tinker was fed up.

Fed up, soaking wet and very, very tired. He'd been running all over the park forever, it seemed, and the creatures chasing him showed no signs of giving up. There were only two of the carousel horses now——the lame one had slipped over again and, with only three working legs, hadn't been able to get back up. The Tyrannosaurus rex was still on his trail, though, and once or twice had almost succeeded in stomping him with its enormous feet. Tinker's own feet were getting sore, and his short legs ached with tiredness.

Where's the smelly kid when you need him? he thought, scurrying through the wet darkness. *A dog could do with a bit of a lift. It'd be nice to get off the old tootsies and be carried around for a bit——not sure how much longer we can keep this up, the old tootsies and me.*

He caught a faint sniff of a familiar scent. Somewhere quite close. The smelly kid had passed this way. There were other, sharper smells, too——odors of dead fish, ancient sneakers and rotting mattresses——but it was the scent of the smelly kid that drew Tinker forward.

All these problems—like the old tootsies getting so sore—perhaps the smelly kid could solve them? The smelly kid didn't seem to mind carrying a little dog before. Perhaps he wouldn't mind carrying a little dog again?

Tinker threw a quick look over his shoulder. *Oops, here come the two horsey thingies—and there, close behind, the roaring monster thingy—off we go again!*

He pushed his exhausted legs back into a gallop and headed fast in the direction of the smells.

"*Eating* her?"

Flicker, flicker went the black forked tongue.

"Arcturion will absorb her well of mana, her inexhaustible well of mana, and it will become his. And *his* mana will become *mine*. Together, we will be unbeatable."

Measle's mind was racing. He had to stop this! Somehow he had to stop it! And, if he couldn't stop this (and there didn't seem to be any way of doing it, other than a miracle) then he had to delay it as long as possible.

"But what for? Why do you want to be unbeatable?"

The Dragodon turned its blank eyes down toward Measle.

"Surely *everybody* wants to be unbeatable, Measlestubbs?"

"Yes, all right—but who do you want to beat?"

The Dragodon lifted one corner of its thin mouth in a sneer.

"Why, *humanity*, Measlestubbs. Humanity. Men are fools, Measlestubbs—stupid beyond belief—and they cannot be allowed to control this world any longer."

"I don't think they're so stupid—"

"Well, of course you don't, Measlestubbs." *Flicker flicker* went the tongue. "You are one of them, after all. One of the cleverer ones, I must admit—which is saying very little. The proof of Man's idiocy lies above us. Who but idiots would spend their time and their riches building a playground for children?"

"It's not just for kids," muttered Measle. "My dad likes it, too."

"You prove my point, Measlestubbs. The mind of Man is a childish mind. That is why I intend to take over. To *run* things again, Measlestubbs, the way we did in the ancient times. That was the Dragodons' destiny—to run things. To rule. To control."

"To control *what?*"

"*Everything*, of course. As I said, it was the Drago-dons' *destiny*. A destiny that was interrupted for a long, long while, but now it can be ours again." The Dragodon smiled a small, black smile. "Well," it whispered, so quietly that Measle had to strain to hear the words, "Well, since I am the last of our kind, perhaps I should say—*mine* again."

Measle thought desperately. "Well all right then, but, how are you going to get out? You and your—your worm? *You* can get out, I suppose, but I don't see any hole big enough to let your dragon out."

The Dragodon laughed, a dry, dusty chuckle.

"When Arcturion's mana is restored, he will reach his full strength again. Look at him, Measlestubbs! He has been growing steadily during all these endless years! He is vast! He will be the largest creature ever to walk on—and fly above—this earth! Do you really believe that a few feet of rock will be able to hold him?"

"Yeah, well—" (*think, Measle! THINK!*) "well, if he does get out—if you both get out—we've got jets— jet fighters—and they've got rockets and machine guns and everything—"

The Dragodon's dry chuckle became a throaty, rasping laugh.

"I have seen them. They pose no threat to either of us. You forget the magic, don't you? I have had a lot of time, Measlestubbs, time to think. Time to develop. Time to practice new skills. I shall not make the mistakes of the past. As for Arcturion, I say again, look at him! Where once his fiery breath consumed an army, now it will incinerate a city! A *city*, Measlestubbs! And you threaten me with puny flying machines?"

The ground (*Not ground! Skin! Muscles! Blood! Bones!*) under Measle's feet shifted almost imperceptibly. It was as if a tiny ripple, no bigger than one caused when you drop a little pebble into the calm waters of a lake, suddenly moved across the surface, passing directly under his feet. Measle's eyes jerked downward and he heard the Dragodon's quiet chuckle.

"He moved, did he? My beloved Arcturion? He must be hungry. Well, perhaps it is time, at long last, to feed him what he needs."

The Dragodon paused and then raised an arm and pointed to a tall outcropping of black rock that rose from the center of the cave floor.

"You asked, Measlestubbs, where your mother is. I choose to tell you now. She is there, on the other side of that rock. You may go to her, if you like."

Measle didn't need any more encouragement than that. Forgetting what he was standing on, he turned and ran toward the distant rock. The ground (*Not ground!*) was smooth but uneven, with short, steep hills and deep, narrow crevasses, and Measle had to cross each one in turn, scrambling sometimes on all fours up the slopes and leaping, if they were narrow enough, over some of the dark fissures that lay between them.

At last he neared the rock. It was tall, at least thirty feet high, its base the size of a big garden shed. There was no sign of his mother. Measle ran around to the far side of the rock, and there she was.

She was slumped down, sitting listlessly on the ground, her head drooped to one side, her long red hair falling over her face.

"Mum?" whispered Measle. He moved close to her and touched her gently on her cheek. "Mum?"

Lee raised her head and looked into Measle's eyes. Her face was thin and pale, with streaks of dirt on her forehead. Her own eyes were blank and puzzled, and she looked at Measle without a trace of recognition.

"Hello," she muttered. "Who are you? Can you help me?"

"Mum!" whispered Measle, fiercely. "It's me—Measle!"

Lee smiled a small smile. "That's a funny name," she whispered. "And I like your hair. But look—I'm in trouble here. Is there any way you think you could you get me out? Or are you in the same trouble, too?"

"*Mum!*"

SHE HAS RECEIVED A DOSE OF MY BREATH, MEASLESTUBBS. SHE CAN REMEMBER NOTHING. JUST AS YOUR FATHER CAN REMEMBER NOTHING. SHE WILL NOT KNOW YOU.

Measle's head buzzed. For a moment he wondered why the Dragodon was choosing to communicate like this again. *Of course, it's on the other side of the cave, I couldn't hear it, even if I wanted to.*

Measle looked into his mother's bewildered eyes. He was about to say something—to tell her who he was and who she was and what was happening to them both—when—

AND NOW, MEASLESTUBBS, ALLOW ME TO INTRODUCE YOU AND YOUR MOTHER TO THE MOST WONDROUS CREATURE YOU WILL EVER MEET. HOW SAD THAT YOUR ACQUAINTANCE WILL BE SO SHORT. A PITY, BUT TIME WAITS FOR NOBODY.

There was a moment of silence in Measle's head. Then—

ARCTURION! ACHMAAL! ACHMAAL! MELACHIN MELOACHIN! ARCTURION! ARCTURION!

The harsh, guttural words were like hammer blows in Measle's head. Lee screwed up her eyes and closed them tight. Then she opened them a crack and peered at Measle. "That hurts, doesn't it?" she muttered through clenched teeth. "What's doing that?"

Measle was about to tell her, but he didn't have time.

There was an upheaval, a massive, rolling, undulating, shifting of the landscape. The entire floor of the vast cave began to move. Slowly, a nearby hill lifted and then shifted to the right. Beyond it, another ridge sank down several feet and then moved steadily to the left. Measle watched, his mouth hanging open, as the floor became a vast plain of moving shapes, valleys sliding past hills, hills sinking and rising like ocean waves.

And then a hole appeared on the far side of the cave. It was a dark, deep hole, formed by the sudden shifting of a line of mounds, and the sinking and parting of an equal number of ravines—all resolving themselves into a huge circular pit.

And, slowly, out of this great pit, rose something

that Measle, for several moments, was completely unable to identify. It was the size of a house. A big house—as big as Merlin Manor at least—and, as more and more of it appeared from the pit, Measle realized that it might even be as big as the White House itself. The top of this enormous object was knobbled and lumpy, a pale, glowing green that matched exactly the color of the surrounding landscape.

And then there was an eye.

Huge. The size of a double-decker bus. Slanted. Yellow. A narrow, vertical pupil, like a cat's. It was an eye that showed nothing—no fear, no kindness, no interest, no compassion. It was just a cold, expressionless, glowing yellow eye, set in the expanse of wrinkled, lumpy skin that surrounded it.

And then, below the eye, there was a mouth.

Long. Grinning. The tremendous jaws parted a little, showing a line of yellow teeth. Each tooth the length of a tall tree. Behind this forest of fangs, a black, flickering tongue, forked like the Dragodon's but a hundred, a thousand, a *million* times bigger.

Arcturion raised his great rectangular head from the pit formed by the endless coils of his body and slowly turned it from side to side.

Measle shrank back against his mother, feeling the warmth of her body. It was a small comfort but, without her being there with him, Measle thought he might have gone mad at the sight that was filling his eyes.

SAY GOOD-BYE, MEASLESTUBBS. TO YOUR MOTHER. TO YOUR LIFE.

Measle pressed himself hard against his mother. He heard her whisper against his ear. "Oh, no—"

ARCTURION! MELACHIN! MELOACHIN!

A long, scaly neck lifted Arcturion's head higher out of the pit, and Measle saw that the creature's glaring yellow eyes were now actively searching the ground in front of it. The immense head glided a hundred feet above the floor, twisting slowly this way and that.

The dead yellow eyes of Arcturion saw them.

For a moment the dragon paused.

But not for long.

The gigantic block of the dragon's head moved down toward them. When the front of the jaws reached a point a hundred feet from the rock, it stopped. The black tongue flickered out from between the yellow fangs, the twin tips hovering in the air. Slowly, the tongue extended, coming closer and closer. Twenty-five feet. Twenty. Ten. Five——

The tips of the forked tongue were shiny with saliva. They quivered in the still air, just a few inches from Measle and Lee. Then the tip closest to Measle darted forward. It almost touched his nose, but not quite. It hung there, trembling slightly for ten seconds, then it withdrew. Out of the corner of his eye, Measle could see that the other fork of the great tongue had darted forward in Lee's direction——but this one didn't pull back from her. It moved over her face, still not quite touching her. Measle realized that (like a snake) it was *tasting* the air that surrounded her. Then the trembling at the tip of the fork began to move faster and faster. Its vibrations increased until the tip of the fork was moving so fast that it was almost invisible. Then, quite suddenly, it streaked backward, joining its twin. The entire length of the great shiny black tongue was drawn away until it disappeared into the forest of fangs in Arcturion's distant jaws.

HE HAS FOUND HER OUT, MEASLESTUBBS. HE KNOWS HER FOR WHAT SHE IS.

SHUT UP! screamed Measle soundlessly, the words

staying inside his head. *JUST SHUT UP!*

VERY WELL, MEASLESTUBBS (came the words back into his brain). **I SHALL BE SILENT. ARCTURION WILL BE MAKING ENOUGH NOISE FOR ALL OF US.**

Measle hadn't taken his eyes off the dragon, and now he saw the creature raise its head toward the roof of the cave. He saw it open its jaws. . . .

A scream, an ear-bending, glass-shattering, ground-trembling scream, like the loudest siren on the biggest ship in the world, came blasting from Arcturion's throat. It made the roar of the Tyrannosaurus rex sound like the squeak of a sickly mouse. Measle put both hands to his ears to block out the deafening noise. With the sound a little reduced, Measle could make out the actual tone of the scream. It wasn't a scream of pain, or anger, or misery. It was a scream of triumph, like a great war cry.

And then the scream ended and Arcturion lowered his head and began to thrust his jaws forward, across the cave toward them.

14

DEEP
IN DARKNESS

Tinker's legs were trembling with tiredness, and his paws were so sore that they were almost bleeding. In desperation, he had adopted a new technique with his pursuers and it was working rather well.

He'd found his way to where the scent of the smelly kid was strongest, in a small area round the Ferris wheel. Nearby, in the shadow of the great wheel, was a large, gaping hole in the ground. Tinker had very nearly fallen into it, but he'd seen it just in time and had managed to skid his way around it, his little paws scrabbling against the slick, wet asphalt. Now, on the far side of the hole, Tinker took a breather and watched as the Tyrannosaurus rex and the two carousel horses emerged from the corner of a low building and advanced toward him.

The dinosaur was incapable of feeling tired; but it could feel *anger*. The same was true of the carousel horses. They all felt fury toward the little white creature that was now crouched down, panting, with its tongue lolling from one side of its mouth, on the far side of a black pit that yawned in the ground between them.

The T. rex and the horses began to move around the side of the pit. As they did so, Tinker got up and moved, too, keeping the same distance between them. The dinosaur changed direction, stumbling against one of the horses and almost pitching it headlong into the hole. Tinker changed direction again and moved back to where he'd been a moment before. Both hunters and prey did this several times and, each time, Tinker simply kept the pit between himself and his pursuers.

The Tyrannosaurus's rage increased. No matter what it did, the little white animal stayed out of reach. In a fury, the great dinosaur stamped its massive feet hard. Tinker could feel the ground trembling under its enormous weight.

Then Tinker heard a very strange noise. It was a scream, an unearthly, howling screech that seemed to be coming from far, far away.

And what was odder still, it seemed to be coming from somewhere deep in the ground *beneath* him. It certainly hadn't been made by the Tyrannosaurus, or by either of the carousel horses.

Neither the Tyrannosaurus nor the horses took any notice of the sound. Once again they began to move around the circular pit—and once again Tinker moved with them. Again, the T. rex paused and showed its rage by stamping on the ground. But this time, its great clawed feet stamped very close to the edge of the gaping pit. . . .

And the ground beneath the clawed feet and the wooden hooves—suddenly gave way. There was a grumbling, rumbling, caving-in sound, followed instantly by a sort of *whooosh!* of rushing air, and that was followed by three high-pitched screams. . . .

A chunk of asphalt the size of a chest of drawers hit Arcturion on the head.

For a moment it seemed that the dragon hadn't noticed the blow. Then a second, even larger piece smashed against the end of his long snout.

Arcturion paused in his forward movement and lifted his enormous head.

There, from a distant hole in the ceiling of the cave, *stuff* was falling down—mud, rocks, more lumps of asphalt—and three solid creatures, too, that screamed as they fell.

And, as they fell down and down and down, dropping closer and closer and closer to Arcturion's great raised head, the dragon instinctively opened his mouth to receive them.

It was this strange, sudden interruption that jerked Measle out of his paralysis. He took in the fact that something was falling toward Arcturion's gaping maw, and that the something—*no, three somethings!*—were distracting Arcturion from his main purpose.

"Come on, Mum!" he whispered frantically. "You've got to get up!

Obediently, Lee began to struggle to her feet.

Measle looked up and saw that Arcturion, who had now swallowed the creatures, was regarding them both, his huge, expressionless eyes boring down on them, as if the great creature was mildly interested to see what these two tiny beings would do next.

Measle's only thought was to put something between Arcturion and themselves. The rock, obviously, if he could get himself and his mother around to the other side of the rock. . . .

Lee closed her exhausted eyes and stumbled against him. Thinking that she had tripped, Measle looked down at her feet. There was something there, resting on the ground—small, oval, a purplish, bluish color.

It was a jelly bean.

In times of extreme stress, Measle's brain worked very well. *Jelly bean. Blue. Not mine. Must be Mum's. Only one reason for Mum to have a jelly bean . . .*

In one swift movement, Measle bent down, scooped up the jelly bean and pushed it into his mother's mouth.

"Wha'?" mumbled Lee, trying to push the jelly bean out of her mouth with her tongue.

"Eat it, Mum!" whispered Measle. He glanced up.

Arcturion's enormous head was on the move again, bearing down on them at the speed of an express train. He could see the jaws beginning to open, he could see the forest of yellow fangs parting, he could see the twin forks of the black tongue flickering deep in the shadows.

"*Eat* it!" screamed Measle. At the same moment that Lee bit down on the jelly bean, Measle pushed himself into her arms and wrapped them tight around his body.

And Lee disappeared right before his eyes.

The only way Measle knew that she was still there was the pressure of her slim body against his. He risked a quick glance down at himself and saw to his great relief that he too had gone.

Thirty seconds! That's all! So move!

Measle held tight to Lee, and together they staggered around the rock, putting its bulk between them and the dragon. Once on the far side, Lee's legs gave way again and she sank to the ground.

Behind them, there was a shattering roar, and this time, there was a very different quality to the sound. This time, instead of a scream of triumph, Arcturion let out a wild shriek of rage. The huge creature had been relishing this moment, and then, without warning—

Where was his prey? It had been there, before his very nose, a second ago! And now it was gone! His precious prey! One of the little creatures was small and insignificant and meant no more to him than a grain of rice might mean to an elephant—but the other was rich in mana! Rich beyond measure! Those three plastic and wooden morsels that had just fallen out of the sky and into his mouth, and the three soft little wriggling creatures before them, they too had been rich in mana and were giving him a small (and short-lived) degree of his old strength. But this temporary strength was nothing to what the tiny thing by the rock would give him! It had more mana (and more *reserves* of mana) than anything he had ever experienced! The little thing was so rich in mana, in fact, that he knew instinctively what ingesting that tiny creature would mean to him! Eternal Power! Endless Strength! Infinite Glory!

And now it was gone!

Measle and Lee huddled together in the shelter of the rock as Arcturion let out another, even louder scream of rage. They felt the ground shudder as the dragon shifted its body. Then Arcturion's palace-sized head appeared from around the side of the rock. The great yellow eyes searched the area, the tall, vertical black pupils passing right across Measle and Lee still huddling against the hard stone wall.

Fifteen seconds gone! Do something!

Frantically, Measle freed one of his hands from Lee's encircling arms. He fumbled against her dress, searching for the pocket that he knew was there.

Ah! There it was! Now please let there be more inside.

Measle's fingers plunged deep into the pocket and touched a small heap of little oval objects. He grabbed a handful and pulled one jelly bean from the little pile in his palm. He pushed it between Lee's lips.

"What are you doing?" mumbled Lee, trying to turn her head away. Her eyes were still closed tight. "I don't like the blue ones—"

"I know you don't, Mum," whispered Measle, "but you've got to eat them! Every time I give you one, you've got to eat it! *Don't ask why!*"

There was such a desperate urgency in Measle's voice that Lee felt a strong urge to do as she was told. There was something about this boy, with his funny, sticking-up hair—something vaguely familiar and, at the same time, something very dear and very comforting.

Lee bit down on the second jelly bean and chose that moment to open her eyes.

She was alone!

No, no she wasn't alone! She could *feel* the boy, pressed against her! But she couldn't see him.

"Where are you?" she whispered.

"Right here, Mum," came back the answer. She could feel the warm air of his breath against her ear. "Keep still. Don't move. Don't make any noise. And keep eating the jelly beans."

Even without her memory, Lee Stubbs was an intelligent woman. She had lost everything—her past, her knowledge, even her identity—and, a moment earlier, she had even been at the point of losing her *life*. And then this strange boy had appeared at her side and, even as the most humongous monster Lee had ever imagined was bearing down on her, this boy had somehow managed to drag her out of the path of the great creature. Not only that, but this extraordinary boy, with the bizarre haircut, had somehow managed to make both himself and her *invisible!* This succession of fast-moving, impossible events all seemed to be holding out some small hope of survival! So, if this extraordinary boy wanted her to eat blue jelly beans, Lee Stubbs was, at the moment, rather inclined to do as she was told.

And now, Arcturion's fury at the loss of his prey was sending the dragon's small brain into a frenzy. His vast head was now darting around the great cave, searching frantically in every nook and cranny, around every projecting rock, all the while keeping up a series of piercing screams, each one louder than the last.

The huge coils were shifting fast, rippling across the floor and up the walls. Measle and Lee, huddled in the shelter of their rock, watched as the endless length of the dragon's body slid past. Their invisible hands were pressed hard to their invisible ears. Conversation was impossible. Every thirty seconds, Measle pressed a jelly bean between Lee's lips.

Then, as Arcturion unwound his endless great body, freeing it from where it had lain so still for so many countless years, he suddenly discovered that he was imprisoned. Imprisoned in a space that was too small! Too small to unfurl his great wings! Too small to move properly! Too constricting! The walls and the roof seemed to bear down on him, seemed to close in on him, squeezing him tighter and tighter.

And then Arcturion's fury turned to mindless panic. The volume of his screeching increased, his movements became more and more frantic as he tried to circle the cave, tried to find a way out, tried to stretch his great, black-membraned wings. He managed to free the end of his tail, dragging it up and out from under the heavy coils of his body, and now he began to swing his tail in wide, sweeping arcs. The tail ended in a huge ball of bone, all covered in spikes, which now began to smash against the walls of the cave. *SMASH!* to one side, then *CRASH!* to the other. The walls shuddered and splintered under the blows, big shards of black rock splitting away from the surface and crashing to the floor. Through all this deafening, thunderous, screeching cacophony of sound, Measle and Lee heard (but only within their heads):

ARCTURION! ARCTURION! SCHKRAAAST! SCHKRAAAST!

But whatever it was the Dragodon wanted, Arcturion's rage and terror were putting the dragon's brain past commanding. If anything, Arcturion doubled his efforts to escape this terrible, confining space, swinging his great tail with ever greater effort, until Measle and Lee could feel the rocky floor shudder and shake beneath them. All they could do was huddle even closer together, with Measle feeding Lee the jelly beans from a fast-diminishing pile in the palm of his hand.

And then, it happened.

The huge ball of bony spikes at the end of Arcturion's tail swung yet again against the rock wall of the cave, and a massive, rough circle of rock crashed and fell from the surface, leaving a black hole in its place.

A black hole, from which came a sudden trickle of water that dribbled over the edge of the hole . . .

There was a distant rumble . . .

The trickle turned to a gush . . .

Another rumble, closer this time . . .

The gush turned to a torrent, that spewed from the hole, the water spreading rapidly over the cave floor. . . .

Another rumble, much louder now . . .

And the torrent turned to a jet—a jet of cold, green water, thirty feet across, that leaped from the hole and smashed clear across the great cave. It roared above Measle and Lee, making a sound like a rocket taking off. Then it hit the far wall, splashing in a huge circle of white foam.

The water began to spread quickly across the floor.

The first shallow wave reached Measle and Lee, washing over their legs and hands. They both struggled to their feet. Measle lifted his right hand out of the chilly water. He touched the ends of his wet fingers to his tongue.

The water was salty.

"It's the sea, Mum!" he shouted. "The sea's coming in!" His voice sounded small and faint over the roar of the water and the screams of Arcturion.

And, suddenly, the screams of the Great Worm sounded different.

Before, there had been the scream of triumph. Then the shriek of fury. Then panic, mixed with rage. Then, just pure panic. To Measle, each earsplitting howl from the throat of the immense creature had been clear in its meaning. And now—now there was another scream, just as clear.

This one was a scream of pain.

Measle carefully poked his head out from the shelter of the rock.

An extraordinary and horrible sight met his startled eyes. Arcturion had somehow managed to drag the endless coils of his body across the cave, heaping them up against the far wall, piling them higher and higher, his head now brushing the roof, all in a frantic effort to keep any part of himself from touching the rising waters. But the waters *were* touching him—lapping against the lowest coils that still rested against the cave floor—and there was nothing Arcturion could do about it.

And where the water flowed against the dragon's skin, the skin turned black. It was as if the water was now acting like fire—or acid, perhaps—burning Arcturion's hide wherever it touched. And, where it touched, the soft, glowing light that shone from the dragon's hide was slowly, but surely, being extinguished. Arcturion's screams of pain were now so high-pitched that they were almost beyond the limits of human hearing. And the only movements from the great creature were his futile struggles to keep his vast body away from the rising waters.

Measle watched as Arcturion managed to free one enormous wing. It was shaped like a bat's wing, with a membrane that was stretched between the long supporting bones that ended in great, curved claws like scythes. Arcturion flapped this freed wing desperately, making a small hurricane of wind that swept over Measle's head with the sound of a train going past. But one wing, in this confined space, was no help to Arcturion. There was no way he could avoid this *wetness*—this terrible wetness that burned wherever it touched and, through his dreadful agony, he began to feel himself gradually weakening. Those parts of his coils which now lay under the water were beginning to dissolve in the corrosive salt water, leaving only the bones behind. As the sea rose steadily, it engulfed more and more of the great body, blackening the outer skin as it went. And as it did so, the strange unnatural light from Arcturion's hide (which had, until this moment, lit up the whole cave with its soft green glow) began slowly to dim.

The huge jet of water continued blasting across the cave and smashing in a great fountain against the opposite wall. It had been compressed through the narrow hole in the cave wall and then released into the cave, with all the force and pressure of the whole ocean

311

behind it. Now the cold green waters were rising faster and faster. . . .

Already the water was up to Measle's knees. He dragged his eyes away from the horrible spectacle of Arcturion's agonized struggles and looked into Lee's face. She was standing now, her back braced against the rock. She looked at him and smiled.

"We're going to have to swim for it!" she yelled, over the roar of the water. "Can you swim, kid?"

Measle nodded. *There's only one problem,* he thought, *where are we going to swim to?* There was only the inside of the cave.

Lee must have seen Measle's eyes as he swept them over the high rocky walls, because she bent her head close to his and shouted, "There must be a way out!"

Measle didn't look too convinced, so Lee yelled, "We just let the water take us up! There's that hole in the ceiling—the one all those things fell through!"

Measle nodded. There was only one problem with this idea: what if the water finally reached the same level as the sea that surrounded the island and then rose no farther? They could be stuck, floating below the hole above them, with no way of climbing out of it.

But there was no more time for thought. The water was up to Measle's neck, so he leaned forward and lifted his feet from the floor. Lee did the same. They clung together, letting the water lift them upward. The water was very cold and, in a few moments, Measle's teeth were chattering. They were careful to keep the rock between them and the dwindling sounds of distress that still came from the far side of the cave. Even half-melted away, Arcturion might be still capable of one last effort in their direction.

And now the seawater, rising unbelievably fast, washed over the tip of their rock. Measle and Lee found themselves floating out in the open, in the center of the cave, with nowhere to hide.

One look told Measle and Lee that the danger from Arcturion was almost past. On the far side of the cave, the dragon was still struggling feebly, but most of his lower coils were gone, dissolved to nothingness in the bitter water, and all that was left of the great creature was his long, long neck and his head the size of a palace. The head was drooping, swaying slowly from side to side and the great yellow eyes were losing their light. In fact, the whole cave was filling with shadows and Measle found he could no longer see the ceiling at all, so dark had it become within the vast space.

MEASLESTUBBS.

Measle felt the word drop into his skull like a small piece of lead. But this time, there was none of the power of command in it. This time, there was a note of pleading—pleading mixed with fear and uncertainty.

WHAT? replied Measle, sending the thought flying across the cave. Was the Dragodon still there, standing on its rock ledge on the far side of the cave?

I AM STILL HERE, MEASLESTUBBS. THE WATER IS RISING. IT IS GETTING DARK. I CANNOT SEE ARCTURION—BUT I FEEL HIS MANA DRAINING AWAY. I AM GROWING WEAKER, MEASLESTUBBS. WHAT HAVE YOU DONE? WHAT HAVE YOU DONE?

Measle paused for a moment, wondering how to respond.

I THINK WE'VE WON, DRAGODON. I THINK MY MUM AND ME HAVE WON!

There was a long pause.

HELP ME, MEASLESTUBBS.

There was no doubt about it. The Dragodon was begging! There was no power in those unspoken words to

314

command any more—just this fearful, defeated begging! And there was something so pathetic in the tone of the request, something so utterly helpless, that Measle, still holding tight to Lee with one hand, began to swim awkwardly toward the distant wall where he remembered the Dragodon's ledge to be.

"What are you doing?" said Lee, finding herself being towed along by this determined boy, whether she wanted to be or not.

Measle didn't reply. He knew what he was doing—he just didn't know *why* he was doing it. He just felt that this was the right thing to do, and that was why he was doing it.

QUICKLY, MEASLESTUBBS. QUICKLY! THE WATERS! THE WATERS ARE COMING! I CANNOT FLOAT, MEASLESTUBBS! I CANNOT FLOAT!

And now there was stark terror in the Dragodon's tone. Measle swam harder, dragging Lee behind him. They swam in silence across the cold, choppy water, the darkness deepening all around them. They could no longer hear any sound from Arcturion, and now there was only a small faint green glow from the far side of the cave.

MEASLESTUBBS! MEASLESTUBBS! MEASLESTUBBS!

The impact of the fear-filled words in Measle's head grew fainter and fainter and fainter.

They swam on. The cave was silent now, apart from the splashing of Measle's arms and legs. The water had long since risen above the hole in the cave wall, risen above the blasting jet, drowning out the deafening roar of its passing. Arcturion had fallen silent some time ago. They were surrounded by a darkness that grew thicker with every passing second. Soon they would be as good as blind.

And then Measle felt Lee's free hand grab his shoulder.

"Measle?" he heard her whisper. "Measle, my darling, is that you?"

Measle twisted around in the water and stared into his mother's eyes.

They had changed.

Before, they had been the eyes of a friendly stranger. Now—now they were the eyes of his mother, staring back into his with wonder—with relief—with love—with bewilderment.

"Mum? You know who I am?"

"Yes! *Now* I do!"

"And you can remember everything again?"

"Yes! *Everything*! I remember now—I was kidnapped in the parking lot—the Wrathmonks brought me here—the Dragodon—I remember it all!"

"But—but how? *How* do you suddenly remember?"

Lee grabbed both of Measle's shoulders and pulled him close to her in a bone-crushing hug. "It means that the Dragodon is *dead*, Measle! That's how most spells are lifted! When the caster dies! That means—that means it's dead, Measle!"

"Dead? The Dragodon?"

Lee nodded, her eyes glittering in the darkness. "There's nothing to go back for, Measle," she said. "The Dragodon's gone. We have to save ourselves now. Come on, we've got to try and get out of here. We've got to swim for that hole in the roof."

Lee took his hand and began to swim back in the direction from which they'd come. As Measle felt himself being towed along by his mother's powerful strokes, his whole body suddenly relaxed. A great tide of relief swept over him. He was no longer in charge. He didn't have to do anything—think of anything—come up with any more ideas—not now, now that his mother was back to herself again. She was his mum

317

again. All he had to do was what she *told* him to do.

The water was very cold. A little wave splashed into his open mouth. It tasted bad—salty, mixed with another strange, metallic flavor. It was like licking an old penny.

And now the darkness was almost complete, surrounding them with velvet blackness, apart from a pale, ragged circle of light high above them. With the Wrathmonks gone from the island, the black clouds had gone, too, and now the moon shone down onto the Isle of Smiles, flooding the whole area with soft, blue light. Some of that light fell down through the hole in the asphalt and cast a circle of blue light onto the water below.

Measle and Lee swam into this circle and treaded water. They watched, shivering, as the seawater lifted them higher and higher toward the ever-closer hole.

And then, a few moments later, their hopes died. They stopped rising. They saw that the hole wasn't getting any closer. Measle and Lee floated together in the circle of moonlight, staring upward. The hole was perhaps ten feet above their heads, but it might as well have been a hundred miles above them; there was no way that they could reach it.

"I think the water's stopped coming in, Mum," said Measle, flatly.

"Yes," said Lee. "I think it has, too. I'm afraid it doesn't look like we're going to go any higher."

And now they were getting very tired. They had been swimming, both fully dressed, in this freezing water, for fifteen minutes, and now they were simply trying to stay afloat. Their legs felt heavy and weak, and their arms ached with cold and exhaustion. Measle got another mouthful of water and experienced once again that strange, unpleasant metallic taste on his tongue.

"It tastes funny, this water," he muttered.

"That's because it's not just water," said Lee. Her voice was very tired, and there was a trace of uncertainty in it as well. "It's mixed up with something else, Measle. Try not to swallow any of it."

"Mixed up with what?"

"Arcturion, love. What's left of him. That's his blood you're tasting. And I have no idea what swimming around in diluted dragon's blood does to you."

They both heard the rumbling noise at the same instant.

*/ */ */*

Ever since Cudgel had lifted Measle out of the swing seat, the Ferris wheel had been hanging on by a thread— *literally* by a thread. A thread of steel—the remains of the axle that supported it off the ground. Most of this axle had sheered away under the strain of Cudgel's enormous strength—strength that had overpowered the automatic braking system that had held the wheel immovable ever since the park had closed for the winter. The entire weight of the ride now rested on this thin thread of metal, which had been steadily weakening under the enormous strain of holding the contraption upright.

The scrap of metal had survived the vibrations from the trampling, stamping feet of the Tyrannosaurus rex. It had survived the shaking and shuddering from the blows of Arcturion's great tail that had caused rippling vibrations, which had traveled up in waves from deep below ground, like an earthquake. It had survived (but only just) the last, massive shake from underground when the powerful jet of water had smashed against the opposite wall of the cave. It had survived all these shocks, but each one had had weakened it more and more, and now it was at the point of breaking.

And then, simply, it snapped in two.

And it was Tinker who, quite accidentally, caused it to snap.

Tinker had been squatting in the shadows of a nearby refreshment booth wondering, in the vague sort of way that dogs do, where everybody had got to. The thingy and horsies were gone, which was good, but where was that smelly kid? He felt a sudden itch behind his right ear—so, up came his back leg and *scritch—scritch—scritch* went his claws on the tickling spot. It was a very persistent itch, so Tinker bent his head sideways and scratched even harder. Then at the end of each stroke, his furiously working back leg began to thump on the ground. *Scritch—thump—scritch—thump—scritch—thump*!

With each thump of his leg on the ground, tiny, almost unmeasurable vibrations began to run through the ground. By the time these vibrations reached the thread of steel—the thread that was all that held the Ferris wheel in position—they were so weak that even the most sensitive of instruments would have had difficulty picking them up.

But, weak as they were, they were enough.

There's a phrase, "the straw that broke the camel's back." Well, the effect on the Ferris wheel of the vibrations from Tinker's back leg thumping on the nearby ground fits that phrase perfectly. The metal thread was, by now, so fragile that these minuscule pulsations, which traveled through the ground and then up the metal frame, were just enough to cause the overstressed thread of steel to snap.

There was a faint *twang!* from somewhere near the axle of the wheel. Then the whole Ferris wheel made a small lurch downward. Tinker watched, puzzled, as the great contraption swayed from side to side. Then gravity took over. With a groaning, creaking sound, the huge wheel slid forward, off the supporting pillars, and the rim of the enormous hoop touched down on the ground. Then slowly, majestically, like a gigantic bicycle wheel, the thing began to roll forward.

It rolled, ponderously, to the edge of the gaping hole.

Then, slowly, it toppled in.

With a grinding, crunching sound, it sank down into the pit. It looked, to Tinker's astonished eyes, as if it was going to continue sliding down into the hole until it disappeared altogether. But then, with a third of itself inside the deep depression, the edge of its leading rim grated against the far side of the hole. Several pieces of asphalt broke away from under the rim and the wheel sank another foot. Then it stopped. Its steel latticework groaned under the strain. It settled another couple of feet and stuck fast.

When Measle and Lee heard the rumbling sound, they both instinctively began to paddle backward as fast as they could, out of the circle of moonlight and into the relative safety of the deep shadows beyond. They watched as the hole above them suddenly filled with darkness. Then they saw the great mass of steel sinking fast down toward the surface of the water. Chunks of roadway fell around them, sending up fountains of water into the air, and it was only by the greatest good luck that neither Measle nor Lee was hit by any of the falling debris.

Then, just as the great mass of steel touched the surface of the water, there was a grinding, crunching, creaking sound and the wreckage of twisted metal came to a halt.

"What *is* that thing?" whispered Lee, her teeth clattering with cold.

"It's the Ferris wheel, Mum!" yelled Measle, his voice echoing round the cave. "I climbed it! All the way up! *So can we*! It's easy! Come on!"

Lee didn't need any more encouragement than that. Ignoring the aches in their arms and legs, they swam quickly to the wheel. They dragged themselves up and out of the icy water and began to climb. Within a few minutes, the hole was just a few feet above their heads.

And that was when they saw the small white head, with a pair of fuzzy ears and a shiny black nose, and an alert and curious pair of eyes staring down at them from the edge of the hole.

"Oh—h-hello, T-t-tink," said Measle, his teeth clattering together from the cold. "I b-b-bet you've been having f-f-fun, haven't you?"

15

THE
WRATHMONKS' REVENGE

A very large and very powerful motorcycle, with a battered old sidecar attached to one side of it, turned off the main road and passed between the open gates of Merlin Manor.

The motorbike was painted a dull black. Under the massive gas tank was a huge black engine, which made a steady *thrump—thrump—thrump* noise through the rusty exhaust pipes that stuck out at the back.

Low in the sky, and directly over the motorbike, hung a black cloud. A gentle drizzle fell steadily onto the machine and its occupants.

For all its power, the motorbike was going very slowly. Cudgel was the driver. Behind him, on the pillion seat, sat Frognell Flabbit. Flabbit's face was still just as red and lumpy as before, and it looked even more like a plate of raspberries than ever. Flabbit was holding tight to Cudgel's waist. Flabbit couldn't get his arms all the way around the enormous Wrathmonk, so he was forced to cling onto the bottom edges of Cudgel's leather motorcycle jacket. His comb-over had long since come unstuck and was hanging long and loose and dripping by the side of his head.

Griswold Gristle and Judge Cedric Hardscrabble sat, squashed together, in the sidecar. Griswold still clutched his umbrella, but it had long since blown inside out and was now no use to anybody at all. All four Wrathmonks were very wet.

Since there was only the single seat in the sidecar, Griswold was perched on Judge Cedric's bony knees, and he was very uncomfortable indeed. He'd been very uncomfortable ever since they had set off. This was partly because he was soaking wet, partly because Judge Cedric's knees were rather sharp, but it was mostly because something very strange seemed to have

326

happened to the sidecar's single wheel. Instead of being round, like a normal wheel, the sidecar's wheel was square. The rim was square and the tire that surrounded the rim was square as well. This meant that instead of running smoothly along the road, the sidecar bounced up and down with every quarter turn of the misshapen wheel. *Thumpsqueak—thumpsqueak—thumpsqueak* it went, jolting Griswold and Judge Cedric up and down so hard that Judge Cedric had to hold tight (with one hand—the other nursed his aching jaws) to his bowler hat to stop it falling off.

The square wheel meant that Cudgel had to drive very slowly. He'd been driving very slowly for a very long way.

"Thisss is all your fault, Flabbit!" he snarled over his shoulder as they crept jerkily up the long gravel drive toward Merlin Manor.

"How's it *my* fault, Mr. Cudgel?" said Flabbit plaintively.

"You let the van run out of gasss, didn't you?" rumbled Cudgel. "There we were, driving along, you lot in front in the van, me following on my bike, then, all of a sssudden—right in the middle of nowhere, *ssssputter—ssssputter—ssssputter*—and your tank is empty!"

"I ssstill don't sssee why that'sss my fault," said Flabbit.

Griswold opened his mouth. Being jolted up and down like this made it hard to say anything, but he was determined to join in this discussion. "You—were—s-s-ssupposed—to—be—in—charge—of—the—van," he managed to stutter. "That—includes—the—g-gasss—tank—Mr.—Flabbit."

Flabbit began to look a little angry.

"Now look here," he said, "what about what the judge did, then, eh? Nobody is sssaying anything about that, are they? All right, I grant you, the van running out of gasss might have been a *bit* my fault—"

"A—*b-bit?*" stuttered Griswold.

Flabbit ignored him. "But thisss ssstupid sssquare wheel was nothing to do with me! Ho, no—thisss ssstupid sssquare wheel was caused by a certain *judge*, wasn't it? Why is nobody sssaying anything about that, eh?"

"Cedric—has—apologized—for—that."

"Not good enough!" snapped Flabbit. "I mean to sssay—ssso, we run out of gasss and—well—thank goodnesss for Mr. Cudgel and his motorbike, that'sss all I can sssay, because our journey is hardly interrupted at all. We all pile on—a bit of a sssquash, but never mind—then a few miles farther on, and through no fault of myssself, nor of Mr. Cudgel, his sssidecar wheel gets a puncture. And Mr. Cudgel is jussst getting ready to mend it, when a certain judge decides to try a bit of his magic on it!"

"Well—he sssaid—he wanted—to change—the wheel," muttered Judge Cedric sulkily and under his breath, so that only Griswold heard him. "He sssaid—he wanted—to *change* it—ssso I—changed it—for him!"

"Yesss, well—never—mind—all—that," stuttered Griswold. "We—are—here—now. Perhapsss—Mr.—C-cudgel—we—might—ssstop—here—and—w-walk—the—ressst—of—the—w-way?"

Cudgel brought the lurching motorbike to a halt and switched off the engine. All four Wrathmonks breathed a collective sigh of relief. Flabbit slid off the back of the pillion, Cudgel swung one enormous leg over his saddle, and Griswold pulled himself shakily off Judge Cedric's knees and then helped the Judge out of the sidecar. Then, their legs wobbling slightly, the four Wrathmonks trudged up the drive to the front door of the big, red brick house.

Griswold Gristle took a deep breath. He looked at his fellow Wrathmonks and said, "Are we all ready?"

The other three Wrathmonks nodded.

"Very well," said Griswold. "Let usss proceed with our final misssion." He raised his hand and pressed his stubby forefinger against the doorbell button. There was a distant ringing sound.

Several seconds passed. Then they all heard the sounds of slow, shuffling footsteps, and a moment later the heavy door creaked open.

Sam Stubbs stood in the doorway. He was in pajamas and a dressing gown and his feet were bare. His hair was tousled, he had several days growth of stubble on his face and his eyes looked sleepy and bewildered.

"Yes?" he said, in a weak voice. "What can I do for you?"

Griswold Gristle stepped forward, rubbing his fat little hands together. He had a beaming smile on his round face and his tiny, piggy eyes were gleaming.

"Hah, Sssam Ssstubbs!" he cried. "It is not what you can do for usss! It is what we can do for *you*! More precisssely, in fact, is what we are going to do *to* you! What do you think of that, eh?"

"Er, I'm not sure I understand," said Sam mildly. He rubbed a hand across his eyes. "Who are you, anyway?"

"Allow me to introduce myssself," said Griswold. "I am Griswold Grisssstle. These are my colleagues, Mr. Buford Cudgel, Mr. Frognell Flabbit and my learned friend, Judge Cedric Hardsssscrabble!"

"Nice to meet you," said Sam. "Now if you don't mind, I think I'd better go back to bed. I'm not very well, you see." He began to close the door, but Cudgel stuck out one huge, booted foot and jammed it in the doorway.

"Not ssso fassst, Ssstubbs," he rumbled. "We've got business with you."

"Indeed we have," said Griswold. He peered up at Sam, his head cocked to one side. Then he said, in a slightly sorrowful voice, "It's sssuch a pity that you have no memory, Sssam Ssstubbs. If you only knew who and what we are! The fact that you don't makes our revenge a little less sssweet, I'm afraid."

"Then why don't we tell him, Griswold?" said Judge Cedric.

Griswold stared at Judge Cedric in wonder. It was

331

the first sensible thing his friend had said in months. In years even.

"Excellent idea, Cedric!" he said. Then he turned back to Sam. "Ssso, Sssam Ssstubbs, my friends and I are Wrathmonks. Vassstly sssuperior beings to mere Wizards, of which order you happen to be a very *minor* member. We are your enemies, Sssam Ssstubbs—and we are here to dessstroy you!"

"Oh, dear," said Sam. "Must you?"

"Yesss! We mussst! We would have done it sssooner but for variousss missshapsss on our way here! Not that those missshapsss have delayed usss at all, sssince it was necesssary, anyway, for usss to wait a day and a night in order to recharge our powers. We *disss*charged our powers on variousss presssing matters, Sssam Ssstubbs—*sssome* of usss disssscharging them rather more effectively than *others*, it mussst be sssaid." (And here Judge Cedric turned his frizzy head aside and stared innocently out into the distance).

Griswold went on, "And now, after a sssomewhat uncomfortable night ssssleeping together on the floor of the van, we are fully recharged! Fully recharged— except for *one* of usss, who unfortunately wasssted all his preciousss mana on deforming an innocent *wheel*.

332

However, that is of no consssequence, sssince there are three of usss absssolutely *brimming* with mana! And we are here, to take our revenge!"

"Oh," said Sam, nodding thoughtfully. He glanced down at Cudgel's boot, which was still stuck in the narrow gap between the edge of the door and the door frame. "Goodness," he said. "What big feet you've got."

Griswold turned to the other Wrathmonks.

"Sssee how ssstrong His Lordship the Dragodon's exhalation enchantment is!" he whispered. "This absssurd wizard doesn't even undersssstand what is about to happen to him!"

"Yeah, well, let's get on with it, Grissstle," grumbled Cudgel.

"Very well," said Griswold. He took a step backward, and the other three Wrathmonks all took a step backward as well. Then Griswold raised his hand and pointed a fat finger at Sam.

"Sssam Ssstubbs!" he cried, "you are sssentenced to death."

Judge Cedric tapped him on the shoulder. "That'sss what *I* sssay, Griswold."

"Be quiet, Cedric!" snapped Griswold. "You have no mana left and are therefore not part of thisss moment!"

He glared at his friend for a moment and then turned back to Sam. "As I was sssaying, you are sssentenced to death, Sssam Ssstubbs, by order of the Great Order of Wrathmonks! Prepare to meet your doom!"

"What, now?" said Sam, smiling a small smile.

"Yesss, now!" shrieked Griswold. Then he narrowed his little eyes and yelled, *"Dwaaargen Ssskaaargen Onglepoise!"* Immediately twin beams of electric blue light sprang from his eyes and flashed toward Sam.

And Sam brought his left hand out from behind the door frame and held it up, the palm of his hand facing the Wrathmonks—

And the twin blue beams smashed against Sam's outstretched palm and then splashed, like a fountain, against his skin, the beams breaking into little glowing blue streams, that slid and dripped from his hand and then disintegrated into nothingness.

Griswold stepped back another pace, his round, white face creased with confusion.

"Ah," he said, uncertainly, "Well, it would ssseem that, while you may have losssst your memories, you have not losssst your abilities, Sssam Ssstubbs. That, I asssume, was an inssstinctive reaction?"

Sam smiled gently and said nothing.

Griswold shook his head. "Well, what a pity," he said sadly. "That was my famous turn-inssside-out incantation. I should ssso like to have watched you turn inssside out—a sssplendidly disssgusssting ssspectacle! However, your low quality, defensssive magic has sssomehow managed to block it. But your magic won't help you—not anymore! You sssee, you have used up your mana, Sssam Ssstubbs! As have I! Neither of usss has a drop of mana left! Of courssse, I could always resort to my exhalation enchantment, but I really feel you deserve more than that. Ssso with both of usss drained, that would mean a ssstalemate, Sssam Ssstubbs. That is, if it was jussst you and I facing each other! But, it is not jussst you and I, is it? No, there are three more of usss!"

Griswold paused and glanced, with a look of irritation, in Judge Cedric's direction. "Well, *two* of usss, at any rate. However, my colleagues, Mr. Buford Cudgel and Mr. Frognell Flabbit, have, between them, more than enough mana to dessstroy you, Sssam Ssstubbs! Ssso, I leave you to them! Gentlemen?"

Griswold gave Cudgel and Flabbit a small bow and stepped to one side. Then Cudgel and Flabbit both stared grimly at Sam.

"My brain-to-porridge incantation, I think," said Flabbit.

"My lightning-ssstrike-to-the-head incantation, I think," rumbled Cudgel.

"Together, my dear Cudgel?" said Flabbit.

"Together?" growled Cudgel. "Yesss, why not!"

Both Wrathmonks opened their mouths and spat out their spells in unison.

"*Groinduckle Groanduckle Ssspinglebunce!*" screamed Flabbit.

"*Bellicoop Zimbaldrum Armitramp!*" roared Cudgel.

A pair of pink beams shot from Flabbit's eyes and sped toward Sam.

A pair of yellow beams shot from Cudgel's eyes and sped toward Sam.

Sam Stubbs raised a finger and tapped it against the outer panel of the front door. Then, in one fluid movement, he simply swung the door shut in the Wrathmonks' faces.

The four beams—two pink, two yellow—smashed against the heavy door, splashed outward across its surface and then dripped and drizzled harmlessly down toward the ground, fizzling away into little tendrils of

336

colored smoke that floated away in the still air.

There was a long silence as the four Wrathmonks stared in bewilderment at the closed door. Then Griswold recovered himself.

"Mr. Cudgel!" he shrieked. "It would ssseem that our foe has sssome unsssussspected reserves! Our only recoursssse now is to use our exhalation enchantments on him! Kindly use your great ssstrength and sssmash that door to pieces!"

Cudgel took a step forward but, as he did so, the front door swung open again.

"Now I'd really rather you didn't do that," said Sam, smiling apologetically. "I'm sorry, but it's a nice door, and I would prefer to keep it in one piece, if you don't mind."

"Breathe on him!" screamed Griswold, dancing furiously from foot to foot. "We mussst all breathe on him together!"

The four Wrathmonks each took a step closer and all of them opened the mouths and prepared to fill their lungs with air.

And then Sam swung the front door wide open——as wide as it would go, revealing everything that was in the great hall of Merlin Manor.

And the Wrathmonks gaped in horror.

Sam Stubbs wasn't alone.

Lee Stubbs was standing by Sam's side. Sam's right hand (hidden behind the door until this moment) was held tightly in her left. Her free right hand rested on Measle's shoulder. Nanny Flannel hovered in the shadows behind the three of them, with Tinker at her feet. Tinker had a large beef bone in his mouth, and he was trying to growl at the intruders and chew the bone at the same time.

At last Griswold Gristle found his voice.

"But—but—but—" he stammered. Then he raised a trembling finger and pointed it at Lee and Measle. "But—you're dead!"

"Apparently not," said Lee. "You must be thinking of somebody else."

"The Dragodon, probably," said Measle. "*It's* dead, I know. Dead as a doornail."

Sam stepped forward, out of the doorway. Lee stepped with him, still holding tightly to her husband's hand. They both stared severely at the frozen Wrathmonks.

"You've all been very naughty little Wrathmonks," said Sam quietly. "You've been making dreadful nuisances of yourselves. You've been bothering my wife and my son, you've turned a whole bunch of innocent people into stone statues. They're all right now, no thanks to you, but you've also smashed a perfectly splendid Ferris wheel—and now you turn up at my house on a horrible, smelly, broken-down old motorbike and start chucking dangerous spells about. Well, we can't have that sort of behavior, you know. We just can't. Sorry, but there it is."

Sam raised both his arms and made a few complicated hand movements in the air. Then he said, *"Circumretio Infragilistum Bolenda!"*

There was a shimmering in the air over the Wrathmonks' heads. Startled, all four of them looked up and saw a shining, silvery net materialize out of nothing. It hovered there for a moment and then, quite soundlessly, it dropped down onto the Wrathmonks. The edges of the net fell to the ground and then slid under the Wrathmonks feet, gathering itself together like the strings of a shopping bag.

"Oy!" yelled Cudgel, punching his great fists at the net. "Let me out!"

The net drew tighter and now the Wrathmonks were beginning to feel the squeeze.

"Griswold, please remove your foot from my face,"

whined Flabbit, struggling to pull himself free.

"I do believe that thisss is sssome sssort of *net*!" shouted Judge Cedric. His bowler hat was being shoved down hard on his head and was beginning to squash his pointed ears. "Are we going fishing?"

"Mr. Cudgel!" squeaked Griswold. "Kindly ssstop waving your great fisssts about! That was my *eye*!"

The net tightened and tightened around them, until it was difficult to work out which of those wriggling hands inside it belonged to which of those wriggling arms and if that shiny bit over there was one of Cudgel's boots or a section of his motorcycle helmet.

Then, with the four Wrathmonks wrapped tightly together in a neat ball of tangled arms and legs and bodies and heads—they were encased so tightly in fact, that they could hardly breathe and certainly couldn't say anything—Sam made another small gesture with one forefinger and the whole silvery mass slowly rose a couple of feet into the air and then hovered there, bobbing gently up and down.

Sam turned his head and called back into the hallway of the house.

"Mr. Needle! Mr. Bland! Ready when you are!"

Mr. Needle and Mr. Bland appeared out of the shadows and walked quickly out into the daylight. Mr. Needle spoke briefly into what looked a little like a walkie-talkie and, a moment later, a large white truck crunched around from behind the house and drew up by the front door.

Measle noted, with interest, that the truck had no driver.

Mr. Needle put on a pair of thick leather gloves. Mr. Bland opened the rear doors of the truck and Mr. Needle carefully pushed the hovering, netted ball of Wrathmonks into the cargo space. Then he and Mr. Bland swung the doors shut with a clang.

Mr. Needle and Mr. Bland turned and looked at the Stubbs family.

"Excellent work, Mr. Stubbs," said Mr. Needle coldly.

"Most efficient," said Mr. Bland, in the tone of somebody who thought he could have managed the whole affair a lot better.

"We'll take it from here," said Mr. Needle, pulling the leather gloves off his hands. Then he walked to the driver's side of the truck and climbed in.

Mr. Bland smiled a wintry smile.

"We shall be making a complete report to the Guild," he said, "and I have no doubt that they will be in touch. I imagine that, in addition to the regular fees, there will be a generous bonus. Allow me to congratulate you all. Good day."

Mr. Bland raised his hat, made a shallow bow and then joined Mr. Needle in the front seat. A moment later the truck moved off, crunching its way over the gravel, and gathering speed as it headed down the long drive to the distant gates.

There was a long silence as the Stubbs family watched it go. Then, when the truck turned out of the gates and was at last lost to view, Measle tapped his father's arm.

"Yes, son?" said Sam, smiling down at him.

"I was just wondering, Dad. . . ."

"What were you wondering, son?"

Measle grinned up at his father.

"Well," he said, slowly, "what I was wondering was this: they've left their motorbike behind, haven't they?"

"So they have," said Sam, shading his eyes and peering down the driveway, where the big black motorbike was parked. "Horrible thing. Well, it's no use to them now. We'll just have to get rid of it."

"Mm. I was wondering," murmured Measle slowly, "whether we could—er—whether we could keep it?"

"No, Measle," said Sam, shaking his head. "No, I don't like motorbikes."

"Don't you, Sam?" said Nanny Flannel, in a surprised voice. "Oh, *I* do. In fact, I used to have one when I was a young girl. I used to go all over the place on it. It was lovely."

"That's beside the point, Nanny——"

"Justin Bucket used to take me on the back of his motorbike," said Lee dreamily. "It was such fun. We'd go really *fast*."

"Yes, well that's why I don't like 'em," said Sam.

"Why?" said Lee, grinning wickedly. "Because they go fast? I thought you liked going fast?"

"I do."

"Why don't you like them, then?"

"Well, if you *must* know," said Sam, in a dignified voice, "I don't like 'em because Justin Bucket took you for rides on his, that's why." Sam turned away, trying to hide the fact that his face was going a little red. He pointed to the distant machine. "Besides, look at that sidecar wheel. It's useless."

"I expect we could mend the wheel," said Measle.

"No, we couldn't," said Sam. "Besides, the whole thing is *filthy*."

"We could polish it up, get it all nice and clean," said Nanny Flannel.

"I daresay we could," said Sam. "But we won't."

"We could buzz around the estate on it," said Lee. "It'd be fun."

"I daresay we could," said Sam. "But we won't."

"But Dad——" said Measle.

Sam held up his hand. "No, no, *no*," he said firmly. "No motorbikes at Merlin Manor. Never! The whole thing is absolutely, completely, utterly——and finally—— *out of the question*."

Well, there's only one thing left to do, thought Measle. *Use the WORD. The extraordinary WORD. The amazing, effective and magical WORD, that sometimes works miracles! The WORD that can change History! The WORD that can move mountains! The WORD that can . . .*

"Please?" said Measle.

There was a very long silence. Even the birds in the trees fell quiet. The seconds ticked by. Everybody held their breaths.

Then——

"Oh, all right then," said Sam.